Fantastic® Four

REDEMPTION OF

THE SILVER SURFER®

Fantastic Four®

REDEMPTION OF

THE SILVER SURFER®

MICHAEL JAN FRIEDMAN

ILLUSTRATIONS BY GEORGE PÉREZ

MARVEL COMICS®

BYRON PREISS MULTIMEDIA COMPANY, INC.
NEW YORK

BERKLEY BOULEVARD BOOKS, NEW YORK

Special thanks to Ginjer Buchanan, Lucia Raatma, Michelle LaMarca, Steve Roman, Mike Thomas, Steve Behling, and Stacy Gittelman

FANTASTIC FOUR: REDEMPTION OF THE SILVER SURFER

A Berkley Boulevard Book
A Byron Preiss Multimedia Company, Inc. Book

PRINTING HISTORY
Putnam hardcover edition / June 1997
Berkley Boulevard edition / April 1998

All rights reserved.
Copyright © 1997 by Marvel Characters, Inc.
Edited by Keith R.A. DeCandido.
Cover art by Steve Fastner & Dave DeVries
Cover design by Claude Goodwin
This book may not be reproduced in whole or in part,
by mimeograph or any other means, without permission.
For information address: Byron Preiss Multimedia Company, Inc.
24 West 25th Street, New York, NY 10010.

The Penguin Putnam Inc. World Wide Web site address is
http://www.penguinputnam.com

Check out the Byron Press Multimedia CompanyWorld Wide Web site
address: http://www.byronpreiss.com

Make sure to check out *PB Plug*, the science fiction/
fantasy newsletter, at http://www.pbplug.com

ISBN: 0-425-16489-6

BERKLEY BOULEVARD
Berkley Boulevard Books are published by The Berkley Publishing Group, a
member of Penguin Putnam Inc.,
200 Madison Avenue, New York, New York 10016.
BERKLEY BOULEVARD and its logo
are trademarks belonging to Berkley Publishing Corporation.

PRINTED IN THE UNITED STATES OF AMERICA

10 9 8 7 6 5 4 3 2 1

For my mom and dad,
who actually thought reading comics was a *good* thing

ACKNOWLEDGMENTS

Where do I start? Who do I thank first?

How about the talented people who first created sequential art (comic strips and books to the uninitiated) . . . and then came up with the wacky idea of people with super-powers? Yeah, that'd be as good a place as any.

Thanks, guys, for opening my eyes—both directly and through your worthy disciples—to the possibilities. Because, at its best, that's what comics are—a literature of possibilities.

Thanks, also, to a guy named Stan Lee, who took the concept of super heroism a dramatic step further by giving his characters real-life problems and personalities. And to Jack Kirby, whose art was so powerful, so textured and immediate, you felt as if you could reach out and touch it. After all, it was Stan and Jack who created the Fantastic Four. Without them and their creations, this book would never have gotten a chance to exist. So, yeah, a really *big* thank-you to those guys.

On a more human scale, I'd like to express my gratitude to my wife and kids, who endured yet another Deadline with Dad. We're thinking of making it into a sitcom where the father figure doesn't say anything for weeks on end; he just pounds on his keyboard and growls.

Also, thanks a bunch to editor Keith R.A. DeCandido (Keith R.A. to his friends), who cajoled and convinced me to do the book in the first place. He said the danged thing would be fun, and whaddaya know? It *was*.

Then there are the guys at Marvel Creative Services, who rode shotgun with nary a whimper as we rumbled hell-bent for leather through the Negative Zone, holding on to the reins of Marvel continuity as tightly as we possibly could.

And George Pérez, artist extraordinaire, who lent vibrant life to each character he touched, demonstrating at every turn that he somehow knew my story better than I did. I tell ya, George, it gave me the shivers.

Finally, a tip of the hat to Ron Marz, everybody's favorite cosmic comic writer, who got me involved with the Silver Surfer to begin with. For those of you who've been wondering, yeah, Ron *does* soar through the cosmos on a surfboard—except on Wednesdays. That night, he plays volleyball.

Adiós, amigos. Enjoy.

One

The Silver Surfer had seen the proud, red star from a long way off. He drank in its beauty for an entire millisecond. Then he pierced its ardent heart like a silver arrow and emerged on the other side, leaving a glowing trail of heavy elements in his wake.

Once, when he was new at this, he would have made his passage through the star more slowly. He would have taken the time to explore the miracle of fusion and bask in its primal light.

Back then, he had taken the time to explore many things. Despite all his newfound power, the yawning chasm of a black hole or the blinding grandeur of a supernova had routinely taken his breath away (metaphorically speaking).

It still had that effect on rare occasions, the Surfer noted inwardly. But not as often as it used to—and certainly, not as often as he would have liked.

He found himself hungering for more and more these days, seeking out the next celestial curiosity and then the one after that with increasing yearning. But no one thing seemed to satisfy his capacity for wonder anymore—only to whet his appetite for something bigger and more sublime.

An observer might have likened the Surfer to a hunter and the objects and events of the void to his prey. That's how eager he was to know every spectacle the universe had to offer.

But a truly astute observer would have noticed he was not only pursuing—he was also being *pursued*. And if the things dogging his trail were not of the visible variety, if they were more memory than substance, that didn't make the pursuit any less real.

The Surfer hastened to leave the red giant behind. In that haste, he almost failed to notice the tiny object falling through space between the fifth and sixth planets in the system. *A vessel*, he thought.

Certainly, there was much to be said for the births and deaths of suns, the frigid majesty of a comet as it sundered the blackness of space, or the staggering vastness of a far-flung nebula. But in all existence, there was nothing quite so curious and compelling as the collection of biological processes called life.

And where there was a vessel, there would be sentient life. Or at the very least, some of its more intriguing artifacts.

Effortlessly, the Surfer willed his silver surfboard into a tight U-turn—the centrifugal force of which would have torn apart the strongest starship imaginable. As he approached the vessel, he slowed.

Of course, there was no friction in space, no sense of deceleration. Only a perception that the shiny blurred streaks around him were shortening, becoming the pinpricks of distant suns.

And then there he was, right in front of the vessel, hovering motionless on his board. His eyes—flawless silver orbs without a sign of iris or pupil—narrowed thoughtfully as he considered it.

On one side, a portion of the hull had been blackened and caved in—the only sign of external damage. But inside, there was damage as well. And because of it, the ship's power source was slowly dying, taking with it all the vehicle's major systems.

One of the survivors was the vessel's weapons array. But it was modest enough that if it suddenly unleashed its fury on the Surfer, he would be able to handle it.

Of more concern to him was the mystery of how this ship had been damaged. He folded his arms across his silver chest as he pondered the question.

Had it been the victim of another vessel, another band of sentients who had seen fit to use their weapons on it? Or had it been victimized by one of the universe's unseen forces—forces about which he himself had learned much to his detriment and chagrin?

There was no way of knowing without penetrating the thing, without going inside it to learn more. His curiosity getting the better of him, the Surfer left his board behind. Melting through the ship's hull like a ghost, he used his mastery over molecular structure to emerge whole on the other side.

The Surfer had expected to find himself in some corridor, or perhaps in a storage area. It was his experience that storage areas and corridors took up most of the volume of spacegoing craft.

However, his search was rewarded immediately. He had inadvertently placed himself in what appeared to be the vessel's control center—a squat, cylindrical chamber with a transparent deck and an equally transparent ceiling, each of them giving him a view of the ship's inner workings.

Nor was he alone. There were two beings within, basically humanoid, ensconced side by side in elaborate, mechanical chairs that seemed to grow organically from the equipment surrounding them. Except for subtle differences in their stature, the two beings seemed identical to each other.

They were tall and pale and hairless, with blotches of purple around their tiny, black eyes and clusters of tiny, fleshy bulbs protruding from beneath long, sharp jawbones. Their digits, three to a hand, were slender, purple-veined tendrils.

Two sets of these tendrils intertwined on a studded console located between the humanoids. The Surfer couldn't help but think this was a gesture of mutual affection, a sign that these two enjoyed each other's company.

Or had, until their recent deaths.

For, upright and composed as they might be, these beings had breathed their last almost two days ago, as Zenn-Lavians counted time. That wasn't merely a guess on the Surfer's part; it was a scientific conclusion based on the lack of viable atmosphere left in the chamber and the degree of decay in the beings' cells.

More curious than ever, he tried to activate the vessel's computer system—to gain some insight into the disaster that had befallen its occupants. However, the system was damaged beyond the Surfer's ability to repair it—not merely lacking a viable power source, but fused in places and still sparking in others.

Again, he turned to regard the corpses in their mechanical thrones. *Did they know they were dying?* he wondered. The Surfer shook his head, wishing he could discern the answer. Unfortunately, even a being as powerful as he had no way of determining that. He couldn't read the minds of the living, much less the dead.

Still, he could imagine, and he chose to imagine that they *had* known. That they had anticipated their fate, if only by a few seconds—and in those few seconds, they had reached for each other's hands, seeking comfort and support in the idea that neither of them was alone.

Perhaps, if they were lucky, that single gesture had provided a sense of closure. A hint that their lives had been worth something, if only because they had shared them, each with the other.

The idea haunted him. To share a life . . .

He had done that, once upon a time. He had been a mere humanoid, confined like others of his kind to a single world—but his mind, at least, had soared, and it had not soared alone.

Shalla Bal. Even now, her name brought an ineffable stirring from within him, a fire that could never be quenched by time or distance. She returned to him in snatches of memory—each one precious in its own way, each one laden with meaning for him.

He recalled the glow of what seemed like perpetual amusement in her eyes. The softness of her skin as she slept, his finger working out a scientific formula on her shoulder. The heavy, fragrant fullness of her hair as it brushed his face, distracting him from his work.

The Surfer remembered those things and more. He remembered one perfect morning, and how still it was as they walked in the park and spoke of their future together.

He remembered how much he had loved Shalla Bal—with all his heart and all his soul. And how she had loved him in return.

No . . .

Not him. Not the Silver Surfer.

It was Norrin Radd she had loved. Norrin Radd, fiery intellectual, one of Zenn-La's foremost scholars despite his youth. Norrin Radd, who had never been able to accept the apathy and sloth that characterized his fellow Zenn-Lavians.

For a while, it had seemed to him it was his destiny to restore Zenn-La's greatness. He had dreamed of the stars, of soaring among them like his star-spanning ancestors. But it had only been a dream.

Then Galactus came and changed everything. His gargantuan vessel had appeared in the heavens above Zenn-La one day, effortlessly piercing the defense network established ages earlier. The citizens' alarm had called for the populace to prepare for invasion.

But how might they have prepared, when Zenn-La had no space fleet—no weapons? And even if they had such things, who among them remembered how to fight? No one, not a single soul. Zenn-La had not encountered a threat from space in ages.

Norrin Radd had not known how to fight, either. But he had resolved to try to learn. He retrieved a spacegoing ship from a museum and flew straight to the heart of the mighty vessel in the sky. Before he knew it, he was drawn inside.

It was then that he met Galactus, a being mightier and more majestic than any he had ever imagined. Galactus, who asked nothing more from Zenn-La than everything she had to give. Galactus, the planet-destroyer.

Legend had it that he drained planets of their energies to obtain the nourishment he needed to survive. And as Norrin Radd stood before him, Galactus confirmed that the legends were true.

There was no way out for Zenn-La. No possibility of escape. Certainly, Galactus would have taken an unpopulated planet before a populated one. But he had no time to seek out a world that was both brimming with energy and devoid of sentient life.

If he had a Herald, he said, many was the world he might have spared. Many were the unique species he may have bypassed. But alas, Galactus said, he had no such Herald . . .

At the time, Norrin Radd had been too frightened, too devastated by the impending death of his race to understand what Galactus was doing—to realize how the great annihilator was manipulating him. But even if he had understood, it wouldn't have changed anything. He would still have struck the same mind-boggling bargain.

One life in exchange for millions. The future of one man in exchange for a world's. There had never been a choice—not really.

Had he elected to remain Norrin Radd, his world would have been forfeit, and all those who populated it. And he and

Shalla Bal would have died along with all the others.

This way, at least, Shalla lived. Zenn-La, its people, and its civilization lived. Only Norrin Radd perished that day, yielding to a transformation no being before him had ever known.

He remembered the crackle of energy that at first seemed to surround him and then became a part of him. He recalled the heat that seemed to sear the flesh from his bones . . . the cold fire within that severed molecule from molecule and atom from atom . . . the flash and focus of titanic forces beyond his meager understanding.

And then it was done.

Where once there had been a creature of flesh and blood, there stood a being impervious to heat and cold, capable of withstanding the terrible extremes of airless space. Where once there had been a man, there was something new. Something more and, sadly, something less.

And the horror and glory of it were that this construct, this personage of almost limitless power, was *him*—was Norrin Radd.

To obtain his Herald, Galactus had agreed to spare Zenn-La. But his hunger was great, and there was no time to waste. Norrin Radd—or rather, what he had become—could perform only one last duty before he took to the heavens. That was Galactus's concession to him.

He could say good-bye to Shalla Bal.

He sailed down from orbit on the gleaming silver board that henceforth would carry him across the skyways. The board took him to her balcony in less time than it took to think about it. At first, she didn't even realize he was there. Then softly, ever so softly, he called her name—and she turned at the sound of it.

On seeing him, her eyes went wide with terror—and perhaps with loathing as well, he thought. But when she realized it was her lover she was looking at under that silver veneer, her gaze softened.

He told her what had happened. He described the deal he had made with Galactus. She accepted all that.

But when he said he had to leave her to keep his bargain, Shalla saw enough of Norrin Radd in him to shake her head. To want him to stay.

Shalla wanted to go with him. She wanted to share his fate,

good or bad. What was left of Norrin Radd ached for her in that moment, ached for what might have been.

But he knew, in truth, he was already gone. Quashing her hope quickly, for it was more merciful that way, he rose into the blood-red sunset sky and put Shalla Bal behind him.

Or so he had believed. But for a long time to come, she was never far from his thoughts. No matter what marvels he witnessed as Galactus's scout, no matter what strange places he visited, Shalla Bal's face was always before him, a reminder of what he had sacrificed.

Still, with the passing of time, the pain of his loss became easier to bear. His loneliness lost its edge. And he became the Silver Surfer Galactus had intended, removed from trivialities like love and companionship.

At least, they had come to *seem* like trivialities. When one had raced light waves and bathed in the awful majesty of the infinite, it was easy to forget the value of simple emotions.

But fortunately, the Surfer had been reminded of it. And now, as he gazed at the two humanoids in the control center of the crippled vessel, he was reminded of it again.

Surely, he thought, it was sad they had perished. But it would have been sadder still if they had not forged a bond that had outlived them—or if he had not been here to marvel at it.

Abruptly, the Surfer became aware of something else on the vessel—another life-form, but not a sentient one. It wasn't in this chamber, but somewhere aft of it. Leaving the two corpses in peace, he moved to the back of the control center and found a door. It slid aside at his approach, revealing a sparsely lit corridor beyond.

He followed the corridor, seeking out the life-form he had sensed. And then, as if it had sensed his presence as well, he heard it emit a high-pitched whine. A complaint, he thought, of loneliness.

Coming to the door from which the whine had issued, he waited a moment for it to open. It didn't. Either it was malfunctioning or it had been locked. No matter, the Surfer thought, and walked through it.

After all, the door was only another configuration of molecules to him. And the Power Cosmic, ceded to him by great Galactus, gave him mastery over all forms of matter.

On the other side of the door, he found what he was looking for—a rust-colored mass of tentacles and tendrils and cilia that was nearly as big as he. Its head was an agglomeration of protuberances, its only recognizable feature a pair of small yellow eyes.

As it caught sight of him, the creature whimpered. Clearly, it was somewhat the worse for wear: hungry, afraid, and it may have been affected by whatever had damaged the vessel. Nonetheless, there was still atmosphere in this compartment, so it still lived.

Kneeling before it, the Surfer saw the mistrust in its eyes—the fear. Never in its life could it have seen anything like him. But of course, he intended it no harm. Quite the opposite.

He reached out to make physical contact with the creature. It started to growl in whatever it had that passed for a throat, but the gentleness of his touch stilled its anxiety. Then, seeking out the nature of its injuries and deficiencies, he applied his healing power.

It was another of Galactus's gifts—the power to mend living things. The ability to see what was wrong with them and fix it.

In seconds, he could see the difference. The animal's ruddy flesh began to shine with new luster. Its eyes grew brighter, more alert. And several of its tendrils curled with contentment.

Perhaps it sensed his desire to help it. Perhaps it was an attempt to bridge its loneliness—an emotion the Surfer understood only too well. In any case, the creature opened its maw and flicked a forked tongue at him, making contact with his dry and poreless skin. And it did so over and over again as he watched.

With the computer files destroyed, he had no idea where its home planet might be. And if he left it here, the creature was clearly doomed to a slow, torturous death. He couldn't allow that.

As Galactus's Herald, the Surfer had aided in the doom of too many worlds to count. At the time, his conscience had been dulled by his master, who believed he was doing the former Norrin Radd a favor. But it had still been the Surfer's fault these worlds were drained of their life energy, and he would carry that guilt forever.

Only one good had come of the experience—the Surfer's

heartfelt belief that life was precious. All of it, in its every guise and variation. There was no way he could make up for all the death and destruction he had caused. There was no possibility of atonement. But he had sworn never to pass up an opportunity to try.

Taking the creature up in his arms, he created an aura about it—one that would keep it warm in the cold of space and supply it with air in the midst of airlessness. After all, it would be journeying with him where few living things had ventured before.

There was only one thing left to determine—where to take the creature. Somewhere close, he decided, to maximize its chances of survival. Somewhere he could be sure there were those who would care for it.

It didn't take him long to figure out where such a place might be. Without another thought, the Surfer melted his way out through the hull and into the void, where his surfboard was waiting obediently for him.

Then he stepped aboard it and headed for Earth.

Two

Johnny Storm was bored. Mega-bored. *Mondo*-bored.

He closed his tired eyes and settled a little deeper into his chair in the Negative Zone watch station. Then, opening them again, he glared at the oversized video monitor across the room.

Using the armrest controls designed by his egghead brother-in-law, he began switching from one view of the starry void to another. And another. And another, just as he'd done for the last half hour or so.

Unfortunately, the Zone didn't have either of the items that intrigued Johnny most in the world.

One of those items was cars—jalopies, Lamborghinis, and everything in between. As long as it had four wheels, a windshield, and a souped-up engine, he was in heaven.

The other item was women—though there, he was a little more particular. No—make that a *lot* more particular.

Ironically, if Johnny had been like any normal young man on this sultry late-spring afternoon, he might have been milling around at the just-opened New York Auto Show, admiring the sight of curve after beautiful curve.

Both kinds.

After all, every ravishing new model at the Auto Show had . . . well, a ravishing new model to point out its unique design features. In fact, as a teenager, he'd always found it tough to decide what to study first—the car or the tantalizing beauty standing beside it.

But of course, Johnny wasn't *like* other young men. Not since he'd taken part in an ill-fated and unauthorized mission to the stars, which had endowed him and his three companions with strange and even monstrous powers.

In his case, the powers of a human torch. The ability to burst into flame at the drop of a battle cry, toss missiles of fire at unsuspecting bad guys, and capitalize on the principles of thermodynamics to soar through the sky like a bird.

Shortly after their transformation, he and his companions had dubbed themselves the Fantastic Four, never imagining they'd become de facto protectors of the Earth within a few short months.

Back then, that kind of title had sounded pretty good to Johnny. *Protectors of the Earth.* And what was that other name the TV news jocks hung on them? Oh, yeah. *The world's greatest superteam.*

Pretty weird. But pretty cool, too.

Still, as someone once said, with great power came great responsibility. No, he thought—make that responsibilities, plural. And one of the worst responsibilities Johnny had was taking his turn here at the watch station, making sure none of the Zone's myriad threats reared its head near his brother-in-law's remote sensor network.

Not that he expected there to be any trouble. The Zone had been quiet lately. And even if it hadn't been, there were scores of automatic backup systems that made it redundant for him to be here.

Except Reed, the brother-in-law in question, always reminded them that mechanical devices could misfire. And if they did, and someone like Annihilus decided to come waltzing by, where would they be *then*?

Johnny ran his fingers through his thick, blond hair and sighed. On Four Freedoms Plaza, outside the FF's headquarters, there had to be dozens of beautiful women who'd have given their eyeteeth for a lunch date with a super hero. And here he was, wasting all that goodwill in some—

Suddenly, he checked himself. Something was wrong here. As a trickle of ice water made its way down Johnny's spine, he leaned forward and adjusted his brother-in-law's controls.

The image on the video monitor changed and magnified, giving him a closer look at the last view of the Zone that had flitted by—one that displayed a section of the debris orbiting Negative Earth.

It was a scene straight out of hell. Maybe a hundred chunks of rock, different sizes and different shapes—and each one had a living being bound to it, chained to spikes driven deep into its surface.

The prisoners were of a half dozen different races. Some

were slender and dark as pitch, some pale and squat with blue markings like tattoos, some green and angular with beaklike faces and feathery crests the color of straw. And there were Baluurians as well—the only ones Johnny could identify.

Each prisoner struggled with his bonds—to no avail. Each one cried out against his fate, eyes wide with pain and fear.

They weren't human, these people, but they were human-oid—close enough for Johnny's heart to go out to them. Sure, they could breathe, because space was different in the Zone. But they were still in deadly danger.

After all, there was something about Negative Earth—a barren sphere roughly the size of Johnny's home planet—that made the debris above it explode when it came near enough. And the occupied chunks of rock were coming nearer with each passing moment.

Johnny didn't know why these people were being subjected to this. He had never seen them before in his life. But as he made another adjustment in the sensor view, he could see that more of them were being chained to the rocks all the time. And if he didn't recognize the victims, he recognized the ones doing the chaining all too well.

They worked for Blastaar—a Baluurian himself, a sadist and a dangerous character if ever there was one. Blastaar had a hunger for conquest, which he always managed to satisfy in the bloodiest ways possible. His subjects once got so sick of his tyranny, they rebelled and imprisoned him in an adhesion suit, then set him adrift in the void.

He'd lived to tell about it, though—much to the chagrin of every living thing in the Negative Zone. Using his ability to generate powerful neutron blasts, he'd freed himself from his suit.

And then, in one of those cosmic coincidences that seemed to follow the Fantastic Four everywhere, Blastaar had caught sight of Reed—who was in the Zone at the time as well. Following the human back to the portal linking Earth with the Zone, he'd caught a glimpse of a new universe to conquer.

Since that time, Blastaar had tried over and over again to seize the Fantastic Four's homeworld—though, in between, he'd found time to conquer half the worlds in his own dimension. A busy boy, that Blastaar.

But what was *this* all about—this slow torture, right under the noses of Reed's remote sensor network? Johnny shook his head, confused. Frowning, he punched the squarish button that would send a call for help through Fantastic Four headquarters. Maybe *he* couldn't figure this out, but he was reasonably certain his brother-in-law could.

That was the value of having a Grade A certified genius on the premises.

Ben Grimm reached down and took hold of the smooth titanium bar.

It fit perfectly in his four-fingered hands—no surprise, since it had been custom-made for him. On either side of the bar sat a round five-ton weight, also composed of titanium.

Under normal circumstances, it would've taken some serious machinery to lift a load that heavy. Certainly, no living thing on God's green earth had been designed to do that kind of work.

No living thing but *him*.

And as for the design part . . . that was a subject for scientists and philosophers, not Ben Grimm. He hadn't asked for his lot in life, not by a long shot. But he wasn't going to waste his time trying to figure out how and why things had happened this way.

They just *had*, he told himself a hundred times a day. All he could do was deal with it and move on.

Bending his knees, Ben set his jaw, took a couple of quick breaths, and jerked the ten-ton weight off the floor. The strain on his back and shoulders was incredible, but he fought his way through it.

Then, just as the bar came up around his chest, he inched forward and made his way underneath it—the way he might have approached a limbo stick as a teenager. Except he wasn't a teenager anymore, and a limbo stick wasn't heavier than a fleet of Volkswagens.

As gravity resumed its claim on the twin weights, the bar bowed slightly, pressing down on him with crushing force. But Ben stubbornly held his ground, resting the length of titanium in the craggy niche between his biceps and his massive shoulders.

Another couple of breaths, even more urgent than the first. If he was going to do this, he had to be quick about it. He had to finish before his muscles realized what he was asking of them.

Giving it everything he had left, Ben tried to lift the bar. For a moment, it didn't even budge. Then, by sheer force of will, he forced it up off his shoulders with a groan.

And pushed it higher, and higher still, his arms and legs trembling mightily with the effort. Pain shot through every muscle in his body. But little by little, he shoved the bar up over his head until he could lock his elbows into place and hold it there.

It didn't have to be for long, either. Ben counted silently to three, the limit of his endurance. Then he heaved the weights off him and watched them crash to the floor, where they bounced a couple of times with a sound like thunder before finally coming to rest.

Fortunately, Reed had thought to reinforce their headquarters, or a weight like that could have gone through the offices beneath them like a bullet through wet tissue paper. But then, there wasn't a lot that got by Ben's old friend and college roommate.

For instance, the lack of mirrors here in the gym, and pretty much throughout their four-story headquarters. Mirrors only served to remind Ben of what he'd become. Over the years, he'd come to hate them.

And not just mirrors. Crowds too.

He recalled that first time he'd gone out in public, shortly after his transformation. He'd tried walking around in a vastly oversized trench coat with specially made shoes and pants and a hat pulled down low over his face. But his size had still made him an object of curiosity.

Then the people around him had taken a closer look. Their eyes had narrowed. And in a fit of rage and frustration, he'd ripped off his coat to show them what he really looked like.

He could still feel the stares of fright and revulsion. Still see the pointing fingers and hear the mutters of disbelief.

Sure, it had gotten better over time. A lot of people had gotten used to him. Especially here in New York, where they appreciated all he'd done for them since the Fantastic Four moved into town—and where strange-looking people had become a dime a dozen.

But there were still the tourists, eager for a peek at a super hero—even one who looked like a walking pile of orange bricks, with four stubby fingers on each hand and four toes on each foot. His only surviving human features were his baby blue eyes, and even those looked grotesque peering out from under a jutting ridge of a brow.

Under the circumstances, he couldn't even blame them for staring at him. If the tables were reversed, he would've stared too. Long and hard. Hell, he wasn't just a monster. He wasn't just a freak.

He was the only one of his kind.

That's why he liked to stay off the streets. He preferred to hang out here, in the solitude and sanctuary of Fantastic Four headquarters. Where he could forget, at least for a few minutes at a time, the great big joke fate had played on him. Where—

Suddenly, a familiar voice intruded on his reverie, only slightly fuzzed by the intercom technology that carried it. "Johnny to Reed and Ben. I need you guys up here at the watch station."

Ben frowned. The pipsqueak wasn't one to panic at the drop of a hat. In fact, he was a lot tougher than he looked.

So if he was calling for help, this was something serious. Having already dropped what he was doing, Ben Grimm—also known as the Thing—made his way across the gym.

Truth be told, he was glad there was something that needed his attention. The idea of facing some superpowered nutcase wasn't half as scary as being alone with his private miseries.

Most of the time, Reed Richards used the elevators and stairways to get around Fantastic Four headquarters, the same as Sue, Ben, or Johnny. But when he was in a hurry, he resorted to an elaborate network of inch-wide tubes that ran from one end of the facility to the other.

At that particular moment, the man called Mr. Fantastic was in a hurry, all right. *A big one*, he thought, as he slithered along through the narrow confines of his tube.

Bad enough Johnny's summons concerned the Negative Zone, which was always one of Reed's major security concerns. On top of that, he had been working on a hypersensitive subatomic test when the call came in. It had taken him a couple of minutes to shut down the experiment before he could even think about leaving his lab.

Unfortunately, the network of tubes didn't go everywhere. With security such a concern at the Negative Zone watch station, they brought Reed only halfway down the requisite corridor. As he emerged from a hole in the wall, craning his head on his elastic neck, he caught sight of a big, orange form lumbering in the same direction.

Again, because he was in a hurry, he didn't stop to say hello to Ben. He just surged by him, his body elongated to the length of a good-sized garden hose and hardly any stouter.

"Wouldja cut that out already?" Ben rumbled at him from behind. "If I wanted ta see rubber bands flyin' past me, I'd go back ta Mrs. Durante's seventh-grade Algebra!"

Reed recognized the Thing's annoyance for what it was—an almost childlike playfulness that belied his monstrous appearance. He'd known Ben long enough to tell the difference between anger and just sounding off.

The door to the watch station slid aside at his approach, revealing Johnny at the main control console. One glance at the massive video screen told Reed why his brother-in-law had called.

Wincing in sympathy for the victims, he was reminded of a place called Execution Rock off Long Island. Hundreds of years ago, men had been chained there at low tide and left to drown by degrees.

This was no better.

"What do we know about this?" Reed asked.

Johnny shrugged. "Nothing, really. Just what you see on the screen—a bunch of Negative Zone–types about to be blasted to bits. And those thugs chaining them to the rocks—"

"Are Blastaar's minions," Reed finished for him. "I noticed."

"Did someone say Blastaar?" Ben growled. A moment later, he swung his bulk into the room. His massive body barely fit through the doorway, even though it was twice the size of a normal door frame.

"I'm afraid so," Reed confirmed.

The Thing glanced at the video monitor. "Wotta creep," he rasped, making no effort to conceal his contempt. "Torturin' innocent people like that. Somebody oughtta tie *him* ta one a' those rocks."

Johnny glanced at Ben, a question in his eyes. "But don't

you think it's funny he'd do it right in front of us? I mean, Blastaar knows we keep an eye on that area. It's almost as if—''

"—he were setting a trap," Reed concluded.

He could feel every thud as Blastaar's soldiers drove their spikes into the rocks. He could feel the tautness of the victims' throats as they gazed wide-eyed at the prospect of death.

"Make no mistake," he said. "The danger to these people is real. But if all Blastaar wanted to do was execute them, he could certainly have found a more expeditious way to accomplish that."

Out of the corner of his eye, he saw Ben stroke his craggy, orange chin. "In other words, he's layin' out a big, neighborly welcome mat for us, hopin' we'll make like the Red Cross."

Reed nodded. "That's exactly right. What's more, we're going to accept his invitation. No matter what this is about, no matter what we're walking into, we can't stand here and watch the deaths of innocent people."

Ben made a sound of resignation deep in his throat. "Y'know, I had a feeling you were gonna say that. I guess I've been watchin' that Psychic Pals show too long."

On his other flank, Johnny nodded. "I'm with you, Reed. Let's crash Blastaar's party."

Reed didn't answer. He just crossed the room to the supply closet, touched a stud on the gray, heavy-duty metal panel, and watched it slide aside. Then he reached inside and took out one of the antimatter harnesses he'd invented.

The harness would allow him to propel himself through the Zone—a necessary capability if he was to avoid becoming a victim of the exploding rocks himself. He'd come close to that possibility once before, and he didn't want to repeat the performance.

"I'll take one of those," said Ben, his voice more gravelly than usual. It always got that way when he was buckling down for a life-or-death struggle, which was almost certainly what Blastaar had in mind for them.

"Me, too," Johnny chimed in. "Can't let two of my favorite teammates put their bacon on the line all alone."

The teenager needed a harness just as much as his teammates did. Though the Zone had an atmosphere all its own, it didn't extend to the area near Negative Earth.

"What about Suzie?" asked Ben. "She's gonna be awful sore when she comes back and sees we bolted on her."

"Maybe so," said Reed. He thought for a moment. "But there's no time to wait for her. The best we can do is leave a message behind, so she'll be prepared in case we don't—"

"Don't say it," Ben admonished him. "Don't even *think* it."

Reed had to smile a little at Ben's unswerving optimism. "All right, old friend. Whatever you say."

Activating a mechanism in the control console, he recorded a message for his wife while Ben and Johnny donned their harnesses. It was brief and to the point—like all his messages. After all, a scientist was nothing if not precise, and Reed was one of the foremost scientists of his day.

Unfortunately, that same precision made him seem distant and cold to people who didn't know him. But he couldn't change for those people—and frankly, he wasn't sure he wanted to.

Pulling on his own harness, Reed headed for the portal sunk into the floor at the far end of the room. It was a good couple of meters in diameter and made of the strongest alloys known. It had to be, to keep the denizens of the Zone from gaining access to Earth.

Pausing by the control console on the wall nearby, Reed electronically unfastened the force field locks that held the portal hatch in place. But even without the locks, it was devilishly heavy.

Reed was about to activate built-in hydraulic mechanisms to open the thing—but Ben beat him to it. Bending over, legs wide, the orange behemoth applied his massive strength to the task.

A moment later, there was a loud creak and a grating of metal on metal. And in the grotesque, faceted hands of the Thing, the hatch swung open—revealing the chaotic light show beyond.

Reed had long ago dubbed it the Distortion Area, being more of a scientist than a poet. But then, he was the same person who had called himself Mr. Fantastic, when there had been any number of more stirring options.

In any case, the Distortion Area had its purpose. As the connecting point between the two universes, it converted the matter of Reed's frame of reference to the antimatter that characterized the Zone—and when necessary, vice versa.

Without this convenience, a traveler between the two dimensions would explode on contact with the first thing he or she touched. Clearly, Reed mused, an inconvenience of significant proportions.

Standing on the brink of the portal, dazzled by the confusion of light and color at his feet, he shifted his harness until it sat more comfortably on his shoulders. Then he looked into the eyes of his teammates.

"Ready?" he asked them.

They nodded. There wasn't the faintest hint of hesitation in either one of them. Of course, they had done this sort of thing before.

"Then let's go," he said, and leaped out over the portal.

For a moment, he seemed to hover there, as Earth's gravity fought with the forces beyond—with Reed himself as the prize. Then the forces beyond the portal won and he was sucked down into chaos.

Three

The Surfer descended through the layers of Earth's atmosphere, using a force field to shield his alien charge from the friction heat that turned the air around him a dull red.

Down below, the irregular line of North America's eastern coast was hidden behind dense, white clouds. Still, the Surfer hardly needed sight to navigate; using his cosmic senses, he steered unerringly toward the city of New York.

Briefly, he passed through the clouds, his force field misting over with their contents. Then he dropped down low enough to discern the spires of what humans called skyscrapers.

They were designed to be impressive—he knew that from experience. But the Surfer, who had seen the Fire Cliffs of Nalidian and the Ice Fountains of Arctur, measured *impressive* with a different yardstick.

In any case, he was interested in only one skyscraper. Adjusting the angle of his descent, he sought the familiar metal-and-glass façade of Four Freedoms Plaza.

A moment later, he spotted it. Slowing down to a glide, he saw the giant numeral made of white marble that graced the side of the building he was facing. In fact, it graced all four sides.

And not just any numeral. It was the simple *four* that had become the Fantastic Four's symbol and calling card.

Of course, the team hadn't always been headquartered here. When the Surfer had first encountered them, they made their home in a place called the Baxter Building—an older, more modest structure that was later destroyed by one of their enemies.

It was just as well, the Surfer thought. The older building hadn't been designed with security or even privacy in mind. The top floors of Four Freedoms Plaza, where the Fantastic Four resided, were a heavily armored fortress protected by the most advanced systems Earth had to offer.

As he descended, he noticed the pedestrians milling about in the plaza and the surrounding streets. A few pointed to him. Others followed their gesture, and before long most everyone was pointing at him.

It was understandable. Even in this city that had become such a nexus for superhumans, an alien on a surfboard was still an unusual sight.

Still, there were those so jaded they only glanced at him and went about their business. Such a thing would never have happened on Zenn-La, where work and ambition were relics of a distant past. Only Norrin Radd might have been driven enough to abandon a public spectacle for the rigors of his studies.

He had that in common with the Earthers. But only that.

Several years ago, the Surfer had turned against Galactus, making a stand alongside the Fantastic Four to save their world. As punishment, he was exiled here on Earth. And in the course of that exile, he had come to know the creatures of this planet all too well.

Certainly, a great many of them were cut from the same noble cloth as the Fantastic Four themselves—but these individuals were clearly in the minority. No matter what part of Earth he visited, he found mistrust, fear, and hostility. He had never seen a planet more blessed with natural beauty, more abundant with life in its infinite variety—or more sick to its heart with the sort of poisons only its inhabitants could inflict on it.

In order to preserve his sense of right and wrong, the Surfer had kept to himself as much as possible, sequestering himself in the more isolated regions of Earth. He had avoided humanity:

Just as he avoided it now, alighting on the roof of Four Freedoms Plaza, where the only prying eyes to which he was subject were in the other skyscrapers around him. After a few moments, he thought, the Fantastic Four's surveillance devices would be sure to pick up his presence there. Then one of his friends would invite him inside.

At least, that seemed like a reasonable assumption. But as the minutes passed, no one responded. The Surfer began to grow impatient—though not half as impatient as the creature in his arms, which began to tremble at the approach of the inevitable news helicopters.

The creature's discomfort made up his mind. Though the Surfer knew it was rude to enter someone's home without an invitation, he felt he had waited as long as he could.

Concentrating on the necessary adjustments in his molecular structure, he melted his way through several feet of protective titanium and entered the Fantastic Four's living quarters, still cradling the alien creature. His board followed closely behind.

Unfortunately, the Surfer didn't find anyone inside. It seemed he was destined to wait, no matter what. But at least he had made it possible for the creature to stop trembling.

Susan Richards had no sooner pulled out some money to pay her cabdriver than she knew something was up.

Four Freedoms Plaza was abuzz. People were pointing to the top of the office tower as if something significant had happened there.

Also, there were a couple of news helicopters. *Not a good sign*, she thought, feeling an adrenaline rush of concern for her teammates.

Suddenly, she was no longer the celebrity chairperson of New York Cares, a charity benefiting the homeless and the needy in the city's five boroughs. She was a member of the Fantastic Four, who benefited New Yorkers in a very different way.

Susan activated her powers, rendering herself invisible— one of many abilities that earned her the name the Invisible Woman. She could hear the driver of her taxi yelp with surprise: "Fer cryin' out loud . . ." He whirled and craned his neck to get a look at his seemingly empty backseat.

Susan didn't stop to hear his further exclamations as she left a $20 bill—enough to cover both fare and a generous tip— opened the door, and slid outside. This was nothing new to her. She'd been astonishing people for years. And as long as she remained the least ostentatious member of the Fantastic Four, she would no doubt astonish them for many years to come.

After all, one could hardly miss Ben in a crowd. Reed, being their spokesman, was also widely known. And her brother, Johnny, hardly went out of his way to avoid the limelight. So when the eleven-o'clock news rolled around, the three of them tended to be more visible than the Invisible Woman.

She could make herself and whatever she was wearing undetectable to those around her. Hell, even to *herself*. It was a handy talent to have at times.

Now, for instance.

Weaving her way through the crowd, she was able to make it across the plaza in under a minute. Only a few bystanders realized something had even brushed past them, and they probably figured it was just a breeze.

Still invisible, Susan made her way through the revolving door into the lobby, drawing only a stare or two from people who had seen the door start up by itself. Then she found the restricted-access elevator that served only the top four floors of the building.

A pencil-thin beam shot out seemingly from nothing, but in fact from her belt buckle. Only Susan and her three teammates had access to this elevator via these special "key" laser beams.

Seconds later, the door slid aside and let her in. And seconds after that, she was soaring past forty-five floors of corporate offices toward Fantastic Four headquarters.

En route, she whipped out a small device Reed had given her. Though it looked like a cellular phone, it had a tiny, built-in video screen and more sophisticated electronics than a NORAD mainframe. Activating it, she saw the flashing red light that indicated an intruder alert.

Whoever—or whatever—it was, the intruder was still inside: on the second of the team's four floors, two from the roof, on the west side of the building. As far as she could tell, it was lingering in one place.

But there was no evidence of anyone else in the building. Neither Reed nor Ben nor Johnny, though they had all been there when she left earlier in the day. Biting her lip, Susan braced herself.

The next step was to get some idea of what she was up against. She called for a video image, as captured by the nearest hidden surveillance camera. Less than a second later, the camera showed her the identity of the intruder.

She saw a masculine form, with what looked like a surfboard hovering in the air next to it. And both were metallic-looking. Silver, in fact, and polished to such a high gloss she could make out Reed's instrument panels reflected in their surfaces.

Susan could feel herself relax a couple of notches. The Silver Surfer was a friend. If he was there, things were under control—at least for now.

But she still didn't know what had happened to the others. Maybe the Surfer would have a line on what was going on— she certainly hoped so. As many times as they'd faced impossible odds together, it was never a comfortable feeling to know her friends—her family—were in some kind of danger.

As Susan thought that, the elevator stopped on the first floor of Fantastic Four headquarters. But according to her device, the Surfer was another floor up. Tapping the appropriate button, she felt the elevator car rise another story. Then she opened the doors and got out.

The Surfer stood right in front of her, waiting. Apparently, he had sensed her approach—or maybe even tapped into the surveillance system. Though she had known him for years, neither she nor anyone else understood the full range of his powers.

"I am glad to see you," the Surfer told her. His voice, soft and expansive, always seemed to have a calming influence on her. "There doesn't seem to be anyone else around. That came as a surprise to me."

"You and me both," she replied. "Come on. We're going to find out what happened to the others right here and now."

The Surfer nodded. "Good. And after that, perhaps—" he tilted his head to indicate something down the hall "—we can find a home for the creature I brought with me."

Following his gesture, Susan saw something on the floor. It was big and lumpy looking, with gnarled limbs and a central mass that seemed to be its head. Its eyes—if that's what they were—looked at her without blinking, while a forked tongue slithered in and out of the thing's maw.

"I rescued it from a derelict spacecraft," the Surfer explained, his silver orbs seemingly devoid of emotion.

"I'm sure we can find a place for it," she told him. Then her thoughts returned to her teammates. "But first things first."

• • •

From his first encounter with the Negative Zone years ago, Reed had been fascinated with the Distortion Area. With good reason—the place was aptly named, for everything was distorted here. Not just his perceptions, but the laws of nature themselves.

Though there weren't any winds or obstacles he could feel, and the propulsion device in his harness was powerful for its size, his progress was full of jolts and unexpected swerves. It felt as if he were riding a roller coaster through a major earthquake.

Lights pulsed around him in every color he could imagine—and some he had never imagined. The effect could be hypnotic if one wasn't careful. He knew from experience to ignore the light flashes.

Instead, he focused his mind on the place beyond the Distortion Area, where the lights grew dimmer and farther apart. Where, if one concentrated, one might see a dense field of debris—the rocks they had seen floating in orbit around Negative Earth.

Only once did he look to his right and then his left to make sure Ben and Johnny were still with him. Fortunately, they were. But then, they were no strangers to the Distortion Area either.

As they bumped and jerked their way through the ever-twisting maze of lights, Reed was glad he'd taken the time to check their harnesses periodically. He would have hated the idea of getting lost here.

In the meantime, the peculiar dynamics of the area were transforming them into antimatter. When they entered the Negative Zone, they would fit right in.

The other good thing about the Distortion Area was that it never lasted as long as one estimated it would. Before Reed knew it, he had reached the limits of the region—the place where its lights were mere will-o'-the-wisps, sparking here and there, barely discernible with the naked eye.

And a moment later, they were gone altogether. Taking a breath of Negative Zone air, which had no harmful effects according to his research, the man called Mr. Fantastic took stock of his position.

Perhaps predictably, his teammates weren't nearly as close as they had appeared. The Thing was a good fifty meters away and Johnny was nearly twice that distance back.

However, as they emerged from the distortion belt, they sighted their leader and used their propulsion capabilities to converge on him. Reed could hear Ben grumbling.

"I forgot how much I hate that place," he said. "I'm gonna be seein' spots for a week."

Johnny chuckled dryly. "Think of how the spots must feel. They've got to look back."

The Thing scowled at him. "You're a regular Henny Youngman in knee pants, y'know that?"

Reed tuned out the banter, as he generally did. He knew it was just his teammates' way of gearing up for the battle ahead. Certainly, there were times when the Torch's ribbing rubbed the Thing the wrong way. But at a time like this, the give-and-take just helped reduce the tension.

As one, the three of them shot toward the debris field. Somewhere in there, in the lower tiers, they would find the rocks to which Blastaar's minions were chaining their captives.

Of course, it wasn't easy to get through the field. As usual, the rocks were packed in pretty tight—sometimes too tight for someone Ben's size to negotiate. And he didn't dare start using his strength to pulverize them, for fear he would start a chain reaction.

Characteristically, Reed found a bright side to the situation. It was good, he told the others, that they weren't encountering their adversaries right off the bat. "It means we can weave our way through the field and sneak up on Blastaar's men."

"Gotta love that element of surprise," Ben mumbled.

"I do," said Johnny, with a little more enthusiasm. "I like it a lot—especially when that's all we may have going for us."

Unfortunately, for reasons Reed still hadn't figured out, the Torch was unable to flame on in this area. Everywhere else in the Negative Zone, Johnny was able to soar through the void like a shooting star and pull out every trick in his fiery arsenal. Here, in orbit around Negative Earth, he was just another man in a propulsion harness.

Not that Johnny wouldn't be of use to them. He was still a seasoned hand-to-hand fighter. It just meant he had to pick his fights carefully.

Slithering past rock after rock, Reed and his companions began to hear something in the distance. Ben turned to him.

"Explosions," he said.

Reed nodded. "The rocks that've crossed the planet's proximity threshold. Let's just hope they're unoccupied."

"Yeah," Johnny chimed in. "Let's hope."

Here as elsewhere in the Negative Zone, physical laws were a mystery to Reed—and therefore a source of great fascination. As long as he could remember, even as a boy, it had always intrigued him when he encountered something he didn't understand. In the universe *he* came from, rocks didn't explode when they approached Earth. But here, they exploded with regularity.

What made that happen, when both the debris and the energy fields surrounding the planet seemed perfectly unremarkable? And why hadn't he seen anything like this phenomenon elsewhere in the Negative Zone? Or, for that matter, anywhere in his own universe?

And where did the rocks come from? There always seemed to be a multitude of them. But if they were always descending and always exploding, how was the supply replenished?

What was different about this place?

He shook his head. To grasp the forces that ruled here, one might have to devote a lifetime to empirical research. And as tempting as that sounded, Reed's responsibilities as Mr. Fantastic had to come first.

He wasn't just a scientist anymore. He was what the newspapers called him—a super hero, one of those empowered by chance or design to stand between humanity and its enemies.

He was still thinking this when he negotiated a particularly big rock and spotted the first of Blastaar's soldiers. Like Blastaar, he was a Baluurian, big and mean and gray-maned. And like Reed, Ben, and Johnny, he wore a harness that allowed him to maneuver in Negative Zone space. Gesturing at his teammates, Reed made sure they saw the soldier too.

"Looks to me like clobberin' time," the Thing rasped as softly as he could. He tapped his harness affectionately. "Here's where we put these babies through their paces."

Reed shook his head. "No. Not yet. Even at top speed, there's a chance he'll see us coming in time to fire."

"You've got a better idea?" asked Johnny.

Reed looked at him. "As a matter of fact, I do."

Ben elbowed Johnny. "Didn'cha just know he was gonna say that?"

As his friends watched, Mr. Fantastic reached through the debris field, his arm growing longer by the moment. It took a while, because he wanted to keep his hand hidden from the guard as much as possible.

Finally, there was nothing but open space between his hand and the Baluurian. Reed extended himself a little farther—

—and tapped the guard on the shoulder. Crying out, the Baluurian whirled. And met with the whiplash force of Reed's fist.

Momentarily stunned, the guard let go of his weapon. Seeing his chance, Reed grabbed it and flipped it around one-handed. Then he found the trigger and fired.

A flash of green energy jolted the Baluurian, sending him pinwheeling into a rock. In the aftermath, he went limp.

Reed reeled the weapon in, then turned it over to Johnny. "We've got to move quickly now," he said. "There may be a perimeter check every so often, and our friend there isn't going to answer when he's called."

Reaching for his harness controls, he propelled himself deeper into the debris field, right past the unconscious Baluurian. Ben and Johnny were right on his heels.

But they didn't get very far before they caught sight of other guards—three of them this time, gathered in a knot. As Reed stopped to consider them, Ben caught up to him.

"Is it clobberin' time *now*?" he asked.

Mr. Fantastic sighed. "So it would appear."

He glanced at Johnny to make sure he was ready too. His brother-in-law nodded and cradled his weapon a little more securely.

That was all the communication they needed. Reed and his partners had been together too long, fought too many formidable enemies as a team, to require anything more detailed.

Reaching for his harness controls, Mr. Fantastic went into action, accelerating to the greatest speed he could muster. After all, he was their leader. And if he'd learned anything since becoming a being of incredible elasticity, it was that leaders *led*.

Taking their cue from him, Ben and Johnny accelerated as

well. They plowed through the debris field on a straight line, hoping Blastaar's men wouldn't catch a glimpse of them and turn around.

As it happened, the Baluurians never knew what hit them. Reed and his comrades plowed into them with bone-crushing force, sending their weapons flying out of their hands.

Before the guards could recover, Ben grabbed a couple of them and smashed their heads together. And Johnny nailed the third one with a quick burst from his weapon.

Reed looked around, to see if anyone had taken note of the skirmish. As far as he could tell, no one had. But if they had a reason to move quickly before, that reason had become a mandate.

There were weapons available for all of them now. But the Thing declined, saying it wasn't his style. Reed felt the same way—especially since their hand-to-hand approaches were less apt to draw attention.

Together, the three of them kept on, heading in the direction of Negative Earth with all due haste. As before, they kept a sharp eye out for their next encounter. It came sooner than they expected.

And this time, they hit the jackpot. Not just a gaggle of Blastaar's guards, but a stretch of perhaps a dozen rocks with a dozen innocents chained to them. As they watched, yet another was added to the line.

Not too far away, closer to Negative Earth, other rocks exploded. Reminders of what Blastaar had had in mind for these prisoners.

Reed felt the muscles in his jaw go tight. It was one thing to witness such cruelty on a remote sensor screen in another universe. It was another to see it up close, in person.

"Set those people free," he told the Thing. "Johnny and I will run interference for you."

Ben nodded his big, craggy head. "It'll be my pleasure."

"I'll circle left," Johnny suggested.

"And I'll circle right," Mr. Fantastic told him.

With a burst of speed, he got out to the left of the guards and set his sights on the nearest of them. Then, flinging his arms out like cables, he grabbed hold of a couple of rocks—one on either side of the Baluurian.

Suddenly, Reed picked up the slack in his arms—and shot

himself forward like a rock in a slingshot. He hit the guard in the face feet first, snapping the Baluurian's head back. Not hard enough to maim him, but certainly hard enough to keep him out of action for a while.

Out of the corner of his eye, he saw another guard taking aim at him. And firing. There was no time for him to drag his whole body out of the way.

But Mr. Fantastic's muscle control was so fine, he was able to move just the section of torso that would've taken the brunt of the blast. Making a dovetail shape, he avoided the blast.

Then he tied up the Baluurian's weapon with one hand and socked him with the other. While the guard was blinking, trying to regroup, Reed tore the weapon free and belted him with it.

By then, Johnny had come around from the other side and was spraying the guards with their own energy fire. The Baluurians shot back at him, but the teenager was too quick, too agile for them.

More accustomed to flying than the soldiers, Johnny twisted and swerved and corkscrewed his way among his adversaries. And when that wasn't enough, he used unoccupied rocks for cover, frustrating them time and again.

And all the while, the Thing was launching his assault on the prison rocks, pulling up spikes and snapping chains to free Blastaar's victims. And when the opportunity presented itself, he took part in the fray as well. At least once, Reed saw Ben snare a guard by the ankle with a length of chain—then whirl him about and send him flying like a hammer thrower.

At last, all the prisoners were free. Tying one chain to another, the Thing made a lifeline for them to hang on to. Then he used the power in his harness to pull them far from the fighting—and the explosions that were getting closer and closer as the rocks spiraled downward.

By that time, Reed and Johnny had the battle well in hand. Snaking around a chunk of rock, Reed walloped a guard with a borrowed energy weapon. A moment later, his brother-in-law leveled a blast at the two remaining Baluurians, knocking them senseless.

And it was over.

One way or another, every one of the guards had been taken

care of. The only sound they could hear was that of debris exploding below them.

"So far, so good," Johnny noted.

"But we've still got a long way to go," Reed reminded him.

"Y'can say that again," Ben chimed in, approaching them with a spurt of propulsion power from his harness.

The words were barely out of his mouth when Reed heard Baluurian voices. A great many Baluurian voices.

And they were getting louder all the time.

Johnny glanced at the rocks above them. As yet, there was nothing to see. But there was plenty for him to hear.

"Reinforcements," he muttered.

"Let 'em come," Ben rumbled menacingly, curling his thick orange fingers into piledriver fists.

"We may not have a choice," Reed replied.

Indeed, the voices were descending on them from what seemed like every point in the rock field. Every point except from below, of course, and that way lay certain death.

Then Reed saw the source of the voices. An army of Baluurians, descending on them with what seemed like the utmost care. And though they bristled with weapons and more than half had clear shots, not a single one of them was firing.

Johnny raised his blaster. "I've still got plenty of charge left," he said. "If you and Ben grab a couple, maybe we can—"

Reed shook his head. "Not just yet, Johnny." But it wasn't just the Baluurians' aggregate might that kept him from battling them. It was something else.

The feeling that there was something to be learned here. A mystery to be uncovered. And all they had to do was wait.

The Baluurians surrounded the humans, then halted their descent. They, too, seemed to be waiting for something.

Finally, that something arrived—in the savage, thickly muscled, lion-maned form of Blastaar.

Blastaar the Warrior. Blastaar the Conqueror. Blastaar, Emperor of all he surveyed—though that had never been enough for him.

The being who had drawn them here with his brutality. The spider who had constructed a web from which they could not escape. And now he had closed his trap on them, as he must have planned to do all along.

The Living Bomb-Burst eyed his longtime adversaries with tiny, bestial eyes. While his minions wore a variation of the blue-and-silver armor he had favored of late, Blastaar himself had gone back to the maroon and silver he had sported when he first invaded the Fantastic Four's headquarters.

"You came," he grated, in a voice that could have sanded the paint off a battleship. "You did not disappoint me."

"Yeah," said the Thing, glowering at Blastaar. "Our mamas taught us better manners than that. If yer itchin' for a fight, here we are."

"Cornered," Blastaar observed. "Helpless."

Johnny grinned. "A cornered animal fights twice as hard."

"What are we waitin' for?" asked Ben, no doubt irritated by all the talk. "Let's rumble, fer cryin' out loud!"

In response, Johnny shifted his weapon in his arms. But Blastaar didn't accept the challenge.

Instead, he held up his big, gray hand—as if he were calling for peace.

"While I look forward to renewing our hostilities," he said, showing his short, sharp teeth, "combat is not what I had in mind."

"Whaddaya talkin' about?" asked the Thing warily. His hands were still clenched into fists the size of fire hydrants. "Don't tell me ya brought us out here for tea and crumpets."

"What I'm talking about," snarled Blastaar, meeting Ben's skepticism head-on, "is a temporary truce—while I explain why I lured you into the Negative Zone."

Reed eyed the dark, imposing figure of their longtime enemy. He had suspected as much. "A truce? That's a first."

"Yes," the Baluurian admitted, "it is. And I wouldn't even have considered it if there had been another way. But there isn't."

The Torch hovered closer to his brother-in-law. "Don't listen to him, Reed. He's got something up his sleeve."

Mr. Fantastic considered the likelihood that Johnny was right. Blastaar had never shown himself to be the least bit trustworthy in the past. But as far as he could tell, the Baluurian wasn't achieving any real tactical advantage by stopping the battle this way—and also, subterfuge wasn't his style.

Besides, Reed wanted answers. And from the look of things, Blastaar seemed only too willing to provide them.

"Very well, Blastaar," he replied, "we'll listen to what you have to say. But if we see the least hint of trickery, this truce will be null and void, agreed?"

Blastaar's lip curled. Clearly, it wasn't easy for him to accept an ultimatum—especially from the likes of his old enemy. Nonetheless, accept it he did. And that made Reed even more curious about Blastaar's motives.

"Very well," said the Living Bomb-Burst. "I accept your terms."

"I don't believe it," Ben rumbled. "We're gonna stand here and *talk* with this jerk?"

Reed nodded, never taking his eyes off Blastaar. "That's exactly what we're going to do—until we find out what this is all about."

"But, Reed—" Johnny began.

"But nothing," he told the younger man.

Ben absorbed the remark, his eyes full of disbelief and indignation. Still, the scientist knew his old friend would fall into line.

It was Johnny that Reed was worried about. His brother-in-law had always been the hothead in the group in temperament as well as fact—and Reed had never seen him hotter than he was now.

For a moment, he thought the Torch might carry on the battle all by himself. Then Johnny's rage subsided and he just hovered there, shaking his head.

"I *still* don't believe this," he muttered. "But it's your party, Reed. Ours is but to do or die."

"Dissension in the ranks?" Blastaar suggested, more than a little amused by the idea.

Ben snarled at him and shot forward in his harness. "I'll give ya dissension between the ears, ya long-haired maggot!"

"Not now, old friend," Reed insisted, wrapping his arms around his teammate and hauling him back—and interrupting what would no doubt have been inspired deprecation. The Thing glared at him but fell silent.

Releasing his friend, the leader of the Fantastic Four turned to the Baluurian. "I believe you had something to tell us, Blastaar."

The tyrant nodded his great leonine head. "Indeed I do," he grated. "But not here. If you'll follow me, we'll continue this in my flagship."

And with that, he used his personal harness to ascend through the asteroid belt. His soldiers began to ascend along with him. All of them—leaving the humans unguarded.

"Wait," Reed shouted after Blastaar. "What about your prisoners? We're not talking until they're freed."

The Baluurian looked down at him. "Done," he roared, and continued his ascent. But with a gesture, he sent some of his men off toward other points in the debris field.

Reed looked at Johnny, then at Ben. They didn't seem ready to trust Blastaar in the least. But neither could they conceal their surprise at having been let off the hook.

"I don't get it," Johnny confessed. "He had us right where he wanted us." His brow crinkled beneath his shock of blond hair. "Didn't he?"

The Thing scowled. "Maybe killin' us wasn't satisfyin' enough by itself. He's gonna show us his home movies first."

Reed didn't know *what* Blastaar had in mind. But if there was a chance to find out, he was going to pursue it. With the help of his harness, he propelled himself after the Baluurians.

A moment later, his comrades came after him.

Four

The Surfer had never seen the Negative Zone watch station. But had he known what it offered, he might have asked to see it a long time ago.

Though he had traveled the length and breadth of the universe, he had never been granted a look at *another* universe. Yet as he watched the monitor that dominated one side of the room, he was treated to perspective after perspective, each one showing him something alien and apart from his experience.

Yes, he thought, stroking the tentacled creature in his arms so it wouldn't tremble, *it is fascinating indeed.*

Susan Richards was at the console beneath the monitor, working a set of controls. "All right," she said at last, standing back from the monitor. "Let's see where everyone went."

A moment later, the image on the monitor was replaced with the visage of Reed Richards. The Surfer could see Johnny Storm and Ben Grimm in the background as well. Both of them were wearing elaborate metal harnesses.

"Sue," said Reed, "we've detected an emergency in the Negative Zone. I'd have preferred to wait for you to tackle it at full strength, but there just wasn't time."

He went on to explain why. He spoke of the people he'd seen being chained to rocks near something called Negative Earth. And he mentioned his suspicion that someone named Blastaar was behind it all.

Reed also said he thought it was a trap—but that they couldn't let that stop them. And he left the coordinates where he believed the executions were taking place.

As the message progressed, the Surfer watched Susan's reaction. For the most part, she was calm and attentive. But her eyes were full of emotion.

He saw disgust there for what Blastaar had done, and perhaps some small measure of resentment that she had been left out of the team's mission. But most of all, he saw concern.

Finally, Reed's message was over. He expressed love for his wife and told her he would come back as soon as he could. Then his image vanished, to be replaced by another view of the Negative Zone.

The Invisible Woman took a breath, let it out. Her lips were pressed into a thin, hard line.

"Susan?" he said. "Are you all right?"

She turned to him and nodded. "Yes. I'm fine." Then she leaned over the viewer controls again. "It'll take a little while to find the debris field," she noted. "And then a little longer to locate the section we want."

"I understand," the Surfer replied.

In a matter of moments, Susan brought up an image of a debris field, just as she had said she would. Chunks of rock in various shapes and sizes wheeled slowly through space, half in sunlight and half out, so closely packed he could barely see the stars between them.

Then a second view of the debris field took over the screen. And this time, the Surfer could see chains attached to the rocks. But there was no sign of the innocents to which Reed Richards had referred. Nor, for that matter, was there any sign of Reed and his teammates, or the forces against which they had pitted themselves.

By that evidence, he judged Susan hadn't obtained the view she wanted yet. But when he glanced at her, her brow was creased with consternation. She seemed dissatisfied. No, more than that—shaken.

"I don't get it," she said, her voice hollow with an odd mixture of dread and anger. "They're gone. All of them."

The Surfer approached her. Tentatively, he placed his hand on Susan's shoulder, hoping to offer her some modicum of comfort. "Are you sure this is the proper perspective?" he asked.

She shrugged. "These are the coordinates Reed left me. And the chains he described are there." She shook her head. "It doesn't make sense. Blastaar's powerful, and he's got a great many soldiers. But we've held our own against him before."

Susan swallowed—hard. She had to be considering the implications, none of them good. "What could have ended the fight so quickly?" she wondered.

The Surfer grunted softly. "A natural phenomenon of some kind? One that drove off the innocents as well as the combatants?"

But as soon as he suggested it, he knew he didn't believe it—and neither would Susan. True, he was unfamiliar with this Negative Zone. But if it behaved anything like his own universe, natural phenomena seldom appeared without warning. There was usually a gradual buildup of forces, easily discernible if one cared to look closely.

No doubt there was a more plausible explanation. However, to discover what it might be, to track down an answer, one would have to enter the Zone itself. He advised his companion of this.

"If you like," he said, "I will search for them. After all, your teammates have shown me kindness when others of your race have shunned me."

"No," Susan replied. She turned from the viewer and looked at him. "I mean, yes—I'd be grateful for your help. But you're not going into the Zone alone. I'm going with you."

The Surfer met her gaze. He was about to ask her if it was wise for her to come, when they didn't know yet what fate had claimed the others. The last thing he wanted was to place Susan in deadly danger.

Then he remembered with whom he was dealing. The Invisible Woman would not be gainsaid when she put her mind to something. Despite her gentle appearance, she was perhaps the strongest of all the Fantastic Four, both in breadth of abilities and in strength of will.

"Very well," he replied. "We will search for your teammates together."

That established, Susan led him to an area down the hall, where they found a suitable compartment for the Surfer's creature, then returned to the watch station. There, Susan found a propulsion harness in a utility compartment and put it on, though the Surfer was more than capable of providing propulsion for both of them.

"Just in case," she explained.

No further explanation was required. The Surfer was well aware of the value humans placed on self-reliance. And few humans were more self-reliant than Susan Richards.

As he approached the heavy hatch door that separated Earth from the Negative Zone, she temporarily deactivated the force fields holding it in place. Then, with a gesture, he flipped it open and glimpsed the maelstrom of color on the other side.

Susan took a last look at the watch station. "I don't like leaving this place unattended," she said. "If someone should try to escape from the Zone while we're away . . ." Her voice trailed off ominously.

Then she looked at the Surfer. "On the other hand, we can't just stay here and do nothing."

He agreed.

Her resolve strengthened, Susan approached the portal. As she leapt out over it, she seemed to hang in midair for a fraction of a second. Then she was drawn down into the maelstrom.

The Surfer and his board came after her.

For the first time in recent memory, he felt himself tingling with anticipation. *After all*, he told himself, *this is a different plane of existence. A different reality, one might say.*

And given the circumstances, neither of them knew exactly what they would find there.

Aggas Ag stood by the side of his tribe's watering hole, outside the ring of their old wooden huts, and shaded his eyes against the flat, yellow sunset. Squinting, he scanned the distant horizon, shimmering in what was left of the day's heat.

There were no clouds—not even a hint of them. Worse, he couldn't feel any wind that might bring any.

Aggas Ag chittered sadly and looked down at the wilted growth that grew by the side of the watering hole. Once, in his father's time, there had been more than a few sprouts here. There had been grasses and brush and towering trees with great, green fronds.

But in those days, rain had been plentiful. The boundaries of the watering hole had been great indeed. Animals had come from far and wide to drink, leaving droppings to fertilize the ground and making easy targets for the hunters of Aggas Ag's tribe.

As a result, there had been no shortage of food. Males had grown tall and females had smiled. Their babies had been so plentiful as to rival the numbers of adults.

That time seemed like a dream now, and a beautiful dream at that. Over the years, the rains had grown few and far between. And even when they came, they brought less and less of their life-giving water with them.

Gradually, the animals had stopped coming to the watering hole quite so often. These days, it was unusual to see more than one in a fortnight. Nor were they the robust beasts of Aggas Ag's youth, able to supply the tribe with meat for weeks afterward. With their own food source depleted, the animals were as scrawny and malnourished as the tribespeople themselves.

Aggas Ag had not visited any of the other tribes on the land—his nest-mother's, for instance, which lay far to the east. But the youths of his tribe had wandered far and wide, and come back with stories of hardships beyond imagining. In one case, where they had expected to find a tribe, they had found only a collection of broken, old carcasses.

The sun dropped out of sight. The stars came out, bright and insistent against the soft, dark blue of the sky. By degrees, the land became shadow and the world cooled.

Something was happening. Aggas Ag would have been a fool not to see it. Something was happening to the land that had been good to them since the beginning of time.

He wished he knew why. If they had somehow offended the gods, they had also done their utmost to make up for it. Even in these difficult times, they had sacrificed what plants and beasts they could. They had fasted and danced and spent entire nights with their foreheads pressed to the ground.

But nothing changed. Either the gods were so angry they couldn't be placated, or they had abandoned Aggas Ag and his people to their fate, finding other lands on which to bestow their bounty. Either way, the tribe was doomed. Another few generations of starvation and they too would wind up skeletons bleaching in the sun.

He had barely completed the thought when he saw something strange—a star moving across the night sky. Aggas Ag nodded. He had once or twice seen a star fall from the heavens and learned later that it was a steaming chunk of rock. No doubt, he thought, this was such a rock.

But as he watched, transfixed, the star stopped moving. Aggas Ag rubbed his eyes, thinking perhaps that there was something wrong with them. Once a star began to fall, it didn't stop. At least, he had never heard of such a thing, nor had anyone else he knew.

Then the star did something else that seemed strange. It began to grow, slowly but surely, until it dwarfed the other stars. And still it grew, until it was larger than the three moons that had just started to enter the sky.

A great, silver object, it filled the heavens with its glory. Aggas Ag's heart pounded in his ears. Clearly, this was the work of the gods. But what did it mean?

The air began to tremble—to vibrate, as if it were full of newborn. But it was night, and the newborn were all safely in their sleeping-holes by then. Then Aggas Ag realized that the object caused the trembling of the air—and he began to tremble too.

Were the gods so angry with his people they had decided to end the world tonight, rather than wait for them to perish of starvation? Could the universe be so cruel after all?

Or was something else afoot? A portent of hope?

Suddenly, Aggas Ag became aware that he was not alone. Others of his tribe had emerged from their huts, stirred by the unusual vibration in the air. Their eyes were wide with trepidation as they stared at the great silver thing in the sky.

Males cursed, females murmured in wonder, and children moaned their misgivings. They had no idea what was happening, but they knew in their soft places it was the biggest event in the history of the world.

Then something else happened. Without warning, long silver shapes dropped from the object in the sky and buried themselves in the land. The ground shivered with the impact.

"What is it?" whispered a female.

"What is it doing?" asked another.

Aggas Ag turned to them, but he didn't answer. No one did—at least at first. Then Mor Maddas, the eldest man among them, spoke up.

"I once heard a tale," he said, the skin around his eyes twitching as he stared at the celestial object, his wrinkled, brown digits kneading one another like two lizards locked in a death-struggle.

"A tale?" Aggas Ag repeated, because males that old often needed prompting.

Mor Maddas nodded. "A tale of a god. One who roams the cosmos in search of lands to feed his huge and appalling hunger." He took a long, tremulous breath and let it out. "This could be him."

Aggas Ag turned again to the thing in the sky. It didn't look like a god to him, or at least what he had always supposed a god might look like. More likely, this was the god's hut, the place where he lived.

Before he could say this out loud, a reddish-gold light burst forth from the bottom of the object. And in the midst of that light, something emerged. Aggas Ag gasped.

Not something, he realized. Someone.

Slowly, the figure began to descend, still bathed in the reddish-gold light. But the farther it got from its hut the less blinding the light became, and Aggas Ag began to make out details.

The figure was massive—perhaps ten times as high as a tribesman and twice as broad across, covered with some sort of armor. On its head, it wore an elaborate headdress that concealed the upper portion of its face.

But it wasn't just its size that made the figure seem so strange to him. Its posture, its skeletal structure, its proportions—none of them were anything like Aggas Ag's.

And it had no tail. He gasped at the idea. How did it balance itself? How did it walk?

Aggas Ag could hear a rustling behind him. He looked back at his people again. They had prostrated themselves in the presence of the god, hoping to avoid the lash of his wrath. Or if he had come for another purpose, a benevolent purpose, to show him in what esteem they held him.

Aggas Ag fell to his knees as well. It was easy, considering how weak they had become. With great sincerity, great longing for salvation, and great fear of annihilation, he placed his forehead on the ground.

And waited.

Five

n all his travels, the Surfer had never seen anything like the Distortion Area of the Negative Zone.

As he and Susan Richards descended into its stormy turbulence and wild random flashes of light, his surfboard tucked under his arm, his first instinct was to create a protective force field around them.

But as it began to form, his companion turned to him with a look of urgency. "Don't," she said, her voice echoing strangely.

"Don't?" he repeated innocently.

"That's right," Susan confirmed. "The Distortion Area converts matter to antimatter and vice versa. It'll enable us to enter the Zone without exploding on contact with its antimatter. But if something insulates us from the dynamics of the Distortion Area—your force field, for instance—we're going to be in serious trouble."

The Surfer understood. "In that we will remain beings of matter in an antimatter environment."

His companion nodded. "Exactly. So . . ."

"I will drop the force field." He caused what he'd made of it—which wasn't much—to vanish.

Then he willed his board to achieve a horizontal attitude, despite the forces breaking against it, and gathered Susan onto it. Finally, he took up a position himself on the front of it.

The board wouldn't make it any easier to negotiate the Distortion Area. The Surfer just felt more comfortable on it than off it. Discerning a place where the flashes of light seemed to thin out, he slashed his way through the tumult to get there.

It took less than a second. But to a being who had sailed a universe at faster-than-light speeds, even a second seemed like a long time. Clearly, the Distortion Area had earned its name.

"The Antimatter Zone is just ahead," Susan told him. She

pointed to a distant accumulation of rock and debris. "Right there."

He closed the gap in the space of a human heartbeat, so quickly it must have seemed to his passenger that they'd teleported. Then he slowed down and wove his way among the rocks.

Farther down, closer to the sphere of Negative Earth, the lowermost rings of rock were exploding on contact with an energy field. But for all the superacuity of his senses, the Surfer couldn't identify the source of the energy.

The last tiny remnant of Norrin Radd was drawn to the mystery. It was a puzzle; on Zenn-La, he had lived for such puzzles. But the rest of him, the cosmic being who had pledged to help find his friends, held on to other priorities.

They made their way deeper and deeper into the debris field, alert for any evidence at all that Reed, Ben, and Johnny had come this way. Debris continued to explode below them, a constant reminder of how treacherous this region was. Finally, they caught sight of an oblong rock with a set of empty chains attached to it.

Then another. And another. On close inspection, one could tell from the savaged links that the chains had been torn apart.

"Ben's work, probably. But no sign of the team," Susan observed ruefully.

The Surfer turned to her. "That is not altogether true."

She looked at him. "What do you mean?"

It was often difficult for him to interact effectively with lesser beings. It was too easy to forget how limited they were in their perceptions.

"Your teammates have left a molecular emanation trail," he explained. "Just as you and I are leaving one. I believe any organism from our universe would do the same in this frame of reference."

"So you can track them through the Negative Zone?" Susan asked.

"Indeed," the Surfer replied.

"Even though we've been transformed into antimatter?"

"We may be antimatter," he said, "but we are a particularly alien variety of antimatter. Hence, the emanation trail."

His companion didn't ask for a more detailed analysis. She

seemed glad to accept the situation, no matter how it had come about.

"Then let's get cracking," she insisted.

"Unfortunately," the Surfer told her, "the trail is a relatively faint one. I will not be able to follow it at my customary rate of speed."

Susan patted him on the shoulder. "Do your best," she said. "That's always been good enough."

Pleased with the vote of confidence, he pursued the humans' emanations. Partway through the debris field, they parted into three separate trails and he had to follow one at the expense of the others.

The Surfer was glad to see them come together again a little while later. And even gladder when they ascended, leaving the deadly explosions around the planet in the opposite direction.

Every now and then, he glanced at Susan's face. It would have been difficult to miss the shadows of concern there. The pain of not knowing what had happened to her loved ones.

The Surfer sighed. It seemed like an eternity since he'd had a loved one—a being who could elicit worry in him.

Once again, he was reminded of Shalla Bal and the way he had said good-bye to her, wrapped up in his need to leave his old life behind. Little had he known, as he followed Galactus out into the cosmos, how lonely he would be. How very lonely.

Perhaps it was better that he hadn't known. It would have made his sacrifice that much more miserable—and it had been miserable enough to begin with.

Fortunately, he told himself, he had allies on whom he could depend, beings with whom he had established certain bonds since leaving Galactus's service. And those allies made him feel he wasn't entirely alone.

Sometimes.

But he couldn't call any of them his friends. In fact, of all the sentient life-forms he had encountered, the Fantastic Four were among the very few who even came close to being his friends.

And the truth was, he didn't know them all that well.

Blastaar's flagship hovered just above the asteroid belt. As they approached it, Reed saw Blastaar and several of his soldiers vanish into a hatch. Warily, he and his teammates followed.

They found themselves in a stark, functional corridor full of alien circuitry. Reed would have loved to examine it, but a Baluurian indicated the way they should go with a jerk of his head. Following the gesture, the human saw Blastaar disappear into a compartment at the end of the corridor.

"The Ritz-Carlton it ain't," Ben grumbled.

"Luxury doesn't seem to be a Baluurian concern," Reed noted.

Johnny wrinkled his nose. "Neither does personal hygiene."

He had a point, Mr. Fantastic conceded. The place seemed to smell of animal musk and perspiration. But then, the Baluurians were an alien species. They were bound to give off an unfamiliar and perhaps—subjectively speaking, of course—unpleasant odor.

Ignoring the stench, he made his way down the corridor. Then he entered the room the tyrant had entered before him.

Blastaar was waiting for them inside, staring out a large observation port with his back to them. To Reed's surprise, he was alone. No guards, no soldiers—though whether it was a gesture of good faith or of Blastaar's overconfidence in his ability to deal with the Fantastic Four, Reed could not tell.

Beyond him, the stars of the Negative Zone gleamed and glittered in all their glory. Reed recognized some of the constellations from previous trips. Unfortunately, they hadn't come here to stargaze.

"Well," he said, "we're in your flagship. The question is why."

Blastaar turned to look at them, his fierce black eyes reflecting the artificial light. "I did what I did," he grated, "to enlist your assistance—against a threat not only to me and my empire, but to every living creature in the Negative Zone."

Ben grunted. "You're just full of human kindness, ain'tcha?"

"A regular Mother Teresa," Johnny muttered, folding his arms across the numeral on his chest.

Reed silenced them with a glance. They weren't going to accomplish anything by antagonizing the Baluurian—especially when they were in a place where he held all the trump cards.

"Go on," he told Blastaar.

The tyrant scowled through the dense tangle of his beard, his eyes darting from one of his listeners to the next. Clearly, Blastaar wasn't used to having to convince anyone of anything. But then, that was always the case with those who ruled supremely.

"There is a ship," he began. "A ship as big as a Baluurian moon. It appeared recently on the fringes of my empire."

Blastaar turned again to face the observation port. He was no doubt more comfortable in the company of the cold, distant stars than in that of the Fantastic Four.

"My people," he went on, "have told tales of such a vessel since our most primitive beginnings. In it, they say, is a godlike entity. A creature of immense size and power."

The short hairs on Reed's neck prickled. Something about this story was starting to sound a bit too familiar.

And then, just in case he had any doubts, Blastaar put them to rest. "A being," said the tyrant, "who wanders the universe. His purpose? To find worlds on which to gorge his terrible hunger."

Reed felt as if he'd been dealt a physical blow. He looked at his teammates. Johnny had paled a couple of shades. And Ben probably would have as well, if he'd been capable of it.

"Hunger?" the Thing repeated.

The Baluurian nodded his shaggy head. He was still facing away from them, or he would have noticed their consternation.

"Yes. And the same myth, or some variation on it, seems to manifest itself in every Negative Zone culture I know of. Obviously, it is based on a seed of truth. So, naturally, when this ship made its presence known—"

"You feared the worst," Reed observed.

The Baluurian looked back over his shoulder, his visage fierce and terrible. "I fear *nothing*, human—not even a god, if that is what lurks in the moon-ship."

"All right," Reed conceded. "You were *concerned*."

Blastaar began to pace. "Concerned," he allowed. "Yes. Now, I could have allowed this entity to begin cutting his swath of destruction—to nibble away at my holdings, as it were—in order to gauge his power before I opposed him with my own.''

His thick, gnarled fingers clenched into fists. ''But that is not my way. Throughout my lifetime, when I have perceived a threat, I have met it head-on—and that is how I intend to meet this one.''

''So you're going to stop him before he can get started,'' Reed suggested. ''But not alone. Because . . . ?''

The Baluurian looked as if he'd just taken a mouthful of rancid meat. ''Because even the mighty Blastaar has his limitations. If the myths are true, even all my legions may not be enough to turn him back. But with the Fantastic Four on my side, I would be unbeatable.''

''You mean *we* would be unbeatable,'' Johnny amended.

The tyrant's eyes narrowed. ''That is what I said.'' He paused. ''I know we have never fought on the same side,'' said Blastaar. ''But as they say, there is a first time for everything.''

''They also say look before you leap,'' Ben pointed out. ''Especially when yer leapin' with the Livin' Bomb-Burst.''

Ignoring the remark, the Baluurian turned to Reed and raised his thickly bearded chin. ''What will it be? Will you join me, to fight this threat side by side? Or will you run— and in your cowardice, abandon the Negative Zone?''

The three members of the Fantastic Four looked at one another. Finally, it was Johnny who spoke up.

''What do you think?'' he asked. ''I mean, could it really be *him*?''

Blastaar eyed him warily from beneath wild, gray brows. ''What? You know this intruder?''

Reed sighed. ''We have encountered someone who sounds a lot like him. But that was in our own universe. And to my knowledge, Galactus has never visited the Negative Zone.''

''But we don't know that for a fact,'' Johnny reminded him. ''Who's to say the Negative Zone doesn't meet our universe at some point? Or that Galactus can't just—I don't know, make the jump somehow?''

Who indeed? Not Reed, certainly. For all his knowledge, he was the merest babe in the woods compared to the cosmic intellect of Galactus—and even that comparison was undoubtedly a kind one.

"Actually," he said, "it doesn't matter if this is Galactus or not. All that matters is whether he operates the same way. Because if he does, there's no overestimating the magnitude of the danger he presents to the native populations here. And their welfare, after all, is what brought us to the Zone in the first place."

"I could not have put it better myself," Blastaar said with a twisted smile.

"On the other hand," Ben noted, "he could be nothin' more than a rumor." He eyed the Baluurian suspiciously. "Or like I said before, ol' Blastaar here could be pullin' the wool over our eyes."

The tyrant shook his head. "This is no deception."

"Sez you," the Thing countered.

Blastaar took a step toward him. "If I didn't need you to—"

Ben got to his feet. "Don't let that stop ya."

Again, Reed had to insert himself between them. "For the time being," he decided, "we're going to have to take Blastaar's word for what's happening here." He considered the Baluurian. "But I think even he would admit we don't have all the information we'd like. And as far as I can see, there's only one way to get it. That's to—"

"—check out our mystery guest—" the Thing suggested.

"—examine the intruder—"

"—up close and personal," Ben finished.

"—with our own eyes," said Reed.

The Thing chuckled dryly. "Ya work with a guy too long, ya start ta think like him."

"Tell me about it," said the Torch.

Blastaar regarded them. "Then you'll join me in my struggle?"

"That remains to be seen," Reed told him. "We'll go along with you—but for now, just as observers. Then, if it turns out the intruder is the threat you think he is, we'll lend a hand."

The tyrant's lip curled and an angry knot grew where his brows met. After all, he was as unaccustomed to compromises as he was to asking for help. Still, he managed to restrain himself.

"Very well, then. I'll make arrangements for you to observe the enemy." Blastaar glared at them. "Just don't wait too long to join the battle—or you may find you are too late.''

Reed didn't like the Baluurian's tone. But he had to concede, there was a certain wisdom in what he said, and an ominous wisdom at that.

If this was Galactus they were going to confront, or someone even vaguely like Galactus, even an alliance with the mighty Blastaar might not be enough to turn him away.

Six

As a being who could expand the spaces between his molecules and make his body stretch to remarkable lengths, Reed Richards's reach was considerable. But one thing he seldom reached for was the controls of a spacegoing vessel.

After all, Ben had served as a test pilot for years before becoming the Thing. Indeed, it was Ben who had piloted the rocket ship containing himself, Reed, Johnny, and Sue that fateful day when cosmic rays changed them into the Fantastic Four. Ben was the one with the experience and the know-how to keep them on course.

That's why the Thing was at the helm as they sailed through the Negative Zone in the small starship Blastaar had loaned them, surrounded by other vessels just like it. In fact, almost every vessel in the tyrant's fleet was just like it.

And though they were strictly observers at this point and not combatants, their vessel—like all the others—boasted force shields and armaments and other tactical systems. While he had the opportunity, Reed was subjecting those systems to close scrutiny.

After all, he knew if both they and Blastaar survived this adventure, they would be at odds again someday. And the more he knew about the technology that went into Baluurian ships, the better the Fantastic Four would fare against them.

"I still don't get it," Ben grumbled, his remark seeming to come out of nowhere. "The idea that Blastaar'd be worried about some innocent species gettin' stomped on." He shook his head. "It's ridiculous."

Reed sighed and turned away from the exposed circuitry he'd been poring over. He was getting exasperated, and Mr. Fantastic wasn't normally an easy man to exasperate.

"For the third time," he told his friend, "I'm not crediting Blastaar with charity, or even concern for others. Clearly, whatever he's doing is in his own interest. However, it seems that, for once, our interests and Blastaar's may be on a similar course.''

The Thing made a sound of disgust. ''A similar course? And what does that say about *us*?''

''Nothing good,'' said Johnny, sticking his head out of the vessel's rear cargo compartment, where he'd been conducting some experiments of his own. His finger, which he'd been using to test the heat resistance of the ship's inner hull, was still aflame.

Reed cast a look of disapproval at him. He was about to defend himself when the young man spoke up again:

''On the other hand, I've been thinking about what Blastaar told us. And if there is a Galactus-type being running roughshod over the Negative Zone, we've got to do whatever's necessary to stop him—including lining up alongside Blastaar. For now, at least.''

The Thing grimaced at him. ''Ya lay down with dogs, Squirt, ya get fleas. Period, end of story. And another thing—''

He stopped himself and made some adjustments on his control panel. Then he turned to look back over his shoulder.

''Well, whaddaya know. It looks like we've reached our final destination. Stow yer tray tables and bring yer seat backs forward, and thanks a bunch fer flyin' Air Blastface.''

Reed stretched his head forward on his neck to get a look at Ben's control console. It didn't take long to see what he was talking about. There was something on his sensor screen, all right.

And it was *big*. As big as a small moon, in fact.

But it wasn't a moon. It wasn't anything created by nature.

In his entire life, Mr. Fantastic had seen only one artificial object of that size and complexity—the Worldship occupied by Galactus when he came to Earth. Suddenly, Blastaar's claims seemed a good deal more real, a good deal more tangible.

''What's all the fuss about?'' asked Johnny.

Moving forward, he peered over the Thing's other shoulder. Then he saw the sensor screen and he whistled.

''Galactus Alert,'' he said softly.

Throughout Blastaar's fleet, Baluurians would be eyeing the same image and remarking on the size of what they saw. But it didn't seem to daunt them in the least. None of the vessels around Reed's ship even slowed down.

"This is Blastaar," a familiar voice said over their communications link. "We've finally caught up with our enemy. If you've got half a brain among you, you'll join the fight."

Reed pressed a rectangular button, allowing the tyrant to hear what he had to say. "For the moment," he replied, "we still prefer to observe. But we'll be nearby in case we change our minds."

He could hear a disgruntled growling on the other end of the comm link. "You still doubt me?" Blastaar roared.

"We see a ship," Reed explained. "But we don't know the intentions of its owners. And until we do, we won't consider taking part in any conflict."

The Baluurian muttered a curse. "Suit yourselves, then," he told them, and severed the link.

By then, they were closer to the artificial object. They could see how immense it was—how badly it dwarfed the vessels in Blastaar's vanguard, rendering them almost inconsequential by comparison.

The tyrant's flagship was bigger and more heavily outfitted than any of the other attackers. But under the circumstances, it looked like a flea attacking the greatest of elephants.

Gradually, the flagship forged ahead of the other vessels, spearheading the assault. And as Reed and his comrades peeled off from the formation, the rest of the armada followed Blastaar in.

They went for the heart of the immense stranger, each vessel opening fire as it got within range—and then veering off in one direction or another lest it collide with its target. The barrage splashed off the object's force shields, however, causing it no harm.

"Doesn't look like they accomplished much," the Thing remarked from the safety of their observation ship.

"Not yet," Reed agreed. "But if they keep it up, they may batter down those shields. Then they'll start inflicting some damage."

"Whoa," Johnny said. "What's that?"

He pointed to one of the other monitors on the console—where a series of red blips had appeared on a pale green field.

Reed studied the blips, which were growing larger and more numerous by the moment.

Suddenly, he knew. "Reinforcements," he said out loud.

The Thing looked at him. "For Blastaar?"

Mr. Fantastic shook his head on his elongated neck. "No, Ben. For the object."

His conclusion turned out to be right on the money. As the newcomers got closer and closer, becoming visible to the naked eye as sleek, black needles, it grew increasingly apparent that they were going after Blastaar's armada.

They weren't as numerous as the tyrant's ships, but they were faster and more maneuverable, and they began wreaking havoc right off the bat. Wherever an attacker vessel was alone and cut off from the fleet, one of the newcomers seemed to find it and pick it off.

There were explosions, fiery red blossoms opening here and there against the backdrop of Negative Zone space. Before Reed's eyes and those of his teammates, the newcomers scored hit after hit, kill after kill.

Before long, the armada was in disarray, pressed just to defend itself—much less to mount any kind of attack on the object. And it was still losing ship after ship, while the newcomers in their ebon vessels went virtually unscathed.

The Thing grunted. "Blastaar's takin' a beating. I haven't seen such a one-sided tussle since I left Yancy Street."

His tone was casual. But his eyes were hard as stones with the sight of all that death.

"It's tough to sympathize with the Baluurians," Johnny said, his face as drawn and as grim as Reed had ever seen it. "But still . . ."

Then, even as they were commiserating with Blastaar's forces, that misery found some company—in them. One of the black needles came about and homed in on the observation vessel.

"For the luvva Pete!" Ben blurted—and spun them out of the way of a blue-white energy blast.

Reed latched on to the bulkhead on either side of him and craned his neck to study the control monitors. He didn't like what he saw there.

"It's coming back for another pass!" he warned the Thing.

"Just tell them we're observers!" Johnny snapped.

Ben glanced at him. "Yeah, *that'll* work." Then he poked some control pads and initiated evasive maneuvers.

But the Torch wasn't giving up. "It couldn't hurt to try!" he yelled—just as the black needle unleashed another blinding volley at them.

The Thing cursed and pulled them hard to starboard. Somehow, he slipped past the volley and activated their weapons systems.

Instantly, Reed put a hand on his friend's shoulder. "Those weapons are lethal," he said.

"So are theirs," the Thing insisted.

"We came here to *save* lives," Mr. Fantastic reminded him, "not to *take* them. There'll be no killing, Ben."

The Thing hesitated, but Reed knew Ben would come around, once he got his temper under control. "Awright, awright," came the Thing's response. "Ya got anything against me shakin' 'em up a little? I mean, I wouldn't wanna offend yer delicate sensibilities or nothin'."

"Shaking up is good," Reed assured him.

"*Very* good," Johnny added.

With his friends' support, Ben fired off a few blasts just to keep their adversary honest. Then he made a beeline for the thick of the battle.

Reed understood the strategy. What's more, he approved of it. On their own, they were an easy target. In the midst of chaos there was a danger of colliding with another vessel, but it would be harder for their pursuer to draw a bead on them.

Bursts from the black needle sizzling all around them, the Thing dropped them into the mess that was the remainder of Blastaar's armada. Suddenly, ships were careening every which way, firing packets of lethal energy as they went—or exploding as the enemy tagged them with a charge of its own.

It seemed impossible to Reed they'd make it through the clutter and confusion. But Ben wove a herky-jerky path for them, taking them up and down and swerving to one side then the other, avoiding crackup after crackup—and in the process, testing their vessel's inertial compensators as they'd probably never been tested before.

Their adversary didn't give up on them, though. The black needle stayed on their trail, twisting and turning right along with them.

At last, the Thing pulled them out of the melee on the other side—right near the immense object over which the battle was being fought. And as he did so, he swung them around in the tightest of turns.

The bulkheads shrieked and the deckplates shuddered, but the little ship held together—and found itself face-to-face with the black needle, which was what Ben had been aiming for all along. As the enemy ship zagged to avoid a collision, he got it in his sights and fired.

Reed checked the rearview monitor and saw that his friend had been true to his word. The black needle had been hit in one of its narrow, curved wings—which was still smoldering with the remains of Ben's barrage—and was rolling through space unceremoniously.

"She's crippled!" Johnny cried. He slapped the Thing on his craggy, orange shoulder. "You did it, you big gorilla!"

"What did ya expect?" Ben retorted. "Ya think yer playin' with kids here or somethin'?"

That's when Reed felt the jolt of an energy strike in their ship's hindquarters, knocking him to the deck. As he got himself up, the taste of blood in his mouth, he saw what the problem was.

Another black needle. And this one was on their tail, firing away as if they were the only target in town.

They were walloped a second time. And a third. Their craft went spinning wildly out of control.

"Ben!" Reed yelled, holding on as best he could. "Pull out, do you hear? Pull us out!"

Bent over his console, clinging to his seat with all his strength, the Thing shook his massive head. "The helm ain't respondin'. Not even Houdini could get us out of here!"

Then Reed caught a glimpse of his friend's eyes. He saw the frenzy in them, the mounting panic. And that alarmed him more than anything.

They had to do something. Otherwise they were sitting ducks, pinwheeling helplessly through space until the black needle delivered the *coup de grâce*.

Reed's mind was racing, desperately seeking a way out, when he saw Johnny go hurtling into the rear compartment. At first, he thought the Torch had been flung there by centrifugal force. Then he realized that hadn't been the case at all.

Johnny had meant to tumble in there. After all, that's where the hatch was—the way out. Reed reached for him, hoping to restrain him—believing their best chance still lay in Ben's regaining control of the ship.

But Johnny was too fast for him. A moment later the hatch flew open and Mr. Fantastic heard the rush of Negative Zone space past their hull—followed by a fervent and familiar battle cry.

"Flame on!"

Then Reed caught sight of a fiery figure, his flames feeding on the bizarre atmosphere of the Negative Zone as easily as if it had been the oxygen-nitrogen variety back on Earth. Spinning free of their vessel, the figure described a tight loop and flung itself at their pursuer.

"Blasted idjit!" Ben roared. "What's he tryin' ta do—get himself killed?"

The enemy ship didn't fall off even a millimeter as the Torch loomed before it. Its pilot either couldn't react in time or wasn't concerned about what he might do.

Johnny showed him that was a mistake. After all, he'd had years of practice controlling his flame. He could make it gentle enough to fry an egg or turn it into a conflagration of near-nuclear force.

As Reed looked on through the observation port of his crippled craft, the Torch glowed white-hot. Then he shot past the black needle and released a series of pale pink fireballs.

The first one stopped a meter from the enemy ship and remained there, caught in the fabric of the vessel's shield. But the next two penetrated the shield and struck the hull.

Instantly, the superhot flames turned the needle's side to slag. A moment later, there was a hole in the craft, still burning at the edges.

And the Torch wasn't done. Trailing white fire through the void, he went after the enemy ship as it came about. Having drawn blood, he was naturally eager for more.

But one skirmish didn't a battle make. Reed knew that. Had he been out there, he might've drummed some caution into Johnny's head.

Unfortunately, he wasn't anywhere near the Torch. He was still hurtling end over end in their borrowed ship, watching

Johnny and his adversary diminish with distance as Ben struggled to get a response from his controls.

Even if they'd been able to get free of the craft, their propulsion harnesses wouldn't have been a match for the Torch's speed—or, for that matter, that of the black needle. They'd have been left hanging in space, just as useless as they were now.

Pressing his face against the transparent surface of the observation port, Reed saw Johnny generate another series of fireballs. And another, as his flame trail carved itself into the heavens. And each time, the enemy's hull flared in response.

Against all odds, the Torch was coming out on top. By dint of courage and skill, the lad was *winning* a struggle in which he hadn't stood a chance.

Then, before Reed's horrified eyes, the black needle pulled a maneuver he wouldn't have thought possible. For all intents and purposes, it slammed on its brakes in the middle of space—and Johnny, who'd been worrying its flank like a hungry predator, went sailing by it.

Right into its weapon sights. Before the Torch could recover, the ship skewered him with a beam of blue-white force. By the time the barrage was over, Johnny's flame had been extinguished.

"Is he . . . ?" the Thing wondered, unable even to voice his fear.

He had given up on his control panel and was lumbering across the cabin in Reed's direction, digging his fingers into the bulkheads to keep from being tossed about.

The leader of the Fantastic Four could barely make out the Torch against the colorless background of space. It seemed to him Johnny was moving as he drifted—not dead but merely stunned.

"I think he's still alive," Reed said, hopefully.

He'd barely gotten the words out when the black needle started to move forward again. Behind him, the Thing pounded on a bulkhead, frustrated beyond his capacity to contain himself.

A hatch opened in the vessel's side and Johnny was taken in. Then, rather than reenter the fray, the black needle approached the mysterious structure that had been Blastaar's objective from the beginning.

A slot opened in the object and the ship slipped through it. Then the slot disappeared again. And the Torch, battered to a degree his brother-in-law didn't want to think about, was a prisoner of whoever—or whatever—had built the thing.

But first, he had done what he had set out to do. He had saved his teammates, whose vessel was spinning slower and slower now as the atmosphere of the Negative Zone hindered its progress.

"The bastards," Ben rumbled.

The other black needles began withdrawing from the battle as well—though it was hardly as a result of the Torch's efforts. They had simply battered Blastaar's fleet to the point where it was no longer a threat. The few Baluurian vessels left intact were hanging back, leery about suffering the same fate as their comrades.

As the enemy ships got closer to the alien structure, other slots opened in its flanks. Like their sister vessel before them, they slipped inside. And as before, the slots disappeared.

Then, with a vibration Reed could feel even at a considerable distance, the object activated its propulsion system—and moved away from the field of battle at a speed the human wouldn't have thought possible.

With Johnny somewhere inside it.

Seven

For some time, the Surfer cut a swath across the unfamiliar cosmos of the Negative Zone, absorbed in its wonders and its curiosities.

But he didn't let his sightseeing slow him down. Part of his mind—all that he needed—was firmly focused on following the trail of Susan Richards's teammates.

Besides, if he had faltered even a little bit, he was certain Susan herself would have let him know it. She stood right behind him, her hand on his shoulder, clearly intent on only one thing as the Negative Zone unfolded before them—and that was the recovery of Reed, Ben, and Johnny.

Such were his thoughts as he noticed something up ahead, in the distance—something more curious than anything he had seen in the Negative Zone to that point. It was a golden glow no bigger than his fist.

And right in his path.

The odds of *anything* being right in his path in a place like the Negative Zone were astronomically unlikely. But that wasn't all he found unusual. As he approached the glow, unswervingly maintaining his course, he saw that it was getting bigger.

"Surfer?" said Susan Richards. By then, she must have noticed his scrutiny of something far beyond her powers of perception. "Is something wrong?"

"That is difficult to say," he answered.

Slowing his surfboard, he came to a stop in front of the glow. It was the size of a man by that time. And it was still growing.

"I don't suppose you have encountered such a phenomenon before?" the Surfer inquired of his companion.

"I'm afraid not," Susan told him, her face bathed in golden light. "But I think I'll put up a force field, just in case."

He waved off the suggestion. "If necessary, I can defend

us. For now, you would do better to conserve your energy.''

The glow continued to expand until it was nearly twice the Surfer's height. Then something darkened in the center of it. As he watched, the darkness seemed to take shape, to solidify.

Finally, a bizarre figure emerged from the glow. The Surfer caught sight of huge, green wings like those of a Terran bat, and a green mask, flanked by spiked, green shoulder plates. The rest of the figure's attire was of a purplish hue, except for a golden cylinder that hung at its neck.

Though the Surfer couldn't see the face behind the mask—a curious circumstance in itself—the thing's insectoid features only appeared to echo the visage beneath it. Also, there was something vaguely insectlike about the newcomer's posture.

Susan's hands clenched instinctively into fists. ''Annihilus,'' she breathed, brow puckering, eyes alert.

It was not the warmest of greetings. The Surfer turned to her. ''You know this one.'' It wasn't a question.

Susan nodded anyway. ''We've run into him in the Negative Zone before. That cylinder hanging from his neck is called a Cosmic Control Rod. It's made him one of the most dangerous antagonists we've ever fought.''

The Surfer absorbed the information. Considering that the Fantastic Four had battled Galactus, legions of the Skrull Empire, and invasions from Prince Namor's Atlantis in their careers as Earth's champions, Susan's description of the interloper was sobering indeed.

Fortunately, the Surfer was confident in his own power as well. He didn't know what a Cosmic Control Rod could do, but he wasn't ready to believe it could eclipse the Power Cosmic.

''If you are wise,'' Annihilus chittered savagely, ignoring Susan's description of him, ''you will speak only in answer to my questions. Tell me quickly, then—what is your business here, Susan Richards? What need is so dire it would compel you to trespass and incur my wrath?'' He indicated the Surfer with an arrogant tilt of his head. ''And who is this? An ally?''

The Surfer eyed him. ''My name is no secret. I am called the Silver Surfer. As for our business here . . . it is just that. *Our* business.''

The chin of the mask lifted in indignation. The golden glow around Annihilus shimmered and flashed, as if with anger.

"You dare speak that way to *me*?" he rasped. "To one who can rend you atom from atom and quark from quark?"

The Surfer didn't so much as flinch. "If you are as mighty as you claim," he replied evenly, "you know I am at least your equal in terms of raw power. Still, it is always preferable to avoid violence. I can only assure you that we have been drawn here by circumstances still opaque and mysterious to us, and that we will depart as soon as the mystery has been solved."

For the span of an uncomfortable few seconds, Annihilus seemed to mull over the Surfer's words. Then he uttered his conclusion.

"You lie, Silver Surfer. You know more than you say. And for your mendacity, I will see you destroyed."

But not immediately, the Surfer observed, because Annihilus made no move against them. Instead, the bat-winged figure withdrew slowly into the golden glow, finally vanishing altogether. Then, by degrees, the glow itself diminished. Within moments, there was no evidence either it or its maker had ever existed in the first place.

Susan grunted. "How about that? I was certain Annihilus was going to let us have it with both barrels." She glanced at the Surfer. "I guess you really are a match for him."

"At least in his estimation," the Surfer responded. "And for now, that is all that matters."

The Invisible Woman smiled at him. "I'm glad you didn't tell Annihilus about my teammates' disappearance—or Blastaar's part in it. I mean, he hates Blastaar as much as anyone, but not enough to help us out."

The Surfer nodded. "I suspected as much." He regarded his companion. "Perhaps there was a time when I was naive enough to trust blindly—as I trusted Dr. Doom, shortly after my rebellion against Galactus." The Surfer had encountered Doom—the Fantastic Four's greatest enemy, though he did not know that at the time—during his exile, and Doom had temporarily stolen the Power Cosmic from the Surfer. "But," he continued, "I am no longer that being."

Susan's smile deepened. "No," she agreed, "I guess you're not. I'm sorry if I implied otherwise." Then she turned again to the open void. "Come on, let's get back on the trail. We've still got our work cut out for us."

The Surfer didn't answer. He merely rode forward on his gleaming surfboard, following the molecular emanations of Reed, Ben, and Johnny across a vast and wondrous cosmos.

Johnny Storm was dreaming. What's more, he knew he was dreaming. But it was such a good dream, he didn't want to wake up from it.

In the dream, he was lying on a beach towel somewhere, a tropical sun warm on his skin, a gentle breeze stirring his hair. A glittering, azure sea lapped at the sandy shore. In other words, paradise.

No Fantastic Four flare in the sky, calling him to battle with the Mole Man, the Sub-Mariner, Dr. Doom, or anyone else. No one calling him at all. Just the sighing of the palm trees off to his right, as they swayed like dancers under the influence of the trade winds.

He watched them for a while, smiling to himself. Then he turned to his left, expecting to see more of the same.

Instead, what he saw was the most beautiful woman he'd ever met, lying there beside him on the towel. Her eyes were a piercing, startling green, her lips full and pouting, her hair a jet black shot through with strands of gold. And she had a scent about her like sweet, pungent wildflowers.

She grinned at him. "He's waking up."

A little confused, Johnny looked at her. Then he looked around. Then he grinned back. "*He?* Don't you mean *you*— as in you're waking up?"

The woman stroked his forehead with her cool, slender fingers. "We still have a significant number of tests to perform. Reinforce his sedation."

Again, Johnny couldn't help but wonder what she was talking about. "You know," he said, not wanting to dispel the tropical magic of the moment, "it almost sounds as if you're talking to someone else. And maybe it's none of my business, but what are these tests you're talking about?"

The woman didn't reply. She just continued to smile. It set his mind at ease. For a moment, anyway.

Then he remembered that other word she'd used. *Sedation.* It was a funny word, one that seemed completely out of place.

Why sedate someone who was already about as relaxed as he could get? And why on a beach, with the sun warming his skin and the scent of wildflowers in his nostrils and the whirring of machinery in the background?

Abruptly, he stopped himself and retraced the steps of his thought. *The sound of . . . machinery?* he mused.

That isn't good, he told himself. *That isn't good at all.* He closed his eyes and made the effort he hadn't wanted to make before.

Like a swimmer ascending through a dark depth of water, he made his way up to the surface with long, increasingly urgent strokes. And when he reached it, he opened his eyes again.

The woman was still there. Her hair was still a wave of jet. Her lips were still full and pouting, and her eyes were still the green of chiseled emeralds. But that was where the resemblance ended.

Her eyes were too slanted to be human, her brows too arched. And her skin was too golden—as golden as the highlights in her hair, maybe more so. To top it off, she wasn't wearing a swimsuit. She was wearing a formfitting black jumpsuit with a green insignia over the left breast.

Taking stock of his surroundings, Johnny saw that he was strapped with metal bands to a large, metal table, in a large, high-tech chamber full of gizmos and gadgets that he couldn't begin to understand—and that might even present Reed with a challenge. Every square inch of wall space was filled with monitors and gauges and readouts of one kind or another, and they were all generating data a mile a minute.

Besides the woman at his side, there were a half dozen others in the same kind of slinky, black outfit. They were clearly of different races, most likely even from different planets, but they were all basically humanoid. Each one, in her own way, was attractive to Johnny's sensibilities.

What's more, he had a strange feeling he'd seen them before. Then he realized that he had.

These were the pilots of the black needle ships. The pilots who had run circles around Blastaar's assault vessels, lashed out at the three human observers, and ultimately taken Johnny hostage. Which went a long way toward explaining where he was and how he'd gotten there.

Except now, the pilots were acting as something else. *Researchers*, Johnny thought, analyzing him with a wide array of arcane scientific equipment—the kind Reed would have drooled over.

A thought came to him unbidden: *Cat Women of Venus.* It was an old science-fiction movie he'd seen as a kid, curled up under his covers, too scared to watch and yet too fascinated to go to sleep.

He had only a vague recollection of the astronauts who had encountered the cat women, and even less of what the story was about. But the cat women themselves . . . these he remembered very well. He remembered how snugly their costumes fit. And he remembered also their not-altogether-scientific curiosity about the astronauts.

Just then, he saw one of the women approaching with what looked like a slim, silver aerosol can. "Here," she told the brunette. "This ought to hold him for a while."

Neither of them looked at him. Neither of them seemed inclined to acknowledge his presence, other than as a slab of meat. And he bet that even if he asked nicely, neither of them was going to free him willingly.

Under other circumstances, Johnny wouldn't have minded being pored over by a flock of alien women, all of them intensely interested in his body. It kind of appealed to him. In fact, it was right up there with the scene on the beach.

But these circumstances included being trussed up like a Christmas turkey and being put under sedation so they could do who-knew-what to him. Not to mention that they worked for a guy accused of Galactus-like destruction.

Then, just in case he had any doubts about what to do next, Johnny heard the *whirr* of machinery change in volume, and a wicked-looking conglomeration of mechanical arms and probes and needles descended toward him from the ceiling all at once. At the same time, the woman with the golden skin moved to press her aerosol thingie against his shoulder.

"Oh no, you don't!" he told her. "Flame on!"

As Johnny said it, he could feel his biochemistry igniting him, turning him into a creature of intense heat and raging flame: the Human Torch.

The woman with the golden skin backed off, raising her arm instinctively to shield her from the sudden blast of heat. But it was nothing compared to what Johnny was capable of when he set his mind to it.

Setting his jaw, he willed himself to blaze hotter and hotter, until even the metal alloy of his bonds melted and sizzled away like water on a breakfast skillet.

And just for good measure, he directed a few fire spirals at the nightmarish mechanism descending toward him. Its probes and needles softened and bubbled and hissed away into nothingness—which was, as far as Johnny was concerned, where they belonged.

Free now, he leapt off the slab he'd been lying on and turned to face his personal "cat women." But they were ready for him.

Before he knew it, one of them leveled a gruesome-looking firearm his way and tapped the trigger pad on its barrel. Blinding bursts of blue-white energy walloped the Torch in quick succession, sending him flying head over heels—until he smacked into the bulkhead behind him.

As he got to his feet, dazed and bruised, he saw that the others had armed themselves as well—though he had no idea where they'd gotten the weapons. Even without their ships, it seemed, these women were pretty tough. But that was all right. The Torch figured he was tougher.

Looking around, he expected to find something at least vaguely resembling an exit—a door, a hatch, even a fair-sized vent. There wasn't any. At least, none he could locate at a glance.

And a glance was all the opportunity the "cat women" gave him. Aiming their weapons again, they fired.

The Torch shot up to the ceiling, trailing flame—just in time to see the blue-white energy bursts pass harmlessly below him. Where they struck the bulkhead, they splattered.

Johnny watched his captors' eyes as they took aim a third time. When they fired, he darted to his right. The women missed. And he kept going, hoping to get behind them.

Unfortunately, they were quicker than he'd hoped. They dropped and rolled onto their backs, lighting up the walls with a devastating barrage. The closed quarters made it seem even more devastating.

Still, Johnny managed to stay one step ahead of the women and even sling a few fireballs at them—not meaning to hurt them, just to melt their weapons. One of his missiles went astray, but each of the others connected with an energy gun, forcing its owner to drop it like a hot potato.

Outracing another couple of energy bursts, he disarmed two more women. And then two more. That left only one—the one with the golden skin, of course. She seemed to be the most capable one in the group, the one the others looked to for guidance.

If he could take her out, he'd have the time he needed to find an escape route. And now that he only had one weapon to worry about, his goal seemed well in sight.

Avoiding an energy blast, the Torch tossed off three fire-balls in quick succession. Overkill, maybe. But he was eager to finish this.

As it turned out, the woman avoided all three of his missiles, then squeezed off a few shots of her own. Surprised, Johnny was barely able to twist out of the way. Remembering how much those energy bursts could hurt, he did the thing he thought his adversary would least expect.

The Torch came straight at her. It was exactly the right move. Before the woman could fire again, he took her weapon barrel in his hands and turned it into slag. As she dropped it, he saw her glare at him.

No, he thought. Not *at* him. *Past* him. At something she saw over his shoulder. He whirled to see what it was.

But he was too late—by a fraction of a second. Johnny felt a series of energy bursts slam into him, one skull-pounding impact after the other.

There was no letup, either. Not until he was down on the floor, his flame all but extinguished, taking huge gasps to replace the wind that had been knocked out of him.

Looking up, he saw the exit—the one he'd been searching for—and the half dozen reinforcements in black jumpsuits who had come through it. Their weapons were still trained on him.

"What took you so long?" someone asked—the gold-skinned woman, he thought. And then: "Put him under."

Before Johnny could figure out what that meant, he felt a pressure against his arm. A moment later, he felt himself drifting off. Spiraling downward into an abyss.

He seemed to fall for a long, long time.

Eight

"Well?" Ben asked.

He was sitting with his back against an unmarred bulkhead—one of the few left in the ship Blastaar had given them. His mood was a black one and it grew blacker by the minute.

Just a few feet away, Reed withdrew his head from the maze of circuitry inside the open control console. "It's shot in there," he replied. "But I think I can repair it. It'll just take a while."

The Thing grunted, dissatisfied. "The squirt may not *have* a while."

Reed nodded. "I know. But it's the best I can do."

"The best you coulda done," the Thing rejoined, feeling a surge of anger, "woulda been to keep the kid inside the ship in the first place."

His friend's expression hardened. "I could hardly have pulled him back with a command, Ben. He's the Human Torch, not Rin Tin Tin."

Ben pointed a thick, blunt finger at Reed. "And you're our leader, fer cryin' out loud! People are supposed to listen to you, right?"

His friend looked at him askance. "So it's my fault Johnny took off? Is that what you're saying?" He paused. "Or is it yourself you're mad at?"

Suddenly, the Thing was on his feet, eyes blazing. "Me? What would anyone be mad at *me* for?"

Reed didn't answer right away. And when he did, it was with a voice full of kindness and understanding.

"That's exactly my point, Ben. You didn't do anything anyone could get mad at. Not this time—and not that other time."

The Thing glowered at him. "What in blue blazes are ya talkin' about?" he growled—even though he knew exactly what his friend was talking about.

"I saw the look on your face," Reed said softly. "The fear. The panic. It was the same look you had the night we changed."

There. It was out in the open. Finally, Ben had to admit it. In the midst of the battle, as he fought for control of their vessel, he had found himself struggling with a memory. And it came back to him again now, just as fierce and just as frightening.

It had been an attempt to break free of Earth's gravity in the smallest, lightest ship yet. A ship that would revolutionize humanity's struggle to reach the stars—or so Reed had said.

Ben had reluctantly volunteered to be his friend's pilot, though he was leery of the cosmic rays they would encounter. And encounter them they had, high above the Earth, in wave after brain-searing wave.

Each of them was affected differently by the rays. In Ben's case, he felt as if his body had become an enormous weight. As he sank to the deck, his arms too heavy to work the controls, he had lost control of their craft. The four of them had been tossed about, helpless.

By then, Johnny had begun to smoke as if he were on fire. Ben remembered that vividly. He hadn't been able to see Reed or Sue very well, because his head felt too heavy to raise off the deck. But he had seen Johnny and he had thought, *Oh my God, what's happening to the kid? What's happening to all of us?*

He knew now. They had been bathed in the cosmic rays he'd feared all along. But they hadn't died. They'd just become monsters. A human torch. An invisible woman. A man whose body stretched like elastic.

And worst of all, a hideous, lumbering thing. A walking nightmare with the strength of a whole blasted platoon, a freak for whom Mother Nature couldn't be held responsible.

His losing control of the spacecraft hadn't killed them. After all, the autopilot had taken over and landed them safely on Earth. But if the autopilot hadn't cut in, they could have been killed.

And what an irony that would have been. The four most powerful champions the Earth had ever known . . . destroyed in a crack-up before they even realized how powerful they were.

All because of him.

"It wasn't your fault," Reed told him, bringing him out of his reverie. "Not what happened that night, and not what happened to Johnny just now. Not your fault, you hear me?"

"I was the pilot," Ben insisted.

"And you did your best, Ben. That's all you can ever do. And it's a lot better than anyone else's best."

The Thing heaved a sigh. " 'Cept when it comes time to dole out blame. Seems whenever I feel guilty, I start heapin' it on you."

Just as he had that fateful night. He'd blamed Reed for what had happened, when they'd all known the risks. Hell, he'd tried to take his friend's head off with a tree trunk.

Reed smiled a weary smile. "Good thing I'm here, then. Otherwise, you might try to heap it on someone who can't take it."

For a moment, they just looked at each other. Ben's real brother had died when Ben was a teenager, but somehow, years later, he'd found another one. A guy who would take any risk, absorb any abuse, if he thought it would lessen his friend's pain.

"Jeez," Ben said. "I guess we're whatchamacallit ... bonding."

Reed made a face. "Yes, it's a real Kodak moment. Too bad we still have a considerable amount of work to do."

The Thing felt a rush of surprise. "Hey, Stretch, ya made a funny."

His friend dismissed the idea with a wave of his hand. "Reed Richards doesn't joke," he pointed out soberly.

"There," said Ben, pointing at him. "Ya did it again."

Reed rolled his eyes and reached for a tool. Then he ducked inside the control console again.

Just as well, the Thing thought. He was a whole lot better at clobbering things than laying his soul bare.

Sue Richards had long ago stopped looking at her fun-house reflection in the muscular contours of the Surfer's silver back. She didn't like the woman she saw in that reflection.

It was a long-faced woman. A worried woman. One who looked like she'd lost something more precious than life itself. *That's not me*, Sue kept telling herself. *That's someone else.*

The someone I used to be before the cosmic rays turned me into what I am—and more importantly, who I am.

Besides, she hadn't lost anything—at least, not yet. As long as her teammates were still ahead of her somewhere in the great beyond of the Negative Zone, still a goal beyond their grasp, she could embrace the hope they were alive and intact.

And so could the woman reflected in the Surfer's shimmering hide.

Suddenly, Sue saw the reflection writhe, taking on a different shape as the Surfer changed his stance. His head tilted ever so slightly to one side.

"What is it?" she asked.

"Something up ahead," he replied.

"My teammates?" she suggested. Her heart began to pound in her chest. After all, possibility was about to become reality. And it might not be the reality she'd desired.

As if sensing her trepidation, the Surfer reached back and brought her forward until she stood alongside him on his surfboard. Then he pointed into the star-flecked darkness.

"The trails lead to a vessel," he told her. "It is small. And damaged. And it is near a collection of other small, damaged vessels. If I were to venture a guess, I would say they had all been in conflict."

Sue peered into the distance. She didn't see anything at first. Only the passage of distant stars on either side of them.

Then she did see something. And a few seconds later, at the speed they were going, they were almost on top of it. As the Surfer slowed them down, she found herself dwarfed by a vast armada.

As he had said, its ships were damaged—dented and charred as if with enemy fire. Still, they weren't so banged up that she couldn't make out Blastaar's insignia on their hulls.

"These are Blastaar's ships," she told the Surfer. "If my teammates are in one of them, they're captives." She turned to him. "Which one did their trails lead to?"

He pointed. "That one."

Following his gesture, Sue saw a vessel much like all the others, but well apart from the pack. Its aft quarters had been caved in pretty badly, but it looked intact. And anyway, it wouldn't have mattered if there had been a breach. Here in the Negative Zone, the atmosphere outside the ships was the same as the atmosphere within.

The Surfer grunted softly. "That is strange." He turned his head slowly, his eyes alive as if following a thread she couldn't see.

"What is it?" she asked.

"Only two sets of emanations lead to the ship. A third leads . . ." His nostrils flared as he tried to follow it. "Elsewhere."

Sue swallowed. Which one of them was missing? She didn't want to know. Not yet. She still had work to do.

"Let's go inside," she said. "But watch out for Blastaar's troops."

"I will do that," the Surfer assured her.

They approached the ship in question and melted through its hull. Even before they were inside, Sue placed an invisible force field around them and also made both of them invisible—something even the Surfer could not do.

It turned out not to be necessary. There were only two people in the vessel. One was Ben. The other was Reed.

In her happiness at seeing them, she dropped the field and the invisibility. Both men did a double take as they saw Sue and the Surfer fade into view.

"Fer cryin' out loud!" the Thing growled. "Whaddaya ya tryin' ta do, gimme a heart attack?"

Her husband didn't say anything. Not at first, anyway. He just dropped the tool in his hand, reached across the cabin with his elongated arms, and folded her into his embrace.

"Reed," she said, basking in his nearness.

"Susan," he responded just as tenderly. Then he held her away to look at her. "You're all right?"

She nodded. "Thanks to the Surfer."

Reed glanced at the silver being standing on his surfboard, hovering just inches above the deck. "It's good to see you again," he said sincerely.

"The feeling is mutual," the Surfer assured him, his voice sounding even bigger and softer than usual in these confined quarters.

"Yeah," Ben chimed in. "*Real* mutual. The way things are goin', we can use a joker with some moxie." He glanced at the Invisible Woman. "You too, Suzie."

Suddenly, she remembered what the Surfer had said. "Where's Johnny?" she asked, though she dreaded the answer.

Reed sighed. "We were caught up in a battle between Blastaar and some mysterious entity. Johnny was trying to save us when he was seized by the entity's people." He gripped Sue's arms a little tighter. "The last I saw him, he seemed unconscious."

Or dead, she thought. But she didn't say it out loud.

The Surfer turned to Ben. "Then you commandeered this vessel for its propulsion capabilities." He took in the control console. "Though its helm does not seem to be responding."

"True enough," Reed told him. "But we didn't commandeer it. It was given to us, believe it or not." He paused. "By Blastaar."

Sue looked at him. "He *gave* it to you?"

The Thing shrugged. "I wouldn'ta believed it either, Suze. In fact, I wouldn'ta believed any of this."

Reed was the one who finally provided the explanation. He told his wife and the Surfer about their truce with Blastaar and the reason for it.

"By the time the battle reached its peak," Reed went on, "we still didn't have enough information to take sides. But we were in one of Blastaar's ships, so the entity's agents chose a side for us."

The Surfer thought for a moment. "To my knowledge, Galactus has never entered any galaxy but our own. I do not believe the entity has anything to do with him."

"Which doesn't mean it's not a threat," Reed reminded them.

"We've got to go after Johnny," Sue insisted. "And with the Surfer here, we won't need a ship to do it."

Ben scowled. "But how're we gonna *find* the squirt?"

"The same way the Surfer found us," Reed said. "By following a trail we make when we enter the Negative Zone." He eyed their silvery ally. "Something like that?"

The Surfer nodded. "Yes."

"Then what're we waiting for?" asked the Thing. "Ol' Blastface ain't gonna be too thrilled with us fer holdin' back during the battle—especially when he considers the result."

"Ben's right," Reed said. "We should—"

Suddenly, their vessel was rocked by a powerful outside force—something that filled the portals with blinding light. Before Sue could create a force field to protect them, she felt something soft surround her and cushion her collision with a bulkhead.

It was Reed, of course. As he uncoiled, freeing her, he grimaced and reached for his shoulder. Unfortunately, being pliable wasn't the same as being invulnerable.

"It's okay," Ben grumbled, extricating himself from under the control console. "Don't bother cushionin' *me*, Stretch. I'll just bounce around down here for a while."

The Surfer, of course, had needed no one's protection. He had remained perfectly upright, unaffected by the jolt.

Curious as to what had happened, Susan peered out an observation port. Her husband craned his neck to look over her shoulder. Neither of them had to look very long to find an answer.

"Speak of the devil," Reed muttered.

A vessel ten times the size of their own hung in the void. Susan didn't have to see Blastaar's face to know it was his flagship.

Reed turned to the Surfer. "Our shields held up under his first attack, but they may not survive another one. As I began to say earlier, we should extricate ourselves and begin our search while we still can."

The Surfer nodded. "As you wish." He indicated the silver board at his feet. "Please. Join me."

Susan was the first to step aboard. Reed and Ben came next. Then the Surfer melted them all through the battered bulkhead and brought them out into Negative Zone space—

—just as Blastaar unleashed another blinding barrage.

Before their eyes, their vessel caved in on itself like a pop can in the hands of a body builder, unable to withstand the massive force of the assault. Nothing inside the ship would have lived through it. They had escaped just in time.

The Surfer hesitated a second or two, as if intrigued by Blastaar's vessel. What's more, Susan understood. Having heard about the so-called Living Bomb-Burst from Reed, he had to be a little curious.

But not so curious that he would endanger the lives of his friends. As the vessel's weapons turrets swiveled in their direction, Susan could feel them start to glide through the void.

Before she could draw another breath, Blastaar's ship—and the rest of his armada—was only a distant speck. Apparently, they no longer needed to concern themselves with what was behind them.

Only with what was ahead.

Standing in front of the oversized monitor that dominated his bridge, Blastaar ground his teeth and cursed. The humans and their strange, silvery ally were speeding off into space.

This was not what he'd had in mind when he decided to lure the Fantastic Four into the Negative Zone. Not even close.

They were supposed to have seen the threat the planet-eater posed to both their galaxies. They were supposed to have added their power to Blastaar's, without stint or reservation. And together, they were supposed to have driven the upstart into the ground.

Somehow, it hadn't turned out that way.

The humans had undermined Blastaar's efforts with their reluctance to fight. They had betrayed him. And in the end, he had failed miserably because of it.

They owed him their pain for that. Their suffering, their humiliation. But now, the fates were trying to deny him even that much. They were trying to place the humans out of his reach.

The fates be damned, he thought. *I'm Blastaar. I take what I want.* And what he wanted at this moment, more than anything else in either galaxy, was revenge on the Fantastic Four.

"Pilot," he growled. "Follow them. Maximum speed."

"Yes, Emperor," came the reply.

Blastaar glanced over his shoulder at his communications technician. "Contact the remainder of the fleet," he spat. "I want them with us when we catch up to the humans."

After all, the silvery being had shown considerable speed and endurance. It might take more than one ship to bring him down.

"Yes, your excellency. The fleet is falling in behind us."

Blastaar turned back to the monitor. It was only a matter of time, he told himself. Then the humans would feel his wrath.

Their strange ally, too—whoever he was.

• • •

Johnny Storm woke up. And this time, he knew he wasn't dreaming.

There was no tropical sun hanging over him, no fragrant breeze caressing his skin. There was only the chamber of techno-horrors he'd woken to the first time, fused here and there with fireballs or scarred with blaster bursts. And as before, no sign of an exit.

Of course, the jumpsuit brigade was in evidence as well. There had to be more than a dozen of them clustered around him, each more attractive than the other. A good half of them were still armed and ready for action.

The woman with the golden skin and the raven hair was standing closest to Johnny. "How do you feel?" she asked.

He looked down at himself. He wasn't bound by restraints anymore. Obviously, his captors had seen how useless it was to tie him down. Experimentally, he sat up on his high-tech slab.

"Pretty good," he replied appraisingly, "considering some of the shots I took." He had a sudden flash of insight. "In fact, a little *too* good. I'll bet you injected me with a painkiller or something."

The woman nodded. "We anesthetized you, yes. But only where it was necessary. We wanted you alert so we could speak with you." Her expression changed, became apologetic. "So we could come to an understanding. You see, it wasn't our intention to alarm you in any way—only to learn more about your unusual cellular structure."

"And to do that," Johnny interpreted, "you were willing to make a pincushion out of me."

The apologetic expression disappeared. "You must remember," the woman said flatly, "you and your fleet attacked our vessel—not the other way around. All we did was try to learn more about our attackers."

Johnny shook his head. "The fleet may have attacked, but *I* didn't. I was in an observer vessel. I only came out when you started shooting at us."

The woman's eyes narrowed. "In that case," she replied at last, "I regret the incident. Unfortunately, our intentions are often misinterpreted by those who don't know us. When we see a fleet approaching, we tend to react reflexively." She paused, her expression softening again. "In any case, be assured we mean you no harm."

"That's good to hear," he told her. It was no lie.

"On the other hand," she said, "we can't allow you to damage our instruments with your flame power. If you agree to refrain from acts of violence, we will do the same. And of course, we will forgo any further analyses."

Johnny considered her. It seemed the woman was sincere. But then, he had always been a lousy judge of character. The one thing he knew was that he had to buy some time—figure out what was going on in here.

"Okay," he said at last. "It's a deal. I'll take it easy on the furnishings." Swinging his legs around, he slipped off the bed and held his hand out. "Johnny Storm."

It took the woman a moment or two to comprehend. Then she clasped his hand in her own. Her grip was even firmer than he had expected.

"My name is Tjellina," she told him. "I am Primary among the Outriders." She indicated her darkly clad comrades with a sweep of her arm. "These are Outriders as well."

Johnny looked at them. "Uh-huh. And if you don't mind my asking, exactly what does an Outrider do?"

"We work for Prodigion," she said, "the master of this ship. Our job is to scout ahead for planets worthy of his gifts— and when we find one, to bring it to his attention."

Johnny hadn't ever heard of Prodigion. But the kind of service the Outriders performed for him sounded exactly like what the Surfer had done for Galactus. In effect, these women were Prodigion's "heralds"—and they didn't seem the least bit ashamed of it.

Geez, he thought. *Maybe Blastaar wasn't so far off the mark with his ravings about a planet-eater. Hell, Prodigion could just be a name Galactus uses when he goes slumming in the Negative Zone.*

Johnny swallowed. This could be big, he realized.

And bad. *Very* bad.

"So," he responded with a casualness he didn't feel, "if your job is to scout for planets, why aren't you off scouting now—instead of running tests on me?"

"There's no pressing need to scout right now," Tjellina

explained. "We had just discovered a suitable planet and were returning to inform Prodigion when we detected your fleet. In fact, our vessel is headed for that planet even as we speak."

Johnny remembered what it was like when Galactus came to Earth. The terrible pit he'd felt in his belly as he—along with the rest of humanity—waited for the axe to fall.

And now Prodigion, whoever he was, was going to do the same thing to some unsuspecting world. Some innocent civilization.

No, Johnny told himself. *I can't allow that kind of death and destruction—not on Earth or anywhere else. I'm going to stop it.*

I don't know how, he added. *But one way or another, I'm going to put a great big monkey wrench in Prodigion's plans.*

Just then, a panel in the wall slid away and another Outrider came in. She had some kind of gizmo in her hand—probably some kind of report for Tjellina. But Johnny didn't really care what it was. His only interest was in the exit that had suddenly presented itself.

"I hope we can put our hostilities aside," Tjellina was saying. "I imagine there's a lot we can learn from one another."

Johnny looked her in the eye. "Don't bet on it," he told her.

Then he made a dash for the opening in the wall, activating his power en route without his customary battle cry. Sometimes there just wasn't time for it—and now was one of those times.

Johnny could hear Tjellina's cry of protest as he straightarmed the Outrider who'd entered and dove headlong through the exit, already crackling with yellow flames. Too late, his captors sent a barrage of energy bursts after him. An abrupt midair turn took him out of harm's way, and the blasts struck the bulkhead instead.

A moment later, he was speeding down the corridor as only he could, his ruddy brilliance reflecting off every surface in sight. The Outriders' shouts of outrage faded quickly with distance.

The Torch had no idea where he was going or what he was going to do when he got there. But he wasn't going to worry about that just yet. He was simply going to scour the corridors of Prodigion's mothership until he found something that looked like an opportunity.

And when he found it, he was going to jump on it with both flaming feet.

Nine

Blastaar brought his fist down on the end of his vessel's navigation console, crushing the delicate circuitry within and eliciting a white-hot geyser of sparks.

Caught in the blinding spray, his navigator fell backward, clutching his face and groaning with pain. The smell of his blackened flesh filled the bridge, drawing the uneasy attention of the other Baluurians.

Especially that of his pilot, who had given Blastaar the bad news in the first place.

"What do you mean you can no longer follow them?" the tyrant bellowed, making the bulkheads shake with his fury.

His pilot couldn't look at him directly. Swallowing hard, he kept his gaze fixed on his controls. "The humans are too fast for us, Emperor. They've disappeared from our sensor grid."

Blastaar turned to the monitor, which showed only a splash of streaking stars. No sign of the cursed Fantastic Four or their ally. Despite his thirst for revenge, they had eluded him.

Eluded him!

He raised his fist to strike the console again, then stopped himself. For what seemed like a long time, he fought the fury burning inside him—fought his blind, unreasoning hatred for the humans.

In the end, he won.

It was a good thing, too. It would only hurt him to destroy his flagship—or, for that matter, any other piece of equipment. He still needed it to fight the planet-eater, who was every bit as much a threat now as before.

Lowering his fist, Blastaar glanced at his pilot again. "It is not your fault they escaped," he declared. "You did what you could."

The Baluurian regarded him, a glint of hope in his eyes. "That is true, Emperor. I did what I could."

Blastaar eyed his fallen navigator, who was being removed

from the bridge, still moaning and clutching at his face. "And my anger has already caused much suffering—has it not?"

The pilot hesitated. Obviously, he didn't want to push his luck.

But Blastaar wasn't satisfied. "I asked you a question. Has my anger not already caused much suffering?"

The pilot grimaced. "I would have to say . . . it has caused *some* suffering, my emperor."

"But not an excessive amount?" Blastaar pressed.

The pilot licked his lips. "No," he ventured. "Not excessive."

"Just the right amount?"

"Yes, my lord. The right amount."

Blastaar glowered at him, his mouth full of bile. "I disagree," he said in a low, dangerous voice.

Then he grabbed his pilot by the throat, cutting off the Baluurian's air supply, and lifted him out of his seat. And kept lifting him, higher and higher, until the pilot's thrashing feet cleared the deck.

The Baluurian struggled to pry his emperor's fingers loose—to no avail. He kicked at Blastaar's knees and belly and groin—also to no avail. And the more he struggled, the darker and more swollen his face became.

Finally, the pilot began to black out, to succumb to the loss of air. Blastaar didn't like that. He loosened his grip just enough to revive his victim, to keep him alive and alert.

Then, with a deft and economical flick of his powerful wrist, he snapped the pilot's neck.

Equipment was in short supply, he mused. But there was no shortage of Baluurians—especially those who could tolerate defeat.

Allowing the pilot's body to hit the deck with a thud, he eyed the rest of his bridge contingent. They were clearly shaken by what they'd seen, as much as they tried to conceal it.

"No one fails Blastaar, you hear me?" His eyes raked each and every one of them as the place echoed with his thunder. "No one!"

"Hail Blastaar!" they chorused in return.

But he didn't care about their homage. He didn't need it. What he needed was another fleet, he told himself—before his empire was rent asunder.

•　•　•

The first time Reed had seen the entity's ship, he was awed by it. After all, he had witnessed something of that magnitude and complexity only once before—and it had been blotting out the sky over Manhattan, an emblem of humanity's imminent extinction.

Now, as the Surfer began to catch up with the entity's vessel, bringing it closer and closer with each passing heartbeat, Reed found he'd gotten over his awe. He was simply intrigued, as he would have been by anything he didn't entirely understand.

But he would understand it, he promised himself that. He would get to know it well enough to free his brother-in-law. And then, one way or another, he would find out the purpose of its mysterious owner.

Though the vessel was traveling at a formidable rate of speed, judging by the urgency with which the rest of the Negative Zone whipped by, the Surfer overtook it seemingly without effort. Then, matching its course and velocity, he turned to Reed.

"There is no evidence of the force shields of which you spoke," the Surfer observed with just a hint of surprise.

Reed studied the vessel's outer hull. "Maybe they only go up when its sensors register an attack. Or at least the prospect of one."

The Thing grunted. "Obviously, those sensors don't know us too well. I say we stop flappin' our gums and start clobberin' our way in."

"Hang on a minute," Reed cautioned him. "Force shields may only be part of the ship's security array. We don't know what we'll run into if we try to barge our way in."

Sue glanced at the Surfer. "Can't we just melt through the hull," she asked, "the way we melted through the hull of Blastaar's ship?"

The Surfer frowned. "Perhaps. But if this is anything like Galactus's ship, there will be undetectable defenses within the structure of the hull itself—some of them lethal, even to me. Likewise, any force we bring to bear will only be met with greater force."

Ben threw his arms up. "So we just camp out in front of it? Maybe tell some ghost stories and roast marshmallows while we're at it?"

"Now that you mention it," Sue said, "that may be the best option we've got." She bit her lip, obviously trying to keep a level head despite her concern for Johnny. "I mean, what if we were to just wait on the doorstep and see what happens?"

"What'll happen is we'll get pounded," the Thing predicted.

"Or ignored," Reed suggested, "which may be worse." He stroked his chin for a moment. "On the other hand, the entity must already know we're here. We're not going to lose anything by demonstrating some patience."

Ben made a sound of disgust. "I still say we clobber our way in."

But he was outvoted. So, despite his periodic protests, they hovered in front of the vessel and made no demands. In fact, they did nothing at all.

Time passed slowly. Long seconds turned into longer minutes. Reed imagined their image on a thousand monitors throughout the ship—and a single, brooding presence trying to decide what to do with them.

After what must have been a good half hour, nothing had happened. No tactical response, no attempt to communicate, nothing.

Ben swore under his breath. "What a revoltin' development *this* is."

"Hang in there," Susan counseled. "Give it a little more time."

"But this isn't gettin' us anywhere," the Thing insisted. He folded his arms across his rocky chest. "I mean, if I had even the slightest suspicion we were gonna get the welcome mat rolled out—"

Suddenly, two sections of the hull lifted and slid aside, revealing what looked a great deal like an empty air lock. Sue turned to Ben.

"You were saying?" she gibed.

The Thing glowered at her. "So I was wrong. So sue me."

"We should enter while we can," the Surfer advised them. "The entity's patience may not be as great as ours."

"Of course," Reed noted, "it could be a trap. But considering the circumstances, I suppose we can cross that bridge when we come to it."

"Amen ta that," Ben rumbled.

"Let's go," Sue said.

Reed nodded to the Surfer. Slowly, cautiously, they slid into the air lock. A moment later, the hull sections slid back into place, sealing them in.

Ten

The Torch had known Prodigion's ship was big—he just hadn't realized how big. But he was learning fast.

Each corridor seemed to stretch for miles, lined with exposed circuitry and conduits and equipment—the purpose of which he couldn't begin to decipher. When a corridor ended and he had to turn right or left, he found another one just like it.

There was no sign of the Outriders. No sign of Prodigion, either. In fact, there was no sign of anyone, just the Torch's flaming reflection in the deck, the ceiling, and the bulkheads as he hurtled by.

The longer his trek went on, the less optimistic he became about succeeding in his mission. After all, the Outriders would have warned Prodigion about his escape as soon as it happened. And, alerted to the danger, their boss would have set up his defenses.

Sure, he thought. That's what anyone would do when they had a threat running around loose on their ship. They would do their best to get rid of it. To eradicate it.

But what if Prodigion didn't see him as a threat? What if he considered the Torch nothing more than a gadfly—someone he could swat at his leisure?

He pondered the possibility as he turned and rocketed the length of yet another corridor. If this were Galactus's vessel, he probably wouldn't have done a thing about the news of his prisoner's escape. He would just have waited until the Torch confronted him and blown him away.

Was that what Prodigion had in mind? Was he planning to blow him away when the time came?

The Torch pressed his lips together. Let him try. Maybe he thought he had just another helpless victim on his hands. If so, he was in for a surprise. Mama Storm's little boy didn't go down without a fight.

Hell, Johnny mused, if he had a nickel for every madman and megalomaniac who had underestimated him in a clinch, he'd have been able to buy Tony Stark a hundred times over. And Prodigion wasn't going to be any—

He stopped himself in midthought as he caught sight of something far down the corridor. Three figures, he realized. And only one of them looked female, so it couldn't be the Outriders.

In fact, as Johnny got closer to them, he saw that one of the figures didn't even look humanoid. He was too broad, too craggy-looking, too—

—orange?

Suddenly, the Torch realized whom he was flying at. It was Ben. And the two figures with him were Reed and Sue. He could barely believe his eyes.

It was them. It was really *them*.

"Reed!" he yelled. "Sue! Ben!"

His brother-in-law pointed to him as the echoes of the Torch's voice filled the corridor. "Johnny!" cried his sister.

Refusing to wait a moment longer to be reunited with them, the Torch accelerated his flight. All around him, the corridor sizzled with the speed of his passage.

This was good, he thought. This was very good. His teammates were here on the ship. Together, they would do what he'd been unable to do on his own—find Prodigion and stop him from destroying that world.

Then Johnny realized that his teammates weren't alone. There was someone with them—someone casting a shadow from a perpendicular corridor.

An Outrider?

Johnny's hands clenched into fists as he bore down harder than ever. Reed, Sue, Ben . . . they didn't know what those women were like. He had to get to them before it was too late.

Then the figure emerged into the Torch's line of sight—and his heart leapt. It was the Surfer, he told himself—the Silver Surfer! The same alien who had confronted Galactus in the skies over New York and fought his boss to a standstill.

Of all the reinforcements Johnny could possibly have hoped for, the dude with the surfboard was tops on his list. In fact, he *was* the list.

Suddenly, the situation had turned completely around. The good guys weren't on the run anymore. Now they were in charge. If Prodigion had had a problem with the Human Torch, his problem had just multiplied dramatically.

Putting on the brakes so he didn't rocket right by his friends, Johnny alighted on the deck in front of them and flamed off. Before he could say anything, his sister ran forward and took him in her arms.

"Oh, Johnny," she said, hugging him hard. "When are you going to learn not to be such a hero?"

"Uh, I don't know." He chuckled. "Never?"

Still hugging him, she gave his head a swat. "I'm serious," she insisted.

"Hey," he responded, "take it easy. I'm okay, see? And I've got some news about the character who owns this rig."

"What kind of news?" Reed asked.

Johnny turned to him. "His name's Prodigion—and Blastaar was pretty much on the money about him. The guy's a threat to the Zone all right, the same way Galactus is a threat in our universe. In fact, this ship is headed for a nice, juicy planet right now, so ol' Prodigion can suck it dry."

"How do you know this?" the Surfer inquired in that strange, soft voice of his. The mention of Galactus had gotten him good and interested.

"Yeah, how?" Ben rumbled, casting Johnny a skeptical glance. "And don't tell me ya saw it on the flippin' Discovery Channel."

"Actually," the teenager told them, "I heard it from—"

His explanation was cut short by the scrape of metal against metal—as slots opened in the ceiling in front and in back of them and a dozen Outriders pelted down like rain.

Each one carried a blaster in her arms. Judging by the looks on their faces, they hadn't come to lay out the welcome mat.

"—them," Johnny finished.

"They don't seem very forthcoming now," his sister remarked, looking from one squad of Outriders to the other.

"We didn't part on the best of terms," Johnny noted.

Then he burst into flame again. After all, the Outriders' blasts had knocked him for a loop as the Torch. He didn't want to have to face them without his flame power for protection.

Suddenly, the Surfer made Johnny's concerns academic. Turning to the Outriders in front of them, he sent their weapons flying down the corridor with a backhanded flip of his wrist. Then he did the same for the weapons of the Outriders behind them.

"If what Johnny Storm says is true," the Surfer told them, "you are murderers in the service of an even greater murderer. And I have sworn never to countenance such evil."

The Torch had never heard such outrage, such hostility in the Surfer's voice. Not for the Outriders themselves, he thought, as much as for the crimes they had committed.

The Surfer held out his hands to the women in front of them. "Stop," he urged them. "Consider the depravity of your deeds—the lives you tear asunder, the civilizations you destroy. Surely, if you weigh these precious commodities against your master's needs, you'll see how wrong it is to oblige him."

One of the Outriders stepped forward—a woman with long, auburn hair and pure white skin, which stood in contrast to the black of her jumpsuit. When she spoke, it was with a trill in her voice.

"You misunderstand us," she told the Surfer. "Some of what your friend told you is true—but also, much is not. You are clearly an enlightened being—one endowed with compassion as well as intellect. Before you pass any kind of judgment on us, we would like you to learn more of our ways. And, of course, of our master's ways as well."

"It's a con job," the Torch argued. "You saw those blasters they brought along. What else do you need to know about them?"

"Johnny's got a point," his sister agreed.

Reed stroked his chin. "Except we've got nothing to lose by listening to them. If they think we're making a mistake, why not give them a chance to convince us of it?"

The Torch muttered a curse. "Reed, you don't know these Outriders the way I do. When I woke up here, they were poking and prodding me like I was a lab rat or something."

His brother-in-law frowned. "If our positions were reversed, I'd have been tempted to do the same thing."

Susan didn't say anything. Neither did Ben. But the Torch had the feeling they were on Reed's side, as usual.

He turned to the Surfer. "These people are dangerous. You can see that, can't you?"

Facial muscles moved beneath that silver skin. "I have only your word in that regard, Johnny Storm."

The Torch couldn't believe this. "What about those blasters you took away from them? Doesn't that make you wonder about them even a little—like maybe they don't have our best interests at heart?"

The Surfer considered that for a moment. "This is their ship," he said at last. "It may be they were only defending it."

Johnny stared at his friends. "Gimme a break here. You're really going to buy this line of bull?"

The Thing grunted. "We hobnobbed with Blastaar, didn't we? I guess we can hang with a buncha Amazons in jumpsuits."

"For a time," the Surfer added. "Just long enough to discern the truth of what they say. And if their testimonies ring false"—he put his hand on the Torch's shoulder, undaunted by the snapping flames there—"then our hosts will rue the moment they met us. I promise you that with all my heart."

Johnny looked at the Surfer and saw the alien's confidence. His self-assurance. It calmed him down.

"Okay," he said, turning to the auburn-haired Outrider. "We're listening. You can start talking."

The Outrider shook her head. "I'm not the one who speaks for the Outriders. That's Tjellina's job."

"Who?" asked Ben.

"Their leader," the Torch replied. He turned to the Surfer. "You're going to love Tjellina. She's *lots* of fun."

The silver being didn't say anything. He just gazed at the teenager.

Johnny hoped the Surfer hadn't taken the remark literally. Sometimes, it was hard to tell with him.

The Surfer had to confess his fascination with the Outriders, if only to himself. They didn't seem like unreasonable beings. And yet, if they were guilty of the crimes of which Johnny Storm had accused them, they were hideous creatures indeed.

But no less hideous than the creature he himself had been while serving as the Herald of Galactus. The acts of destruction they accommodated could not have been worse than the acts he had accommodated.

And that was what fascinated him.

For if Prodigion was another Galactus, and these females his Heralds, the Surfer had a chance to make up for his misdeeds in some small measure. He had an opportunity to relieve the burden of guilt he carried with him always, if only by the weight of a single stone.

If he could stop Prodigion's cadre of advance scouts, make them see the error of their ways, he could stave off the destruction of millions of precious lives. And if he could stop Prodigion himself . . . would that not go a long way toward balancing the scales?

Would it not redeem him in some way? Make him whole again? Or, if not quite that, at least represent the beginning of his redemption?

Of course, this all presupposed that Johnny Storm was right, and that Prodigion was as awful a force as Galactus. There was still a possibility that the Outriders' claims were true.

In any case, he had agreed to reserve judgment, to keep an open mind. And that was what he would do until the truth became apparent to him.

Such were the Surfer's thoughts as the Outriders guided him and the Fantastic Four through the byways of Prodigion's vessel. They fell upward through throbbing antigravity arteries, sped along on high-velocity walkways, spiraled down through wells of shimmering light.

Finally, they reached their destination—a well-appointed chamber, in which abstract form and subtle colors worked together to create a most admirable harmony. And in the center of the chamber, between two elegant fountains, stood a woman with raven hair and flawless, golden skin.

She approached her visitors—the Surfer first of all. "My name is Tjellina," she told him. "Primary among the Outriders."

Her voice was soft, melodious. Yet a thread of strength ran through it, a vitality for which he had not been prepared. He found the combination quite pleasant—but no more so than the lustrous blackness of her eyes.

"I am called the Silver Surfer," he replied.

Tjellina looked into his eyes, unable to hide her curiosity. "You are a remarkable being, Silver Surfer."

"All beings are remarkable," he said.

Her eyes crinkled slightly at the corners. "Most remarkable indeed." She turned to the Fantastic Four. "Please, make yourselves comfortable. It may take a while to answer your questions."

"Unless you answer them directly," Johnny Storm interjected. "Then it won't take long at all."

Tjellina regarded the Torch. "I attempted to be direct with you earlier. Perhaps this time, I'll find a way to make my meaning more clear."

Johnny Storm inclined his head. The Surfer recognized it as a traditional Terran gesture of respect, though he suspected it was rendered ironically in this case.

"All right," the Torch said, his flame burning even hotter. "Make *this* clear, Tjellina. Tell me how you can live with yourself knowing the things you've done for Prodigion."

The woman lifted her chin. "I've done nothing wrong in serving Prodigion. In fact, I revel in the knowledge of all I've done right."

She scanned each face in turn—first the Surfer's, then Reed's, Susan's, Ben's, and Johnny's. "Contrary to what you seem to think, the Outriders' motives are pure. Just as Prodigion's are pure."

"Pure devastation," the Torch persisted.

Tjellina shook her head. "Not at all. Prodigion doesn't bring death to a planet's inhabitants. Far from it." She smiled reverently. "What he brings them, my friends, is life."

Eleven

Blastaar walked up the steps of his Council Building in a very bad mood.

He felt the clammy heat of the Baluurian night. He drank in the sweet scent of twice-blooming firethorns and listened to the cannibal worms chirp in their sticky web-sacs.

Normally, these things had a calming effect on him. Normally, they eased his nerves. But not this night.

The only thing that would subdue his anxiety now was a plan for rebuilding his mighty armada. Which was, after all, why he had roused his council from slumber. If the twelve wisest men on Baluur couldn't come up with a scheme for him, who could? That was why he let them continue to live, after all.

Coming to the top of the steps, he flung open the heavy wooden doors of the Council Building. Inside, a single rectangular chamber took up the entire edifice, illuminated by huge, standing torches.

Its walls and vaulted ceiling, made of rare northern shell-stone, reflected the firelight in shimmering iridescences. Its bloodmarble floor was bisected by a path of volcanic black-facet, which ended in a massive, raised throne also carved from bloodmarble.

On either side of the blackfacet path stood a semicircle of more modest stone chairs, arranged to face the throne. And before each chair stood an aged, bleary-eyed Baluurian, dressed in the plain gray robes of a councillor.

"All hail Blastaar!" they cried as one.

Making his way along the line of blackfacet, the tyrant ascended the several steps that led to his seat. Then he turned and sat and eyed his ministers with contempt—the same way he eyed all his fellow Baluurians.

"Here is the problem," he rasped.

Then he went on to describe his defeat at the hands of the

world-destroyer and his need for another fleet. No, he amended, not just another fleet—a star-spanning force whose power was many times that of the first. A juggernaut against which even the planet-killer couldn't prevail.

"What I want to know," he said, leaning forward on his throne, "is where I'm likely to obtain such a fleet."

For a moment, there was only silence. Then Haggan, the eldest of his councillors, spoke up.

"Before we respond," he said, "we need some assurance that you will not blast us."

Blastaar looked at him. "Assurance?" he spat.

"Yes, my liege. As you'll recall, the last time you put a question of this magnitude to the council, you didn't like the answer you got. As a result, you blasted your councillors into bits and pieces—which is how we came to sit in their places."

The tyrant scowled. "So you want me to promise I won't destroy you with a neutron blast?"

Haggan nodded. "Yes, my lord. Or strangle us or beat us to death, or cause others to."

Blastaar ground his teeth together. "I should blast you now, for your impudence."

The councillor paled noticeably. "You could," he conceded, his voice a bit more shaky than before. "But then you would not have had the benefit of our wisdom. And you would have to comb Baluur for suitable replacements, as you did the last time."

With an effort, the tyrant swallowed back his fury. Haggan had a point there. He needed answers—and quickly. This was the wrong time to cut himself off from the likeliest source of them.

"All right," he said at last. "You have my word . . . I won't blast you." And he couldn't go back on his word, lest his pact with his people fall apart. His eyes narrowed. "Now what can I do about my problem?"

The councillor sighed. "Precious little, I'm afraid. As you must know, none of the other powers in known space will agree to ally themselves with you, no matter the magnitude of the threat. To put it simply, they don't trust you. They believe you'll turn on them, as you have on other occasions."

Another councillor, a portly specimen named Gruuth, found the courage to speak. "Pinda of Toraxis would be an example, my lord. As would Uroq of Esanaia. As you'll recall, both monarchs have had cause to rue their dealings with you.''

"Under different circumstances,'' said a councillor called Norux, "conquest would be an option. In other words, my liege, the assimilation of smaller forces into our own. Unfortunately, we no longer have a big enough fleet to accomplish that.''

"True,'' Haggan agreed. "No battle would be lopsided enough to serve our purpose. We would end up in a prolonged conflict, spending the last of our strength for no real gain.''

Blastaar shook his head. "What are you saying? That I should give up? Allow the planet-destroyer to consume my empire—maybe Baluur itself?''

The councillors didn't like the sound of that. It was evident in the way they kneaded their hands and exchanged glances.

"Actually,'' Gruuth ventured, "our astronomers are now questioning their original conclusions. It appears the world-eater may not cut through the heart of our empire after all. At worst, he may claim a dozen tributary planets.''

The tyrant could feel his fingers curling into fists. "And what if he decides to change course? What do our astronomers say about that?''

More kneading of hands. More nervous glances.

"I don't know,'' Gruuth admitted, in a decidedly smaller voice than before.

Blastaar glowered at him. "Do we sit here and watch as all we've built comes crashing down around us? Do we applaud politely as the world-eater tears apart our civilization?''

Haggan held his hands out, frightened now beyond his ability to conceal it. "But what else can we do, my liege?''

The tyrant was on his feet before he knew it, propelled by white-hot rage. His hands opened and closed, eager for a windpipe to crush.

"That's what I came here to ask *you!*'' he bellowed, making the chamber shake with his fury.

Then another councillor, the youngest of them, raised a tremulous voice. His name was Jonat. "My lord,'' he said uncertainly, as if the idea were still forming in his mind, "I think I may have a suggestion.''

"And what is that?'' Blastaar roared, still caught up in the blistering heat of his wrath.

Jonat swallowed hard. "The Bolovite Union," he replied.

And the councillor went on to explain the opportunity he saw there. The chance for the tyrant to achieve what he needed to achieve, and quickly enough for it to make a difference.

Blastaar considered the option Jonat had presented. He turned it over in his mind, seeking a flaw. And he could find only one—the possibility that his strength wouldn't be sufficient to the task.

But if that was the only variable, he mused, the Bolovite Union was as good as his. And with something like that under his belt, combined with the threat of the world-eater, he could easily force others to join his cause.

The tyrant considered Jonat. "I believe we have formulated a plan," he announced. "But how is it you know so much about the Bolovites, Councillor?"

Jonat shrugged. "My cousin's cousin has traded with a freighter captain who knows them. I've been regaled with tales about the Bolovites for years."

Blastaar winced. "If I were you, I would hope my cousin's cousin and his friend the captain were sober when they passed these tales along. Because if the information is unreliable, we will all live to regret it—you most of all, Councillor."

Jonat's eyes went wide. "Yes, my lord."

The tyrant turned to Haggan. "As for you . . . you knew you would be useless to me when you extracted my pledge not to blast you."

"Or to strangle us or beat us to death," Gruuth reminded him. "Or to cause others to."

"Yes," Blastaar spat. "All that. You knew you would have no answers for me, yet you demanded my pledge anyway."

"The truth," Haggan admitted, "was we demanded it *because* we had no answers." He smiled. "But Jonat seems to have done the impossible, providing you with an answer after all. We should all be pleased."

The tyrant regarded Jonat. "Come here," he grated.

Jonat paled. "Yes, my lord." Trundling forward in his gray robes, he made his way up the bloodmarble steps to stand before his master.

Blastaar looked past him at the other councillors. "It seems to me your wisdom has abandoned you," he said, "in more ways than one. Otherwise, you would also have extracted from me a promise not to redecorate.''

And before any of them could figure out what he was talking about, the tyrant pointed to the vaulted ceiling. Then he seared the air with a mighty blast of raw neutrons.

The shellstone cracked under Blastaar's onslaught and came away in huge chunks. And as they came away, they smashed whatever was below them—whether it was the floor or some flesh and blood that happened to be in the way.

Seeing the fate that had been decreed for them, the councillors screamed, but they were too old to get out of the way. And before their screams had stopped echoing, ten of them had been crushed to death.

Other than Jonat, only Haggan still lived—though in Haggan's case, the lower half of his body was little more than a stain amid the rubble. He groaned in his pain and pleaded for his liege lord's mercy.

"A quick death is all I ask," he whispered, stretching a bloody hand toward Blastaar's throne.

"Sorry," the tyrant told him. "I've promised not to blast you or strangle you or beat you to death or . . ." He thought for a moment. "Oh yes, not to cause others to. And I always keep my promises."

As Haggan continued to plead and claw at the floor beneath him, Blastaar turned to a stricken Jonat. "Gather eleven of your wisest friends," the tyrant told him. "And be quick about it. I'll need a new council as soon as the ceiling is repaired."

Jonat nodded. "Yes, my lord."

Blastaar started down the bloodmarble steps. "If anyone asks," he threw back over his shoulder, "I'm on my way to Bolov Prime."

The Surfer considered the raven-haired Outrider. "Life?" he repeated, taken aback by the claim.

"That's correct," Tjellina said.

"Ya mean your boss doesn't go around sucking planets dry? Depletin' 'em of their energy?" the Thing grumbled.

"He does nothing of the sort," the woman confirmed.

"Wait a minute," Johnny interjected. "You told me he goes from planet to planet and 'bestows his gifts upon them.' "

"Again, correct," said Tjellina.

"Well," the Torch went on, "we know someone back in our universe who does the same thing. His name's Galactus. And believe me, no one wants the kind of gifts he's giving."

The Outrider tilted her head slightly as she gazed at him. "I see," she said finally. "You believed our reference to Prodigion's 'gifts' to be a euphemism for something sinister. I assure you, nothing could be further from the truth."

"Then what is the truth?" Reed inquired. "Who is this Prodigion, and what, specifically, does he do to these worlds you find for him?"

The Outrider turned to him. "No one knows where Prodigion came from or when his life began. Even Prodigion himself claims not to know. However, for as long as he can remember, he has been a mysterious component of the universal balance—one who distributes the force of life on planet after planet throughout the galaxy."

She gestured to indicate the bulkheads that rose all around them. "That is why Prodigion built this incredible ship. As you must know, planets are few and far between, and worlds capable of sustaining life even farther.

"Of course," she went on, "there are always those who rise to oppose Prodigion, failing to understand him—or motivated by self-interest to stifle his life-giving impulses. However, Prodigion does what he must, always and invariably, despite their opposition."

Johnny grunted. "Uh-huh. And speaking of motivations, what's in it for him? A nice card at Christmastime?"

Obviously, Tjellina didn't understand the reference. But she must have gotten the gist of it, because she smiled tautly.

"Prodigion doesn't act out of need or desire," she explained. "He simply does what he must. That's his role in the universe. It's his destiny."

"Right," Johnny replied. "And I suppose it's our destiny to snap this up hook, line, and sinker."

"You may believe what you wish," Tjellina told him. "All I can do is give you what you asked for—the truth."

There was something about the intelligence with which she spoke, the utter confidence with which she carried herself, that made it difficult to mistrust the Outrider.

Nor was it only trust Tjellina evoked in the Surfer. There

was something else, he realized. And it surprised him that it should be so.

After a moment, he realized he was staring at her. What's more, she was returning his scrutiny. Had he been capable of blushing, he would no doubt have done that.

"The problem with the truth," he noted, "is it signifies different things to different people. It would be more convincing if you could provide proof of your claims."

Tjellina seemed to ponder his suggestion. "Very well," she responded at last. "I'll make accessible all the proof you require. But it will be up to you to find it."

Reed looked at her. "What do you mean?"

The woman shrugged. "I will open this vessel to you in its entirety—with the exception, of course, of Prodigion's private compartments. You may examine our equipment, pore through our data banks, inspect our operating logs—whatever you wish. And you will have Outrider escorts to explain what you do not understand."

"To make sure we see what you want us to see," Johnny countered.

Tjellina sighed. "You may take advantage of the escorts or not. It is completely up to you."

The Surfer glanced at his companions. Reed seemed eager to take the Outrider up on her offer. Neither Susan nor the Thing appeared ready to object. Only Johnny seemed outwardly skeptical, but even he wasn't expressing his doubts out loud.

"We accept your offer," Reed told the Outrider.

She nodded. "Good. It would displease Prodigion if his guests misinterpreted his motives." Her features softened. "And to be honest, it would displease me as well."

She looked directly at the Surfer as she said it. Again, he was inclined to blush, though perhaps a bit less so than before.

Norrin Radd would not have felt so awkward in the presence of this Outrider. Norrin Radd would have taken her scrutiny in stride. But then, in so many ways, he was no longer Norrin Radd.

Twelve

The amphitheater that surrounded Blastaar and his opponent was ancient and bone white, with walls that climbed a thousand feet into a dense, ocher-colored storm front. Clouds trundled across the sky like shaggy, brown beasts crowding to get a better look inside.

The arena boasted fully half a million seats, and every one of them was occupied by the slick, scaly carcass of a hulking, blue-skinned Bolovite. In the streets that radiated from the arena like the spokes of a wheel, the government had set up remote viewscreens, so that several million additional Bolovites could witness the event as it unfolded.

And unfold it would, Blastaar told himself. Just as his adversary's intestines would unfold when he freed them from their lair in his adversary's stomach cavity.

His lip curled as he caressed the edge of his Bolovite ceremonial blade with a blunt, powerful finger. Across the barren stretch of land that made up their battlefield, the gigantic Krona of Bolov Prime did the same, muscles rippling sinuously beneath his scarred serpentine hide, ruby-red eyes slitted with barely contained fury. His long, forked tongue darted in and out of his mouth in anticipation.

Krona wasn't just the most powerful being on his world, he was the most powerful being in the entire Bolovite Union, which included six planets full of Bolovites, several dozen outposts, and some thirty subject populations stretching over seven star systems.

However, what interested Blastaar most about Krona's holdings was the fleet he had used to seize and secure them. It was nearly twice the size of Blastaar's own—even before Prodigion decimated the Baluurian armada.

The Living Bomb-Burst didn't like losing. He was determined not to lose again—not to Prodigion or anyone else.

Which was where Krona came in—and the information

Councillor Jonat had provided about him. According to Bolovite custom, anyone could challenge the reigning monarch at any time, even an offworlder. Of course, such challenges were few and far between these days, considering the size and strength and quickness of Krona—a one-warrior army who had taken the throne from the previous monarch, his late and unlamented father.

But Blastaar wanted the Bolovite fleet. And if getting it meant clawing the crown away from Krona, so be it.

There was only one catch. Blastaar was restricted to the conventional use of his arms and legs and teeth. No application of his natural ability to generate massive and deadly neutron blasts or his victory wouldn't count, no matter how decisive. He would then have to conquer the Bolovite Union world by world if he wanted control of its fleet, and he wasn't equipped for that kind of strategy at the moment.

So he would rely on his other talents to carry the day. No doubt Krona thought he would have a chance in such a circumstance. Blastaar would have to show him the error of his ways.

Abruptly, a rasping, grating cheer went up in the seats all about him, wave upon wave like the crash of a titanic surf on a rocky shore. It drowned out even the mumbling thunder.

The Baluurian turned and saw the reason for it. The aged official who would oversee the contest, draped in flawless white robes, had emerged from the single arch that let out onto the battlefield. His head bobbed on his spindly neck with each uncertain step.

Clearly, he had done this before. But never when the challenge had been posed by a Baluurian, who could annihilate him with a single gesture—and would, if sufficiently provoked.

The official made his way to the center of the area. Up above, threads of lightning as white as his robes, as white as the amphitheater itself, began to stitch the clouds. Thunder droned, audible now as the crowd noises abated.

"This is the challenge," the official said, his voice thin and reedy—yet amplified to resounding proportions by some technology Blastaar neither knew nor cared about. "The challenger is Blastaar of Baluur. The challenged is our monarch, Krona of Bolov Prime. This is the challenge." His old eyes slitted with the seriousness of his announcement—though why he had to say it twice was another thing Blastaar neither knew nor cared about.

"Get on with it," Blastaar spat, his every word a weapon.

But the Bolovite didn't move. At least, not yet. He raised his eyes to the crowds in front of him.

"If the mighty Krona is defeated, he yields all his lands and possessions to the challenger. And if Blastaar is defeated, he yields all *his* lands and possessions to the mighty Krona."

"What?" the Baluurian bellowed, the arena echoing with his fury. "I never agreed to that!"

The official turned to him, his eyes wide with fear. He swallowed hard, a lump crawling up and down the length of his scrawny throat.

"It . . . it is our tradition," he murmured.

Blastaar thought about it for a moment. If he lost—which he had no intention of doing—what did he care who ruled Baluur? His subjects had exiled him into space once before. They deserved whatever they got.

On the other hand, he didn't like the fact that no one had informed him of this particular tradition until now. But he could deal with such matters after the Bolovites were added to his empire.

"Leave," he told the official. "While you still can."

The robed one didn't have to be told twice. He backed off as quickly as he could, headed for some painless form of ritual suicide if he knew what was good for him. A couple of seconds later, he disappeared through the arch.

That left Blastaar and Krona staring at each other across a span of a hundred meters. The Bolovite hefted his axe above his head, screamed his war cry, and came hurtling at his opponent.

Blastaar's nostrils flared with anticipation. A smile spread across his face. He hadn't undertaken this exercise for pleasure—but a pleasure it would be. He had forgotten how good a fight to the death could make him feel.

Then he charged, too. The ground trembled with the force of it.

He could hear a sharp intake of breath—that of half a million Bolovites—as he raised his axe and closed with Krona. They converged in the middle of the field like two unstoppable forces of nature, the Bolovite trying to cut Blastaar in half from the top down.

For the moment, all the Baluurian wanted to do was ward off his enemy's attack. He almost didn't even accomplish that. For as he brought up the haft of his weapon to catch Krona's stroke, the cursed thing splintered under the impact. If Blastaar hadn't been quick enough to sidestep the blow, it would have likely been the end of him.

As he tossed the remains of the axe away, he wondered at his own stupidity. Clearly, it had been designed to fall apart in his hands.

Why should he have expected the Bolovites to give him an even chance? This was their civilization he was after. The last thing they wanted was to be ruled by an alien—particularly one with a reputation like his.

Grinning at the prospect of facing an unarmed adversary, Krona lifted his axe again and charged a second time. Blastaar crouched on the balls of his feet, hands moving in front of him like a wrestler's, waiting for the right moment.

Then he saw Krona shift the axe in his hands and realized where the stroke would be coming from. Shuffling to his left and ducking, the Baluurian let the axe head graze his right shoulder—just to get himself good and mad. Then he lashed out with his right foot, driving it into Krona's side with enough force to shatter a boulder.

As it was, it only fractured a rib or two. But it had the effect of driving the Bolovite off course—and that was all the opening Blastaar needed.

Before his enemy could recover from the blow, he lowered his head and bowled Krona over. They hurtled half the distance to the stands and went down in a mass of arms and legs. In the process, Blastaar managed to grab his adversary's wrist—the one that held the axe.

Somehow, Krona came out on top—but only for a moment. With his free hand, Blastaar smashed him across the face— once, twice, a third time. By then, he had loosened the Bolovite's grip on him, though he still clung fiercely to his axe. Krona's nose and mouth were running yellow with blood, and there was a dazed look creeping into his eyes.

Above them, lightning danced and thunder bellowed, resounding in the amphitheater. But the half million people in the seats around them were deathly still. *How appropriate,* thought Blastaar.

Reaching back, the Living Bomb-Burst put all his strength into the next blow. It caught Krona under the jaw with a mighty crack and sent him soaring backward. He landed on his back a good fifty feet away, then tumbled a few times before he came to a halt. A cloud of dust rose around him where the dirt had been disturbed.

Blastaar got to his feet slowly, as if he didn't have a care in the world, and dusted himself off. Fifty paces away, his opponent gathered himself as well. Krona moved even more slowly than Blastaar, though not for the same reason. From the way he held his head, it was apparent that Blastaar had broken Krona's jaw in several places.

But that didn't stop the Bolovite from spreading his feet in a warrior's stance and hefting his axe as if he meant business. The challenger grinned. And why not? His favorite part was coming up.

Closing the gap, he watched Krona's eyes. They had narrowed with a mixture of anger and apprehension. Without a doubt, he knew that this was his last chance. If he got lucky and gutted the Baluurian, he would outlive his injuries and remain on his throne.

If not . . . well, no one was meant to live forever. Or so it was said. Blastaar himself had other ideas.

Lightning zagged. Thunder rumbled long and loud. The wind swirled in the arena, bringing the first fat drops of rain. The challenger was all but oblivious to it. His world had narrowed to the task at hand.

With a cry of rage and pain, Krona flung himself at Blastaar. This time, he swung his axe from the hip, hoping to spill the Baluurian's guts. But Blastaar had seen the axe head drop in plenty of time. Timing his maneuver perfectly, he leapt into the air and let the blade pass harmlessly beneath him.

A second time, Krona swung his axe. And as before, Blastaar took to the air to avoid it. But when he came down the second time, his adversary still halfway around, Blastaar launched into an attack.

In his battered state, the Bolovite was neither quick enough nor strong enough to ward off the Baluurian's onslaught. Blastaar drove his shoulder into Krona's damaged ribs, eliciting a howl of agony. Then he delivered a blow with the heel of his hand that struck the point of Krona's chin.

It snapped the Bolovite's mouth closed, his teeth snipping off the end of his long, forked tongue. The fragment fell in the dirt between them as Krona staggered backward, still hanging on desperately to his weapon. But Blastaar was far from done with him.

Pressing his advantage, he struck again, sending the Bolovite spinning like a top. And again. And again, each blow echoing within the confines of the amphitheater, until Krona was more bloody pulp than living being.

But the supreme ruler of the Bolovite Union would not fall. He stood there, legs trembling, axe dragging on the ground as the rain pelted harder and harder—but he refused to give Blastaar the satisfaction of collapsing at his feet.

In someone else, that might have spurred a grudging sort of respect. But not in Blastaar. He didn't care how his enemies died, as long as they were no longer around to plague him.

Grabbing Krona by his thick, scaly throat, he lifted the Bolovite off his feet. Krona sputtered and choked, and tried to claw Blastaar's hand away. But it was no use. He'd expended the last of his strength.

Lightning blazed, turning them white with its fury. Thunder crashed as if in protest of what was about to take place. After all, it was Bolovite thunder, wasn't it?

The challenger reached down and pulled the axe handle free from Krona's hand. Then he looked into the Bolovite's eyes— or rather, the part of them that hadn't swelled shut yet. Rainwater ran in rivulets along the contours of Krona's face.

"When you arrive in your Bolovite hell," Blastaar told him, "remember who put you there."

Before Krona could attempt a response with the mangled ruin that had been his mouth, Blastaar let go of his throat. Then, before he could fall very far, the Baluurian brought back Krona's axe and swung it with all the force of his right hand.

There was a *slitch*, and Krona crumpled to the ground, a geyser of yellow-green blood where his head used to be. As for his head itself, it sailed high in the air, end over end, trailing gore and shreds of scaly flesh. It seemed like a long time before it came down, and even longer before it landed in the lap of a surprised and horrified Bolovite in the tenth row.

Lightning lashed the dark, sullen heavens. Thunder groaned, as if in mourning. And the rain came down in earnest, sizzling around Blastaar and Krona's fallen form like a swarm of nightmarish insects.

For emphasis, Blastaar raised his foot and put it down on Krona's massive chest. The rain streamed over his face and matted his great, gray mane against his head.

Mission accomplished, he thought. *I have my fleet, or at least the beginnings of it. And soon enough, I'll have my revenge on the Fantastic Four.*

From his position on the catwalk in Prodigion's ten-story-high biogeneration chamber, Reed regarded the rows upon rows of milky, rectangular packets lining the chamber from top to bottom.

He scrutinized the shimmering silver energy writhing in the chamber's immense containment vessel. And he considered the apparatus on the floor below the vessel.

Finally, he inspected the control console beside him, bringing up screen after screen of complex calculations and detailed schematics. He hadn't yet finished when he heard the soft hiss of a door sliding aside and turned in response.

Sue, Ben, Johnny, and the Silver Surfer floated in on the Surfer's board. Stopping before him, they descended to the catwalk.

"What did you see?" Reed asked.

The Thing looked around. "A place a lot like this one," he replied. "Milk pillows coverin' the walls, big lightbulb in the middle, the whole nine yards. 'Cept I didn't have the slightest idea what it was for."

Johnny shrugged. "I didn't get a whole lot out of it either, to tell you the truth."

Reed looked at Sue, and then the Surfer. "And you visited chambers like this one as well?"

"*I* did," his wife said.

The Surfer shook his head. "I was encouraged to examine the underside of the ship, where I discovered perhaps a hundred apertures—each a meter or so in diameter. However, there was no sign of the mighty collection conduits built into Galactus's Worldship."

Reed absorbed the information. It all seemed to fit.

"So?" the Thing prodded. "Don't keep us in suspense, Mr. Wizard. Tell us what it all means."

Reed stretched out his arm to indicate the energy cells on the wall behind him. "These milk pillows, as Ben calls them, are storage batteries—except they're not charged with electricity. They hold several different kinds of raw energy, none of which I've ever seen before."

The Thing grunted. "Something you haven't seen before? That alone is worth the price of admission."

Retracting his arm and tilting his head toward the containment vessel, Reed went on, undaunted. "When the time comes, the energy from the cells is injected into what Ben calls the lightbulb—actually, an incredibly durable force-container—where the various energy components are mixed and refined."

"And then introduced into a planet's biosphere," the Surfer added. "Hence, the apparatus under the containment vessel and the apertures I found on the ship's hull."

"That's my guess, too," Reed responded. "The energy mixture would descend to earth in elongated silver globules and sink into the ground. And after a while, probably not very long at all, the biosphere is invigorated—instilled with new energy and new life."

"Then Tjellina was telling us the truth," Sue said.

Reed was reluctant to say for sure. "It seems that way, yes. Still, I'd like to see more of the ship. Check out the equipment a little more thoroughly, conduct a few tests . . ."

"But for the time being," the Surfer observed, "Prodigion seems innocent of the crimes we attributed to him. In fact, unless Reed's analysis is completely off the mark, Prodigion is more than innocent. He is a creature of unparalleled benevolence."

"Yeah," Ben said. "And Blastaar was lying through his teeth. Playing us for fools, just as I thought."

"Or maybe," Susan suggested, "he was just misguided. Too quick to judge, relying on rumor and legend."

"Yer givin' him too much credit," the Thing insisted. "Once a scumbucket, always a scumbucket."

"Either way," the Surfer declared, taking in Reed, Ben, and Johnny with a glance, "it appears you were fighting on the wrong side."

"Hey," the Thing pointed out, "it wasn't our idea. Those Outriders came after us, remember?"

Johnny made a T sign with his hands. "Hold on a second. Didn't anybody hear what Reed said? It *seems* Tjellina's telling the truth. It *seems* Prodigion's a heck of a guy. But we all know appearances can be deceiving." He looked around at his comrades. "And I still don't trust Prodigion any farther than I can throw him."

"I would not expect you to trust him," the Surfer answered. "Your experiences with the Outriders were not pleasant, after all."

"That's got nothing to do with it," Johnny insisted. "I've just got a feeling we're getting suckered here—and not by Blastaar."

"Let's simmer down," Reed advised. "We don't have to make a judgment right now, anyway. As long as we've got the run of the ship, let's take advantage of it—find out whatever we can."

He looked at Johnny. "And if we find out Prodigion's the salt of the earth, we'll wish him good luck and be on our way. Agreed?"

The Torch frowned. "Agreed," he said reluctantly.

Aggas Ag stood at his tribe's watering hole and smiled. He was living in miraculous times.

All around him, everywhere he looked, there were grasses and brush and towering trees—just as in his father's day. The watering hole itself was filled to its ancient limits and beyond. And if the dark blue storm clouds on the horizon were any indication, the hole's boundaries would soon swell even more.

On the other side, where the trees hadn't yet grown quite so tall or so broad, a wind stippled the surface of the water. There were animals there, a greater number than Aggas Ag had ever imagined possible.

They were fat, satisfied animals, taking their time as they drank. But he didn't go back to his hut for his hunting implements. He and the other tribesmen had hunted enough. Their bellies and their larders were full. To hunt any more would have been wasteful.

Instead, the tribesmen were spending their time rebuilding their village—knocking down their old ramshackle huts and putting up new ones. With trees growing everywhere, wood was plentiful. And with the people's bellies sated, so was the tribe's motivation.

Besides, with the rainstorms that seemed to come through every few hours, they really needed a sturdy roof over their heads. Otherwise, he laughed inwardly, they might find rainwater mixed with their stew.

And it was the same at all the other villages, as far as he could tell. It rained everywhere and flowers, trees, and vegetables grew—even things they had never seen in their lifetimes—and the tribes were prospering accordingly.

There would be other generations, a great many of them stretching from this moment to the end of time. And they would be tall, not hunched over, and their hard parts would shine with sublime iridescence.

Looking about, sniffing the green scents on the wind, it was difficult for Aggas Ag to remember how bad it had been. It was hard to remember the hardship and the despair he had felt only a few short days ago.

But it was not hard to remember the night things had changed. He would never forget the star he had seen traversing the heavens or the way the air had trembled or the long, silver shapes that had dropped to earth.

Or the majesty with which the god had descended into their midst.

Nor was he a destroyer, as Aggas Ag had feared. As they learned almost from the start, the god was a being of great benevolence. A traveler, as Mor Maddas had said, but one who was kind and generous and brought life to lands like their own.

Now he was gone, in search of other places needful of his bounty. As the god had told the tribesmen, he would never see them again. But as long as his storms slaked the land's thirst and his trees nudged the heavens, the name of Prodigion would be worshiped here.

Thirteen

Blastaar stood on the bridge of his flagship and surveyed the graphic on the oversized monitor before him. His armada, made up of Bolovites, K'choqtoc, Esanaians, and Toraxisi, as well as the remnants of his own Baluurian fleet, now boasted more than a thousand vessels.

What's more, his tacticians had had a chance to mull over the enemy's capabilities. Unlike the last time, the tyrant was going to war knowing what to expect—and how to deal with it.

When the black needles appeared, they would be destroyed. Then the armada would peel back the planet-eater's ship like the skin of a skullfruit and destroy him as well. And Blastaar would once again be undisputed ruler of all he surveyed.

Chuckling, the Baluurian made a mental note to reward Councillor Jonat. For his invaluable assistance in obtaining the Bolovite fleet, which had in turn enabled Blastaar to seize the other fleets in the sector, Jonat would receive a hero's medal. It would look good on his gravestone.

After all, a wise man could be as dangerous as a planet-eater sometimes. And Jonat had proven himself to be a wise man indeed.

"Your excellency?"

Blastaar turned to his new pilot. "Yes?"

"We have arrived at the site of our earlier battle, my lord."

"Let's see it," the tyrant demanded.

A moment later, the monitor showed him the debris of his earlier armada—a hundred or so vessels too badly burned and battered to be of any further use to him. They hung there in space just where he'd left them, filled with their dead, silent testimony to the planet-eater's potential for destruction.

And to Blastaar's potential for failure.

In fact, this floating graveyard was one of the two reasons he had come here. "Weapons officer—target one of these hulks. Relay the order that I want another dozen ships to do the same.''

"As you wish, Lord," the weapons officer replied.

Blastaar allowed a minute for the command to be passed along and positions established. Then he raised his bearded chin.

"Maximum power," he rasped. "Fire!"

Thirteen lurid energy blasts emerged from thirteen different weapons banks—and thirteen crippled vessels scattered their atoms across the void. But the tyrant wasn't done yet.

"Target again," he ordered. And a second time: "Fire!"

Thirteen beams lanced through space. Thirteen ships exploded into nothingness. Blastaar was beginning to feel better.

It took nine vicious, dazzling barrages to eliminate all traces of his defeat, all evidence of his undoing. Only then did he turn away from the monitor and regard his navigator—who, like the pilot, was new to the tyrant's flagship.

"Well?" he demanded.

"I've picked up a free-electron trail, my lord. It appears to have been produced by the planet-eater's propulsion system."

Blastaar nodded his shaggy, gray head, pleased. This was the other reason he had visited the site: to obtain a clue as to the entity's heading or destination. And it seemed he had found what he was looking for.

He turned to his pilot. "Follow the destroyer's trail, maximum speed. I'm impatient to feel his throat constrict in my grasp."

For emphasis, Blastaar closed his fingers into a fist in front of the pilot's eyes. The Baluurian nodded a bit too quickly.

"As you wish, my liege."

Before he had taken another breath, the tyrant felt his ship surge beneath him. He didn't have to consult a monitor to know the rest of his armada was doing the same thing—leaping through the cosmos with a single mission, a single goal:

To avenge their master's defeat and put an end to the planet-eater.

And when that was done, Blastaar would scour the Negative Zone for the cursed Fantastic Four. For he owed them a debt as well, and Blastaar always paid what he owed.

•   •   •

Reed sat at the control station that dominated one of Prodigion's tactical centers, Sue, Ben, and Johnny clustered behind him. He was surrounded by perhaps two dozen monitors of various shapes and sizes.

Some of them were freestanding, some positioned on the bulkheads. Some were one-sided and some two-sided, some curved and some flat. Some showed views of Negative Zone space and some showed interiors.

And then there was the one right in front of him, with its image of the biogeneration chamber Reed had visited days earlier. Since that time, he'd had a chance to visit a great many facilities on Prodigion's vessel, as had his teammates.

Just as Tjellina had said it would, everything checked out. Everything supported the thesis that Prodigion was a giver of life, not a taker—a nurturer, not a destroyer.

But there was one thing they hadn't seen, one piece of the puzzle Reed hadn't had an opportunity to examine. And he couldn't give Prodigion's operation a clean bill of health until he accessed that piece as well.

In other words, until he saw Prodigion.

For all he knew, there was no such being. The Outriders' master could have been created from whole cloth, based on the legend that seemed to have traveled from planet to planet. Reed didn't actually believe that, but he had no evidence to the contrary.

At least, not yet.

Out in the corridor, their auburn-haired Outrider escort peeked in on them periodically to see how they were doing. Or as Johnny had suggested, *what* they were doing. But the Outrider, whose name was Amalyn, didn't impede them or try to regulate their efforts. She just maintained her position at the door in accordance with Tjellina's orders.

Reed wasn't sure the Outrider would have entirely approved of what he was doing. After all, Tjellina had declared Prodigion's private chambers physically off-limits to them. But she hadn't said anything about the security footage that pertained to those chambers.

"Here goes nothing," he said.

The image on his monitor changed. No longer was he looking at an empty biogeneration chamber. Suddenly, he was gazing at a being of tremendous magnitude and majesty, whose every gesture seemed full of portent as he moved from one bank of equipment to another in a chamber that dwarfed the one Reed now occupied.

In his entire life, Reed had seen only one other personage of such size and bearing—and that had been Galactus. But where Galactus displayed stony indifference, there seemed to be a spark of humanity in Prodigion, a hint of compassion.

It was difficult to know for sure without meeting their host in person. But at least on the face of it, it seemed this piece fit the puzzle as well.

"Hey, Stretch," the Thing growled behind him.

Reed was too intent on the monitor to do more than grunt. Still, he knew his friend would understand. It wasn't the first time Ben had seen his teammate absorbed in study.

"Stretcherooney," the Thing pressed. "I think you oughtta see this."

The man called Mr. Fantastic sighed and turned around. "What is it, Ben?"

The Thing jerked a big, orange thumb over his shoulder. "It's this," he replied simply.

Reed followed the gesture . . . and groaned. The big monitor in back of Ben showed an image of Prodigion as well—the same one, in fact, that graced Reed's small screen. The monitor beside it displayed the image as well. And so did the monitor beside that.

In fact, Prodigion's likeness was manifest on every screen in the place. And, for all Reed knew, on every monitor on the ship. Clearly, he had, as Johnny might say, goofed big time.

"You see the problem?" Sue asked.

"It would be difficult not to," he sighed. "I must have activated one datalink too many."

Johnny wasn't the least bit embarrassed. In fact, he seemed amused by the whole thing. "I guess the Outriders are going to know you hacked into Prodigion's security records."

"I guess so," Ben rumbled.

Reed glanced at Amalyn, who was frowning as she took in the sight of Prodigion on all those monitors. She couldn't have been too happy about it, but she had orders not to interrupt.

"Anyway," Sue noted, "I think we've accumulated all the information we were looking for. It still looks like Tjellina was telling the truth."

Reed turned to his screen again and regarded Prodigion. He leaned back in his chair. "It looks that way, doesn't it?"

Johnny folded his arms across his chest. "I still say we're making a mistake. There's something fishy in this bowl."

"But we haven't found it," the Thing reminded him. "So odds are, the Negative Zone's got nothin' ta fear from Prodigion. An' Prodigion can obviously take care o' himself, judgin' from the way the Outriders kicked Blastaar's tail. All in all, a nice neat package that doesn't need us meddlin' in it. Ergo and to wit—it's time to blow this pop stand."

Sue looked at him. "You mean go home."

"I mean go directly home," Ben answered. "Do not pass 'go,' do not collect two hundred dollars. Just get the heck outta here." He glanced at Reed. "Unless Einstein here wants to caress a few more fancy circuit boards. I mean, that's my idea of a good time."

Still staring at the image of Prodigion, Reed shook his head. "No, I think you're right, old friend. It's time we made tracks." But he couldn't help continuing to stare at the monitor.

Sue put her hand on his shoulder and whispered in his ear. "Something's still bothering you, isn't it?"

She would know that, of course. She was his wife.

"Only that we haven't met Prodigion in person," he explained. "I know it's not very likely that someone would create these records just so I could hack into them, but . . ."

"But you're not gonna split this haystack till we meet the Big Cheese," the Thing translated.

Reed glanced at him. "Something like that."

Ben heaved a sigh. "So what're we waitin' for—Guy Fawkes Day? Let's go request us an audience with the great an' powerful Oz."

And before Reed or the others could respond, the Thing went out into the corridor and voiced his request. Sue chuckled.

"Ben'll be all right once he gets over his shyness," she commented.

Reed grasped her hand and smiled. And hoped their request wasn't denied out of hand.

• • •

The Surfer entered the chamber on his surfboard at precisely the time to which he had agreed.

It was not unlike many of the other chambers on Prodigion's ship, which he had explored at some length by then. It was the same generous size, the same rectangular shape. And each of its bulkheads displayed the same ribs of raised circuitry.

Yes, very much the same as any other chamber on the ship—except for one thing. Tjellina was in this one.

She stood at the far side of it, working at a control console. Though her back was to him and he made no sound, his board hovering an inch or so above the floor, the Outrider nonetheless seemed to sense his arrival.

Glancing back over her shoulder at the Surfer, she indicated a spot in the center of the room. "Please," she said. "I was delayed on the hangar deck, but I'll be with you in just a moment."

Descending from his board, he whisked it to a place by one of the bulkheads. After all, it was the Surfer himself in which Tjellina had expressed interest, not his accoutrements.

A few seconds later, the Outrider turned to him, finished with her adjustments. "Thank you for coming," she told him, her tone noticeably more businesslike than before. "I'm certain your friend the Torch warned you against it."

"That's true," the Surfer responded. "But I told him I didn't expect my experience to be anything like his. Besides, knowledge is always a worthwhile goal. And while you are learning about me, who knows? Perhaps I may learn something about myself."

Tjellina's head tilted slightly to one side. "You speak like a scholar."

"As it happens," he told her, "I was a scholar once. In fact, I was one of the few such on my planet."

The Outrider seemed surprised. "If there were so few, you must have been held in great esteem."

The Surfer shook his head. "My people didn't care much for those who would expand our stores of knowledge. They were too absorbed in shallow pursuits and trivial pleasures."

"You speak of them in the past tense," Tjellina said. "Did something happen to them?"

The Surfer hesitated. "More to the point," he finally said, "something happened to me." And in broad strokes, leaving out the details he thought she would find uninteresting, he described the circumstances that had made him the Silver Surfer.

"Remarkable," the Outrider murmured. "Then you are unique. There is no one like you on Zenn-La or anywhere else in your galaxy."

"Galactus has created other Heralds," the Surfer pointed out. "But it is correct to say none of them is exactly like me."

Tjellina grunted softly. "All the more reason to learn about you. To understand what makes you so different."

With that, she tapped a stud on her console. A section of bulkhead slid aside and revealed a storage space full of equipment. Removing some of it, the Outrider approached the Surfer.

"These are energy sensors," she said, separating one from the others.

The Surfer saw a dark plastic oval mounted on a metal stand. The oval had a single narrow aperture.

"They're designed to measure and identify output in routine safety checks." Tjellina began to set them up around him. "However, they will also measure and identify the output you generate."

Finally, when she was done positioning the sensors, the Outrider handed the Surfer an object. He turned it over in his hands. It was roughly the size and shape of a flashlight, with a few small protuberances at the end where the bulb would be.

"What is it?" he asked.

"Nothing of any importance," Tjellina replied. "Just a tool we used to recalibrate our navigational equipment. We have since developed more efficient tools to accomplish the same objective."

"I see," he said. "And what would you have me do with it?"

"Several things," Tjellina told him.

She retreated to her console and pushed some buttons. Tiny lights in the sensors lit up, indicating that the system was active.

"First," the Outrider said, "I'd like you to put your hand through the recalibrator. That is, if it doesn't cause you any discomfort."

"None," the Surfer assured her. Then he did as she had asked, using his mastery over molecular physics to melt one hand through the instrument as he held it in his other.

Tjellina consulted her console, her face bathed in the green light of its monitors. "Very interesting. You seem to impart a certain amount of energy to the object through which you're passing. Did you know that?"

He told her that he did. He was acutely aware of every interaction between his power and the world of matter.

"Now," she requested, "withdraw your hand and create a force field around the recalibrator."

Again, the Surfer did as the woman asked. When he was done, a faint, shimmering aura surrounded the object—an aura that would have withstood a burst from the Outriders' hand weapons.

Tjellina studied the sensor results, then looked up. "I'd like to test the strength of it," she said.

The Surfer shrugged. "Go ahead."

Opening another panel on the bulkhead near her console, she exposed a second storage compartment. Removing a palm-sized device, the Outrider brought it to him. He took it, examined it.

"It appears to be a weapon," the Surfer observed.

Tjellina nodded. "It's a miniature version of the blasters we use for security purposes. Just as powerful, but it holds a smaller charge. Would it be a problem for you if I fired it at the recalibrator?"

"Not at all," he replied.

He waited until she had withdrawn to her console, then fired the blaster at the recalibrator—or, more accurately, at the force field he had erected around the recalibrator. The beam of destructive energy splashed off, leaving the instrument completely unscathed.

At her console, her face cast in emerald light, the Outrider nodded. "Interesting. Your force field distributes the force of the assault over its entire surface." She turned to him. "Are you doing that consciously?"

The Surfer shrugged. "I am aware that it is happening, but I do not wish it to happen. It simply does."

Tjellina regarded him. "You wield such immense power."

The comment seemed to come out of nowhere. "Yes," he

said finally. "It's considerable, I know. But I make every effort not to abuse it."

"Yes," the Outrider replied. "I can see that." She stared at him a moment longer. Then she asked, "Would it be all right if I used a full-sized blaster on you?"

As before, the Surfer shook his head. "Do as you wish. I won't be harmed, I assure you."

Going back to the storage compartment, Tjellina extracted a weapon of the sort he had seen the Outriders carry. Then she trained it on him.

"You're certain?" she inquired, just to be sure.

"Certain," the Surfer confirmed.

A moment later, she speared him with a tightly focused beam of pure energy. He could see how it would have had a nasty effect on the Torch.

But to the Silver Surfer, it was less a threat than an annoyance. With a simple application of will he fashioned a shield of cosmic force, stopping the beam in midair.

"Amazing," the Outrider remarked, her blaster at her side as she studied the monitors on her console. "Absolutely amazing."

Truly, the Surfer had come to take his powers for granted. But seeing Tjellina's fascination with them reminded him that others did not.

She conducted other tests, gauging his response times, his accuracy, even his ability to direct the actions of his board. And she recorded everything she could about the Power Cosmic—its wavelengths, its polarities, its every measurable dynamic.

In fact, the Outrider's research went on much longer than the Surfer had expected. At first, he believed it was attributable to her zeal. Then he wondered if it didn't have a basis in something else.

He couldn't escape the feeling that Tjellina was prolonging their time together. Stretching it out longer than was necessary. But why would she do that?

And why did he not find it tedious? Why did he welcome her curiosity to the point of encouraging it? Was it because it reminded him of another who had displayed great curiosity?

A being called Shalla Bal?

He remembered arguing metaphysics with Shalla long into

the evening, while the luminous strips in his study automatically compensated for the dying light. He remembered her wit, her willingness to try new things, her delight when they stumbled onto some new piece of knowledge together.

Tjellina looked at him, as if she had noticed some change in his expression. "What are you thinking about?" she asked casually.

"I was thinking of Shalla Bal," he replied.

She hesitated for a moment. "Who's that?"

The Surfer told her. He spoke plainly of the love he and Shalla Bal had shared—and of how his transformation had pulled them apart. As he did this, he saw Tjellina's brow wrinkle.

"I'm sorry," she said. "I didn't mean to pry."

"You were not prying," he assured her. "Nor would I have answered if I had not wished to do so."

Tjellina paused. For the first time since he had met her, she seemed awkward to him—as if she were venturing into unfamiliar territory.

"Have you ever thought of returning to Zenn-La?" she asked. "And of trying to resume your relationship with Shalla Bal?"

The Surfer frowned ever so slightly. "I have returned to Zenn-La several times. But resuming my relationship with Shalla Bal is no longer a possibility. Both she and I have changed too much for us merely to pick up where we left off."

Tjellina didn't comment on his remark. She just regarded him for a moment, her expression unreadable—though the Surfer sensed emotions warring under the surface. Then she turned back to her console.

"You know much about me," the Surfer noted, surprising himself with the remark. "But I know so little about you."

She looked at him. "What would you like to know?"

"Everything," he told her. "For instance, where you come from. What it was like there, what your life was like. And how you came to serve as one of Prodigion's Outriders."

Tjellina shrugged, as if it weren't a matter of very great importance to her anymore. "I come from a world called Bathandia," she told him. "A world of great thinkers and philosophers, scientists and inventors. Unfortunately, no one ever actually *did* anything on Bathandia. They only talked about it.''

''But you said there were scientists,'' the Surfer reminded her. ''And inventors. Surely these did more than talk.''

The Outrider sighed. ''Their inventions were impractical. And our scientists dealt only in theory, never sullying their hands with experimentation.''

He absorbed what Tjellina had said. ''Then your world and mine had a lot in common. Their maladies were different, but the symptoms were the same—a stagnation of society. A perpetuation of the status quo.''

''And worse. We had never learned to synthesize what we needed, only to take what nature made available to us. In our foolishness, we depleted our resources slowly but inexorably— made wastelands of our wildernesses and prisons of our cities.''

The Surfer nodded. ''Foolishness indeed.''

''But I was different,'' Tjellina noted. ''I wanted to do something with my life. I wanted to make something, to create. Unfortunately, there was no venue in my society where I could satisfy these urges. That is, until an Outrider landed her vessel outside our capitol.''

He thought about that. ''I didn't know it was your custom to make contact with the cultures you're helping.''

''Normally,'' she told him, ''it's not. But Outriders aren't immortal. We die in accidents or at the hands of those who would oppose us, like Blastaar. Or, in some cases, we succumb to advanced age.''

''I see,'' the Surfer said, sobered by the prospect. ''Then the Outrider was looking to replenish your ranks. To recruit new Outriders.''

''Exactly,'' Tjellina responded. ''She sent out a call for those who would like to dedicate themselves to Prodigion— and all he represented. But even if no one came forth, she said, he would make our world a paradise again.''

''Were you the only one who answered the call?'' he wondered.

''The only one,'' she confirmed. ''Out of nearly a billion people. And much to my surprise and—yes, I admit it, my fright—I was accepted. I left with the Outrider to pursue a new life among the stars.''

The Surfer shook his head. "Your recruitment, then, was a bit different from mine. Your world wasn't hanging in the balance."

"No," she agreed. "It wasn't. And I have been an Outrider ever since." She turned back to her controls. "We're almost done now."

He found himself saddened by the prospect—saddened more than an experimental subject had a right to be. Perhaps, he told himself, there was a way in which he could make this not an ending, but a beginning.

Sue turned to Reed as she and her teammates followed Amalyn down the corridor. "What do you think Tjellina will tell us?"

Her husband shrugged. "Hard to say, not knowing how zealously Prodigion guards his privacy."

"If she wanted us to meet Prodigion," Johnny insisted, "she would've introduced us already. There's something about him she doesn't want us to see."

Ben rolled his eyes. "Give it a rest already, will ya, squirt? We know ya don't like the guy. Ya don't have to remind us every chance ya get."

"Stuff it," Johnny told him. "*Someone's* got to open your eyes."

By then, Amalyn had stopped outside a set of doors. As the Fantastic Four approached, the doors slid open. A burst of light came through them.

"What's going on in there?" Johnny wondered out loud.

Sue grabbed her brother by the arm. "Easy," she told him. "It's probably nothing, Johnny."

But the teenager wouldn't be restrained. "Flame on!" he snapped.

His body bursting into flame, he went flying down the corridor and made a sharp left turn into the room. As he sizzled past her, Amalyn cried out a warning—though Sue couldn't be sure whom she was trying to protect.

There was another flash of light, followed by a cry and an even brighter flash. As Sue skidded to a stop at the threshold, Reed and Ben just behind her, she got her first glimpse of the situation.

The Surfer was standing amid a circle of strange devices,

his hand extended toward the Torch—who was lying on the floor near the doorway, still in his flame-state but looking a little dazed.

"My apologies," the Surfer said, walking out of the circle to help Johnny to his feet. "I saw you attack Tjellina and I simply reacted. I hope I did not shake you up too badly."

The Torch shook his head. "I don't get it." He pointed to Tjellina, who was standing on the other side of the room with a blaster in her hands. "She was firing at you."

The Surfer nodded. "Yes, but with my permission. It was part of a test."

Amalyn had what looked like a weapon in her hand. Seeing there was little chance of further violence, she put it away.

"Obviously," Tjellina noted, "there has been a misunderstanding." She addressed the Torch. "I am sorry. I mean that sincerely."

Johnny frowned. "Whatever you say."

"We came here to make a request," Reed informed Tjellina, circumventing the Torch's error and the Surfer's reaction. "Thanks to your kindness and hospitality, we've seen all we need to see here—and we believe what you've told us about Prodigion."

"I'm glad," Tjellina replied.

"Since you don't seem to require any assistance turning back the likes of Blastaar, we'd like to go home," Reed went on. "However, we wouldn't feel right doing that until we've thanked our *real* host."

"In other words," Amalyn interpreted unnecessarily, "they would like an audience with Prodigion."

Tjellina considered the request for a moment. Then she shrugged. "I don't see why not. Of course, it may take a little while, but I'm sure Prodigion can find the time to meet with you before you depart."

Johnny seemed surprised. "He can?"

The Outrider nodded. "I will make him aware of your desire and arrange a meeting as soon as possible." She turned to the Surfer. "No doubt you would like to meet Prodigion as well. Before you go, I mean."

Sue saw something in Tjellina's gaze. A twinge of regret, perhaps. An expression of sorrow, of loss. It was fleeting, but unmistakable nevertheless.

"Yes," the Surfer replied, his eyes fixed on the raven-haired Outrider. "I would like very much to meet Prodigion. However, I will not be departing with the Fantastic Four."

Ben's jaw dropped. "Huh?"

"Wanna run that by us again?" the Torch asked.

The Surfer didn't turn as he answered them. "I would like to remain here," he said. "With Tjellina."

The Outrider stared at him, as incredulous as any of her guests. "Do you know what you're saying?" she asked.

For the first time, Sue saw a hint of a smile on the skyrider's face. "Yes," he said. "I know precisely what I'm saying." He paused. "Would I be welcome here, do you think?"

Tjellina flushed a little. "Very welcome."

Reed shook his head. "I don't understand."

He wouldn't, Sue mused with an indulgent smile. But then, he was a man. And for all his scientific brilliance, not a very perceptive man sometimes.

The Surfer regarded the Fantastic Four. "Fate has given me an opportunity," he explained. "A chance to rid myself of the burden of guilt I carry. You see, as my former master destroyed life, Prodigion nurtures it. By assisting him in some small way, perhaps I can make amends for the crimes I committed as Galactus's Herald."

"What would you do here?" Reed asked. "Prodigion already has all the help he seems to need."

"I was a scientist once," the Surfer reminded him. "I know there will be a great deal for me to learn, but maybe I can do some of Prodigion's work someday. Even a being of his power can use a respite now and then."

There was more to it than that, Sue observed. It was clear to her the Surfer was smitten with Tjellina. Though even if he weren't, the chance to redeem himself would no doubt be motivation enough.

Still, that didn't mean it was the right choice. The Surfer tended to be impulsive, to act sometimes without thinking. And he had been through enough suffering, enough turmoil in his life.

"Surfer," she said, "are you sure about this? I mean *really* sure?"

He nodded. "I know, Susan Richards. I swore once never to serve another master as long as I lived." He remembered the vow, made in the heat of shame and guilt after he learned how he'd served Galactus. "But to my mind, this is not servitude. It is a labor of love. Of redemption."

Johnny frowned. But even with his suspicion of Prodigion intact, he didn't try to talk the Surfer out of it.

And the Thing was actually encouraging. "You tell 'em, Surf. Ya see the brass ring, ya gotta go for it."

There was a wistfulness in his gravelly voice that Sue understood. After all, Ben had had his share of heartaches and disappointments. It was not easy for one so grotesque to find love and contentment. No easier than for someone like the Surfer, who had been an accessory to the murder of entire planets. In a way, they were very much alike, the Surfer and Ben.

"Indeed," the skyrider assured the Thing, "I will go for the brass ring." Then he glanced at Tjellina, with her raven hair and her golden eyes. "And I will not easily relinquish it."

"Well, then," Reed declared, "the Surfer seems taken care of. But it leaves the rest of us with a problem."

Johnny snapped his fingers. "That's right. We've got no way of getting back to Earth."

Tjellina spoke up. "Perhaps I can be of some help in that regard. You see, we have more defense vessels than we really need."

"Won't Prodigion mind?" Reed asked.

The Outrider smiled a subtle smile. "Prodigion is a magnanimous being. He will have no objection. In fact—"

Suddenly, the chamber filled with the sound of sirens. Alarmed, Sue looked around. "What is it?" she asked.

Tjellina turned to her console and cursed softly. "We're under attack," she told the others.

"Attack?" the Surfer echoed. "But who—?"

The Outrider looked up at him, her eyes hard and grim. "It's Blastaar. And he's got twice the fleet he had before."

Fourteen

T he Surfer watched Tjellina stow her blaster and head for the doors. "I'll be back," she told him, with a glance over her shoulder.

"Wait," he insisted. "I can help."

Tjellina turned to him and shook her head. "It won't be necessary. I'll meet you back here when we're done."

Then she hurried off through the doorway without another word. A moment later, Amalyn vanished in her wake.

The Surfer looked at the Fantastic Four. "Twice the fleet he had before. That's what she said."

Reed returned his gaze. "Obviously, Tjellina believes they can handle it."

The Surfer felt a jolt through the deckplates. And another. And then a third, even more immediate than the first two.

He turned in the direction of their attackers. "We shouldn't have felt those assault beams. The shields should have protected us."

The Thing grunted. "You'd think so, wouldn'cha?"

Reed stroked his chin. "It may be that Blastaar's combined forces are simply too much for the shields. Or maybe it's more than that. But in any case, that should change when the Outriders are placed in the mix."

It didn't. Not after a minute or even two. After a particularly jarring impact, the Surfer shook his head.

"Something's wrong," he decided. "And not just with the shields."

Ben looked at his teammates. "Surf's right. Last time, the Outriders took Blastaar apart lickety-split. If he's still blastin' away at us, they musta run into trouble."

"So what do we do?" Johnny asked. "Go to bat for a guy we're still not a hundred percent sure about?"

"A guy *you're* not a hundred percent sure about," the Thing corrected.

"When it came to Blastaar, we hung back and observed," Reed noted.

"Prodigion's not Blastaar," Ben reminded him. "And we're not with the attacker now. We're with the attackee."

The Surfer frowned. "Debate if you wish. I know what I will do."

Summoning his board, he mounted it and prepared to use his power to pass himself through one of the bulkheads. But before he could get there, he heard someone call his name. Turning, he saw that it had been the Invisible Woman.

"Hang on," she told him. "We're coming with you."

"Yeah," the Thing added. "We can't letcha go out there by yerself. Ya might catch yer death o' cold."

The Surfer regarded his friends. "I appreciate your concern. Come, then—we will go together."

"Fire!" cried the Living Bomb-Burst.

A hundred ships approached the planet-eater's massive vessel. A hundred energy beams burst from a hundred different weapons banks, splattering against the ship's force shields.

"Again!" Blastaar snarled.

Another hundred ships unleashed a deadly barrage. Like the first one, it hit the shields and splashed away.

"And again!" he roared.

Another hundred ships speared the void with their fury. And this time, some of the beams got through. The huge vessel shuddered visibly with impact after impact.

There, thought the tyrant. *I've thrown down the gauntlet. Now it's time for the cursed planet-eater to respond.*

Right on cue, a series of slots opened in the vessel's flanks—and its black needle fighters shot out like a swarm of dark, deadly insects. Its pilots came right at the armada, just as they had the first time.

And why not? Blastaar's forces were more numerous than before, but not much more intimidating. The Bolovite ships and the other new additions were superficially different from those crewed by Baluurians, but in no way superior to them.

All in all, it must have seemed like target practice for the black needles. But Blastaar knew better.

As one of the needles bore down on the flagship, the tyrant turned to his weapons officer. "Shield frequencies?"

"The same, my lord. Weapons are programmed accordingly."

"And their speed?"

There was only a split second's worth of hesitation. "Tracking and extrapolating," the officer assured him.

Blastaar smiled. "Fire when ready."

He watched the smaller monitor in his armrest, where the black needle was represented as a red blip with a yellow overlay of shifting geometric shapes. In the corner of the monitor, a ten-digit numeral changed faster than his mind could follow, displaying calculations and predictions.

Suddenly, the black needle was speared with an energy beam. Then another. And another. And all before it could get off a shot of its own.

What's more, the energy blasts had gotten through, only partially blocked by the needle's force shields. The narrow, black ship was smoking from a trio of puncture wounds in its hull.

Blastaar grinned. He knew it would be different this time.

His Baluurians had had time to analyze the needles' tactical systems. With his propulsion capabilities recorded and measured, the enemy's speed was no longer such an advantage. And with their shield frequencies laid bare, the needles might as well have had no shields at all.

Of course, the needles' pilots would eventually adjust their frequencies and restore their defenses. Likewise, their mother ship. But by then, the tyrant mused, it might be too late for them.

As he watched, the needle in front of him tried to retreat. But Blastaar's weapons officer wouldn't allow it to. He hammered the vessel with blast after merciless blast, poking hole after hole in it.

Finally, unable to endure any more torture, the needle's shields gave way altogether—and the ship exploded in a flash of parting atoms. It was gone as if it had never existed.

The tyrant rubbed his hands together, eager to see the other needles fall victim to the same fate. He had expected his revenge to be sweet, but he was only beginning to appreciate *how* sweet.

• • •

With the Fantastic Four gathered behind him, the Surfer melted through the hull of Prodigion's ship.

There was no resistance, as there would have been if he'd tried this with Galactus's vessel. No hidden defenses to circumvent. The four of them simply slid through on his board until the great void of the Negative Zone opened up to them.

At the moment, that void was filled with ships striving to destroy one another. And those taking the decidedly greater beating were the vessels piloted by the Outriders.

The Surfer didn't know what had swung the battle in Blastaar's favor—nor did he have time to find out. All he could do was try to turn the tide the other way and hope his efforts amounted to something.

He turned to Reed Richards. "We will do better if we split up."

"You got that right," Johnny answered.

As the Torch soared off on his own, leaving a trail of yellow flame, the leader of the group clapped the Surfer on the shoulder. "You're right," he said. "Good luck."

And then the other three members of the Fantastic Four shot off into space, propelled by their harnesses. Free to act on his own, the skyrider set his sights on the nearest dogfight.

A couple of Blastaar's assault ships were pursuing the slender black form of an Outrider vessel. The Outrider was clearly faster than the other two, but they seemed to be able to hit her almost at will—and each shot was taking its savage toll.

Surging forward on his board, the Surfer brought his own power to bear—the Power Cosmic granted to him by Galactus. It shot out from his fingertips like the purest silver light—but when it hit one of the Outrider's attackers, it did so with titanic force, crippling the vessel instantly and sending it flying end over end.

As the first attacker rolled away, the second took note of him and wheeled in his direction. A moment later, it released a searing burst of energy.

Had the Surfer been almost any other being, the blast would have torn him atom from atom. As it was, he merely met it with a blast of its own, the two discharges hungrily canceling each other out.

Then he unleashed an ever-greater fury, wrenching the craft off course and ripping up its engine relays in the process. Like the other attacker, it spun away helplessly, no longer a factor in the conflict.

And more important, the Outrider was free.

The Surfer would have advised her to return to Prodigion's vessel if he'd thought it would do any good. Unfortunately, he knew it wouldn't. He watched as she executed a tight loop and leapt to the aid of a sister ship.

Then he sought out another target.

The Torch still had conflicting thoughts about defending Prodigion against anyone. But the fact that he was going up against Blastaar made the task much easier to swallow.

Targeting one of the larger ships, a flagship maybe, he noted that it wasn't Baluurian. More than likely, then, it belonged to some race the tyrant had taken over. Peeking through a portal, Johnny confirmed it.

They looked like lobsters, not big gray guys with lion manes. That made him a little less eager to pound on them, though for all he knew they might've been even fiercer than Blastaar's people.

The first step was to dazzle their external sensors—if he could find them. Coming up alongside the ship, matching its speed, the Torch noticed a series of circular grids positioned all around the hull—and they didn't look anything like weapons clusters.

As an experiment, he launched a succession of big, blinding fireballs at the grids. For a moment, they didn't seem to have any effect. Then the ship slowed down to a crawl, its pilots having to rely on what they could see through their portals.

Of course, having a couple of big, bloodshot eyes on flexible stalks might have helped a little. But not enough. The vessel's occupants would have to recalibrate their sensors to get them working again.

In the meantime, the Torch mused, he had an easy target for step two. Finding the ship's weapons banks, which wasn't difficult at all, he fired blast after red-hot blast at them. And after a while, they began to melt.

Seeing what he was up to, the lobster people tried to target manually and fire back at him, maybe drive him away. But it was a mistake. Johnny had already slagged all the weapon barrels on that side of the vessel.

The energy stream got so far and no farther. And without a release point, it was forced to turn back on its source. Like electrical feedback, the Torch thought, except a thousand times more vicious.

The result? An explosion in the craft's aft quarters, with a big boom and lots of fireworks. By the time the lobster people got the fire under control, their ship would be a wreck.

Unfortunately, Johnny didn't have time to hang around and watch. He had a lot more work to do.

The Thing applied the afterburners on his harness and went after the belly of a Baluurian ship.

It wasn't an easy target, however. The vessel slowed down, sped up, and changed direction as it fired this way and that. Twisting his body as well as his directional controls, Ben tried to adjust accordingly—but it was like diving out of a plane and trying to hit a penny on the ground.

Finally, he caught up with it. Reaching out, he dug his powerful fingers into the hull and hung on through a gut-wrenching turn. But as soon as it was over, he got his revenge on the thing, drawing his fist back and driving it into the ship's tough metal hide.

There was a loud crunch. And suddenly he was through, his powerful fingers positioned just where he wanted them.

If he'd calculated correctly, and he was right below the helm controls, he'd be able to grab a fistful of energy linkages and make the vessel impossible to steer. If not . . . well, no one ever said being a super hero didn't have its share of risks.

The Thing probed and probed some more—and finally found a bundle of stuff that felt like what he was looking for. Tugging down as hard as he could, he ripped it out of place.

Suddenly, the craft went out of control, bucking like the bronco to end all broncos. Ben could likely have held on, but there didn't seem to be any point. So he released the crippled vehicle.

And watched it slam into another of Blastaar's ships, where it did a bunch of damage. A moment later, the second vessel was spinning like an out-of-control top as well.

Two for the price of one, the Thing observed. He'd take that kind of bargain any day.

• • •

The Invisible Woman didn't bother to live up to her name.

It wouldn't have done her any good anyway. Even if she had turned transparent, the sensors in Blastaar's ships would have detected her by virtue of her mass. So she forgot about turning invisible and put her other talents to use instead.

The ability to create invisible force fields, for instance. Approaching a Baluurian fighter with a burst of harness power, Sue saw it turn its blaster turrets in her direction. But before they could fire, she erected an invisible barrier around the turrets—one considerably denser and smoother than her usual creations.

So when the Baluurians did fire, their barrage bounced off her shield and reflected back at them. Unfortunately, the beams missed the weapons placements but managed to poke a few holes in the vicinity of the cockpit.

That gave Sue a chance to wedge smaller versions of her super-barrier into the blaster barrels. They were little more than slivers, really—but she was confident they would do the job.

Then she held her hand to her head and feigned the effects of having been stunned. After all, the Baluurians were a proud, male-dominated race. They'd have no trouble believing some of their beams had gotten through to her, "frail" female that she was.

Sue could almost see them leering at her as they placed her in their sights. She could imagine the vengeful glee with which their captain gave the order to fire.

This time, she didn't need a shield. Because when the energy beams tried to emerge from the gun barrels, the tiny wedges she'd driven into them did their jobs. Instead of skewering their target, the beams were deflected.

They sliced through the void, striking and maiming Baluurian vessels unfortunate enough to be in the vicinity. In a couple of cases, the beams split open the blaster barrels, spraying energy even more haphazardly.

But thanks to Sue's impeccable concentration, a talent she'd honed over the years, the invisible wedges survived—and not a single burst reached her. In fact, none of them even came close.

All of which must have irked the Baluurians no end.

Then, as the barrage stopped, Sue executed a graceful *coup de grâce*. Driving her slivers deeper into the gun barrels, she reached into the energy sources that drove them and wrought havoc with them as well.

In a burst of light and heat, the weapons overloaded, sending spikes of unfettered power throughout the vessel. Before its crew could do anything about it, their ship shut down—every system at once.

Sue smiled a lethal smile. That would teach them to underestimate the likes of the Invisible Woman.

It was easier for Mr. Fantastic to latch on to one of Blastaar's ships than it was for any of his teammates.

Even with the Torch's speed, he couldn't reach out over a vast distance and grab on to a projection on a vessel's hull—then, using the handhold as an anchor, reel himself in until he was sprawled over a section of the hull.

Not knowing whether the occupants of the ship had noticed his arrival, Reed acted quickly. Lowering himself into position over the forward observation port—the spacegoing equivalent of a windshield—he swung his leg out and down and kicked a hole in the transparent surface.

With shards flying in the faces of the vessel's pilots, Mr. Fantastic flowed in through the jagged hole. Not as quickly as he would've liked, of course, because he had to be careful not to cut himself on the edges. But quickly enough to catch his adversaries by surprise.

As he'd expected after seeing the ship's design, these weren't Baluurians against whom he'd pitted himself. They were beings he'd never run into before, tall and powerful looking with blue, serpentine scales and angry eyes the color of rubies.

With unexpected speed, they reached for the pistols they carried at their sides. But Reed beat them to it, drawing their weapons first and tossing them out the hole he'd created. Then he grabbed the pair and knocked their scaly heads together.

As they slumped to the deck, he took a look at the controls. But he didn't concentrate on them so hard that he forgot about the rest of the vessel—or the possibility there might be a crew hiding in the aft compartment.

Out of the corner of his eye, he saw another adversary edge out of hiding and take aim. As the cockpit was bisected by a scarlet beam, Mr. Fantastic flung his midsection out of harm's way—and watched the energy stream sizzle through a bulkhead instead.

As the pistol wielder tried to take aim a second time, Reed gathered himself into a ball and bounced—first off a bulkhead, then the ceiling, the deck, and the opposite bulkhead. All over the ship, in fact.

Each time he struck something, he gathered speed, making it harder for his adversary to follow his progress. Finally, when the fellow looked as if he'd watched one tennis match too many, Mr. Fantastic bowled him over.

Restoring himself to his original form, Reed disarmed the unconscious alien, then checked to make sure no one else was aboard and sat down at the controls. With a few quick strokes, he isolated the energy core that powered the engines and ejected it into space.

Turning to one of the unconscious pilots, he said, "Sorry, friend—but this vessel isn't going anywhere."

His work there successfully completed, Mr. Fantastic slithered out the hole in the observation port and climbed up onto the roof of the spacecraft. Then he took hold of a couple of weapons ports, drew himself back as far as he could, and selected another of Blastaar's ships.

Reed waited patiently for just the right moment. When it came, he slingshotted himself across the void and caught hold of the vessel.

And began his sabotage all over again.

Having dispatched another of Blastaar's ships to the junk heap, the Surfer scanned the battle zone for his next objective. But as he did so, he was impressed again with the enormity of his task.

He didn't have the luxury of disabling the enemy's craft one at a time—or watching his allies do the same. The armada was simply too big, its component parts too numerous. And with Prodigion's ship under fire, time was a rare and precious commodity.

So he chose another tactic, one he would never dream of using in his own universe, but which was quite sound in the Negative Zone with its odd, oxygen-bearing space. Using just a fraction of the speed with which he traveled from star to star, the Surfer homed in on one of the tyrant's vessels. Before the ship could fire at him or get out of the way, he ripped through it, board and all.

Despite his haste, he had been careful not to take any lives—only to sever some of the links that allowed the vessel to operate. The lack of explosive decompression simplified that task. Of course, he would never know the exact extent of the damage, because he was already rocketing through the next vehicle.

And the next. And the one after that.

And on and on, wreaking havoc with his passage, slashing through circuit after circuit and power coupling after power coupling. The Surfer didn't bother to count the critical systems he had destroyed; he just punched his way through them.

And hoped that when he was done, it would be enough.

Blastaar couldn't believe it. As he eyed the monitor in his flagship, he saw ship after ship whirl out of control or suffer some crippling explosion or simply die in its tracks.

He had expected to see such chaos when he came here. He had expected a spectacle of pain and destruction. What he hadn't expected was that his ships would be on the receiving end of it. It wasn't the planet-eater's fleet that was reeling in disarray—it was his.

What's more, it wasn't the black needles that had proved the tyrant's undoing. When he'd had them alone to face, the confrontation had gone all his way. No, his troubles were the work of the cursed Fantastic Four.

Almost immediately, they'd tipped the balance in the planet-eater's favor. And the longer they continued to fight, the farther it tipped.

Worst of all, there was nothing Blastaar could do about it. His blood burned to confront his enemies one on one—but if he yielded to that impulse, his armada would be left without a leader. There would be no one to coordinate their actions, no one to maintain discipline.

Either way, it seemed, he was bound to lose again, bound to taste the bitter brew of defeat. A wise man, he knew, would pull back his forces while he still had them. A wise man would withdraw and fight another day.

The Baluurian didn't fancy himself the wisest of men. But

he wasn't stupid either. His mouth twisting in disgust as he spoke the words, he called for a general retreat.

"Pull back!" he snarled. "Get out while you still can!"

His forces seemed surprised but eager to comply. After all, to them, the planet-eater was only a threat in the abstract. The planet-eater's champions, on the other hand, were punishing them here and now.

Then, as Blastaar endured the humiliation of watching his ships abandon the field, he saw a familiar figure stretch from a crippled vessel to another that was still intact. His lips pulled back in a wolfish grin.

"Richards," he said out loud.

No doubt the human hadn't realized a retreat was under way. He was still working his way from one target to another, wreaking as much havoc as he could.

The tyrant signaled his weapons master. "There's something I want to do before we go," he growled.

"Yes, my lord," the officer responded.

Blastaar pointed to the vessel Mr. Fantastic had just entered. "You see that ship? The Bolovite?"

"Indeed, your excellency."

"Destroy it," the tyrant commanded.

He sensed that the weapons officer was looking at him. Still, the man had the intelligence not to question Blastaar's order.

A moment later, a tightly focused beam of energy lanced through space and struck the vessel in question. As the tyrant's smile grew wider, the ship's engine exploded, creating an inferno of expanding plasma.

It didn't destroy the vessel completely, however. So for good measure, the weapons master fired a couple of beams through the cockpit, creating a second and somewhat smaller display of fireworks. Then the ship dropped out of sight as a wave of retreating Esanaians cut in front of it.

But Blastaar was satisfied that Richards had perished. It was almost worth all the ships he'd lost to accomplish that.

Sue Richards watched Blastaar's ships wheel one by one and head for open space. Was it possible they'd turned the tyrant back? That they'd won?

She'd expected to have to do a lot more fighting. After all, Blastaar was a savage being, a creature driven by pride and anger. And more than anything else, he hated to lose.

Before this, however, Sue had mostly seen him battling on his own, not at the head of an armada. She conceded she may have underestimated his strategic skills. It was also possible the Baluurian had something else up his sleeve—something she couldn't even begin to imagine.

No matter what, they'd won a respite. Scanning the void, Sue searched for her teammates. She spotted her brother first. And at what seemed like the same moment, the Torch spotted her.

He looped around and came blazing in her direction. There was something about his posture that communicated a sense of urgency. And by that sign, she knew something was amiss.

"What is it?" she asked as Johnny pulled up in front of her.

"It's Reed," he told her. "He's been hurt, Sue. I saw one of the Outriders scoop him up and take him into Prodigion's ship."

Sue didn't have to ask how badly Reed had been injured. She could tell from the pained look in Johnny's eyes.

"Take me to him," she said, her heart pounding against her ribs.

The Torch didn't hesitate. Knowing Sue would protect herself from his flames with a force field, he swept her up in his arms and cut a fiery swath through the void. In Prodigion's vessel up ahead, slots were beginning to open for the Outriders' ships, which had taken a terrible beating.

Halfway there, Sue and her brother were intercepted by the Surfer and Ben, both of them riding the Surfer's board. Ben called to Johnny and Johnny yelled back, and soon the four of them were heading for Prodigion's vessel together, sharing a common pain and a common fear.

nlike the Outrider ships, the Surfer didn't use one of the slots that had opened in Prodigion's vessel. He simply melted his way back in, following Reed's molecular-emanation trail as he had before, taking Susan, Ben, and Johnny along with him.

They came out in one of the myriad corridors that circum-navigated the core of the ship. Reed's trail was stronger here, more focused, more recent. The Surfer could hardly have missed it.

Speeding down the corridors on his board, negotiating bend after bend, he moved so quickly the bulkheads on either side of him became a blur. Susan, Ben, and Johnny clutched at one another for support.

But they didn't ask him to slow down. After all, they were in as much of a hurry as he was.

Abruptly, the corridor widened and the ceiling slanted away from them, as if attempting to accommodate a being much larger than they were. Up ahead, the Surfer spotted a mammoth set of doors he hadn't seen before in his travels. They were at least a hundred feet high and five times as thick as any other door on the ship.

But that didn't mean anything to one who wielded the Power Cosmic. With barely a thought, he passed his molecules and those of his friends through the metal-alloy surface, bringing them safely to the other side.

Then and only then did the Surfer slow down—and finally stop—because it was clear to him they'd reached their desti-nation. Like ants at the feet of a human, they looked up.

And saw the entity called Prodigion.

He towered over them just as Galactus had, with the same nobility, the same mountainous grandeur. Clearly he was a being apart, a force of nature as much as a creature of flesh and blood.

And Reed lay in the palm of his hand—a ravaged and broken Reed, his flesh blackened and the rags of his clothing soaked with blood. He wasn't moving, either.

Slowly, but without the least hint of clumsiness, Prodigion's head turned and his eyes took in the sight of them. As black as ebony, they had silver pupils that seemed to pierce the Surfer to his soul.

Susan gasped at the sight of her husband and clutched her brother for support. "My God," she said.

Johnny shook his head, as if in denial. "Reed?"

"Yeah," said the Thing, his voice little more than a whisper. "It's him, all right."

Susan turned to the Surfer. "Can you—?"

"Help him?" he finished.

He floated upward on his silver board, leaving his comrades behind. At first, he feared in his heart that Reed was dead—that they had returned to Prodigion's ship moments too late to save him.

Then he saw the human's eyelids flutter and heard him groan softly in pain, and by those signs he knew his friend was still alive. He held his hands out to the gigantic entity called Prodigion.

"Let me have him," he said. "I can heal him."

But Prodigion shook his massive head. "It is not necessary," he said, and the chamber, large as it was, resounded with the power of his voice. "The healing has already begun."

As the Surfer looked more closely, peering beyond Reed's appearance to his molecular reality, he could see that Prodigion was right. The human's body was repairing itself at a great rate, feeding on an energy that was at once similar to the Power Cosmic and quite different.

An energy that came directly from Prodigion.

"Hey," Ben grunted. "Reed's gettin' better."

Indeed, the restoration being carried out within the body of Mr. Fantastic was making itself known even on the outside now. His bones mended, his wounds closed, his blackened flesh turned pink before their eyes.

And little by little, Reed regained consciousness, became aware of his awesome surroundings. He stared up at Prodigion with wonder in his eyes—for above all, even in the throes of his re-creation, he was still a seeker after knowledge.

"Thank God," Susan sighed. She approached Prodigion. Looking up at him, she said, "And thank *you*."

The colossal figure's eyes moved to take note of her. At first, he seemed impassive, hardly even curious. Then he spoke.

"No," Prodigion replied. "It is I who should be grateful. You risked your lives for me—though truth be told, you need not have intervened."

"We couldn't just sit and watch," Susan explained. "Your Outriders were taking a beating."

By then, Reed's recovery had reached its final stage. He sat up in Prodigion's hand, rotating his arms in their sockets and kneading his shoulder muscles, as if he'd undergone nothing worse than a demanding workout.

"I have other lines of defense besides my Outriders," Prodigion explained to Susan. "Once I had analyzed Blastaar's forces, I would have brought these defenses to bear."

As he said this, he gently lowered Reed to the ground. Susan ran to meet him. As soon as the leader of the Fantastic Four descended from Prodigion's hand, he met his wife's loving embrace—an embrace he returned with gratitude and wonder.

The Surfer eyed Prodigion, humbled by the giant's last remark. "Surely, our efforts were of some value to you."

Prodigion fashioned a benign smile. "Precious little," he replied.

The Thing snorted. "Sheesh. Now he tells us."

"Nonetheless," Prodigion went on, "I am grateful for your concern and your allegiance. And I would like to demonstrate my gratitude."

"No problem there," the Torch responded. Even now, his brother-in-law healed, there was still a note of cynicism in his voice. "Just lend us one of those black needles so we can get home."

Prodigion considered him. "Black needles?"

"One of our ships," Tjellina explained.

The giant absorbed the information. "Unfortunately," he said, "we have but one spaceworthy vessel—and we require it to locate our next planetary destination. If we were to give it up, my life-energy would be wasted." He lifted his chin. "I could not tolerate that."

Tjellina turned to Reed. "If you don't mind waiting awhile," she suggested, "until some of our other vessels can be repaired . . ."

In that moment, the Surfer made a decision. "That will not be necessary," he interjected.

All eyes turned to him. "And why is that?" Prodigion inquired.

He lifted his chin. "Because I can guide you to an appropriate planet myself. In fact, I have some experience performing such a service."

As before, the Surfer saw Susan Richards shoot him a questioning look—a look that reminded him of his vow never to take another master. But as before, he told himself his vow didn't apply here.

How could it be wrong to act as Prodigion's scout? To seek out places where life was faltering or had faltered and invigorate them? Indeed, in what nobler cause could he invest his time and energy?

"In that case," Prodigion announced, "I see no reason to retain the Outrider vessel." He gazed benevolently at Reed. "It is yours, to do with as you see fit. You will find it on our hangar deck."

Mr. Fantastic inclined his head to his mammoth benefactor. "Thank you—from all four of us. And if there's a way to get it back to you, perhaps via some homing device . . . ?"

"It already has such a device," Tjellina promised him. "Wherever you leave the vessel, we will find it."

Reed nodded. "Good." He turned to his wife, then his other two teammates. "Then it's all settled."

He regarded the Surfer and extended his hand. Familiar with human customs, the skyrider took it.

"I hope you're happy here," Mr. Fantastic told him.

"I will try to be," the Surfer replied. Again, he looked at Tjellina. "Though I trust I won't have to work too hard at it."

Susan took his hand next. "Don't be a stranger, all right? You know where our remote sensors are in the Negative Zone. You can always contact us—if only to say hello."

"I will do that," the Surfer assured her.

The Thing rolled his eyes. "Awright awready, we get the idea. Hug hug, kiss kiss, don't ferget ta write. Now let's haul our keesters outta here before someone starts bawlin'."

"Man," Johnny declared, "you're just the soul of sentiment, aren't you?"

"Ya want sentiment," the Thing grumbled, "go watch a soap opera. Me, I'm outta here." With that, he turned his broad, rocky back on them and headed for the exit.

Johnny turned to the Surfer. "Like it or not, I guess I'm out of here too," he said. "Good luck, buddy." Then he glanced at Tjellina. "I hope you don't need it."

"I'm sure he won't," Susan commented, taking her brother's arm. Then she, Reed, and Johnny followed the Thing out into the corridor.

In the silence that followed their departure, the Surfer felt as if he had lost something valuable. He might never again find friends as loyal and true as the Fantastic Four.

But as he regarded Tjellina, he knew he had gained something just as valuable. New friends, for instance, and a mentor, if all went well and Prodigion consented to share his knowledge with the Surfer.

And most important of all, a chance to make up for the evil he had done as Galactus's Herald. For that alone, he would have sacrificed anything and everything.

Sixteen

The Thing sat alongside Johnny at the controls of the borrowed Outrider ship, daydreaming about the home cooking he'd consume when he finally got home.

"A couple o' dozen burgers," he said. "Nice an' rare an' smothered with onions, just the way I like 'em. And a plate full o' those crinkly little french fries."

His teammate glanced at him. "How can you think about food at a time like this? We may have just let the biggest monster in the Negative Zone off the proverbial hook."

The Thing scowled. "Listen, Junior, all that stuff is behind us. We made our decision, so get over it. Move on."

Abruptly, he saw a familiar head float past him on an elongated neck. Ben sighed. *As if it ain't cramped enough in the cockpit already,* he thought.

"Whatcha doin'?" Ben asked. "Checkin' ta see if I'm goofin' off?"

"Nothing of the sort," Reed replied. "You never goof off. You're one of the most dependable people I know." But as he said it, he was scanning the vessel's control panel.

"Then what is it?" the Thing prodded, craning his neck to try to look his friend in the eye. "Ya get tired of sittin' in the aft compartment and playin' footsie with Suzie?"

"Actually," said the Invisible Woman, joining the rest of them in the cockpit, "we were just waiting until we had put enough distance between ourselves and Prodigion."

Reed nodded. "And according to my calculations, which are admittedly a little rough, we should be just about"—he pointed an elasticized finger at the sensor monitor—"there."

The Thing looked at him. "No offense, good buddy, but what in blue blazes are you two yammerin' about?"

"Here you go," said Reed, fiddling with the navigation controls. A set of coordinates came up on the adjacent monitor.

Ben glanced at the monitor, then at his friend, then at the monitor again. "Here I go what?"

Reed smiled. "It's a course change, Ben. One that'll take us to a planet known as Nicanthus Prime in Prodigion's stellar cartography files. Mind you, I'm not sure who gave it that name or even who originally mapped the sector in question, but—"

The Thing held up a huge orange paw. "Hang on, Stretcho. I don't give a rat's fat patootie about Prodigion's computers or who mapped what. I just wanna know what's so important we gotta make a detour for it."

"Because," Reed said, "despite all the evidence to the contrary—despite the impulse to oppose Blastaar that led me to risk my life for Prodigion earlier—I couldn't help feeling there was something eerie about Prodigion's operation."

"I had the same feeling," Sue remarked. "So when I was helping Reed complete his analysis of Prodigion's equipment, we lifted the name and coordinates of the last planet he visited in his travels. We wanted to see for ourselves that he's as benevolent as he claims."

"We'll check out the results of his labors there," Reed explained. "And if we're satisfied Prodigion is as good as his word, we'll turn around and head for home."

"How about that?" said Johnny, no doubt feeling vindicated by this turn of events. He grinned. "I guess I'm not the only oddball who got a creepy feeling from ol' Prodigion."

Ben glared at Reed. "So you and Suzie had this plan all along and you never mentioned it to yours truly? How come I'm always the last to know these things? And while we're on the subject, what else are ya keepin' a secret? Maybe there's a party on the way home ya forgot to invite me to?"

Sue patted him on the shoulder. "It's my fault, Ben. Reed suggested that we alert you and Johnny, but we didn't want to get into a debate on Prodigion's premises. We didn't know what kind of security devices he might have planted around his ship."

The Thing glanced at the course change represented on the monitor. "But what's the point? I mean, even if he was keepin' something from us—even if he turns out to be another Galactus—what're we gonna do about it?"

"If it's something serious," said Reed, "we do what we

did with Galactus. We show him the error of his ways. And even if it's something not so serious, we owe it to the Surfer to establish the truth. After all, without him we wouldn't have a home to go back to.''

"Hey," said Ben, "don't get me wrong, I'm just as grateful to that oversized hood ornament as anybody. I just think we're bein' a lot more suspicious than we need ta be.''

Sue shrugged. "So we go to Nicanthus Prime and we find out Prodigion's a prince after all. No foul, no harm. And we can feel good about leaving the Surfer in the Negative Zone.''

The Thing frowned. "It's still a waste of time, if ya ask me. But as usual, nobody's askin'." Studying the map on the monitor a moment longer, he turned to his navigational controls and made the requisite adjustments. "And here I was hopin' to get back in time for *Oprah*.''

Reducing power to the engines, he brought the craft around. Starlight glinted off the starboard exhaust assembly. It was a smooth maneuver, if he said so himself. Not a single bump or jostle.

Inwardly, Ben patted himself on the back. *What were ya thinkin', ya big lug? Ya still got it in spades. No matter what happened a few years back, yer still the best pilot in the flippin' business. In fact, if ya didn't look like a pile o' orange rocks, life'd be perfect.*

That's when a ruby red energy blast came out of nowhere and sent them pinballing through space. The bulkheads shrieked under the impact. Ben was wrenched free of his seat but managed to hold on to his control console by digging his fingers into its crevices.

For a single, terrifying moment, as he saw the others thrown around by forces beyond their control, Ben had that hideous sense of déjà vu again. He felt as if he were reliving the fateful flight that had given the Fantastic Four their powers.

For that moment, he was afraid there was nothing he could do about it. As on that most bizarre of nights, he felt as if he was up against something too big for one man to beat.

Then the moment passed and he wasn't Ben Grimm anymore. He was the ever-lovin' Thing. And the Thing could beat *anything*.

With renewed determination, he dragged himself back into his pilot's seat. He eyed his monitors. And he did his best to locate the source of the energy blast that had blindsided them.

The Thing's monitors didn't let him down. But when he realized where the attack had come from, his baby blues opened wide. Avoiding another blast might not be as easy as he'd hoped.

"This isn't good," he muttered. "This isn't good at all."

"Ben," gasped Reed. He slithered back into his seat like a rush of water running upstream. "What is it? Who's after us?"

"See for yourself," the Thing suggested.

He watched his friend crane his neck around to peer into the monitor. Reed's eyes narrowed with concern. "Blastaar," he said.

"Correctamundo," Ben confirmed. "And he's got his whole fleet with him—or what's left of it."

It didn't really matter that Blastaar's armada had been knocked down a peg. Even in its torn-up, ragged condition, it was still plenty big enough and strong enough to destroy a single Outrider vessel.

On the other hand, the Thing reminded himself, this wasn't just any Outrider vessel. This one had the toughest man-monster in the galaxy at the helm. And he wasn't giving up without one helluva fight.

"Hang on!" he growled. "They ain't seen nothin' yet!"

And with that, he gunned the engines, hoping to elude pursuit by virtue of speed alone. It only took a few seconds for Ben to realize that wasn't going to work. Blastaar's opening blast seemed to have knocked free some of the vessel's power couplings—so while they could still go fast, they couldn't go fast enough.

On the other hand, speed wasn't the only card they could play. The Outrider ship could still turn on a dime. All Ben had to do was work his way into the midst of Blastaar's fleet and he could tie them up all day. Besides, they'd be scared to fire for fear of hitting their own buddies.

Anyway, that was the theory. In practice, it worked out a little differently.

For one thing, the possibility of hitting their own buddies didn't seem to deter Blastaar's weapons officers in the least. In fact, if Ben didn't know better, he would've sworn they enjoyed it.

For another thing, Blastaar was smarter than the Thing had

given him credit for. Just as he wove his way into the Balu-urian's ranks, the armada began to break up—to scatter. Before Ben knew it, he was out in the open again.

Exactly where he didn't want to be.

He gritted his teeth. It was a setback; that was all. He was still the Thing. He still had the strength and the skill to win, he told himself, if he just kept plugging away at it.

Because of that strength and that skill, it was a long time before he took a second energy blast and then a third. And by that time he'd scored half a dozen choice shots of his own.

Funny, he told himself. He'd expected those energy beams to knock them around a little harder. Then he caught a glimpse of Sue's face and he realized she was shielding them with a force barrier.

A sheen of perspiration on her brow, she managed a smile. "Keep going, Ben. I'm with you all the way."

For a while, that was enough. The Thing wrenched them through maneuver after gut-twisting maneuver and the Invisible Woman kept them from buckling when Blastaar's minions got in a hit.

But they couldn't keep it up forever. They all knew that. The handwriting was on the wall.

It was Reed, naturally, who volunteered to read it out loud. "That's enough, Ben. You've done your best, but we can't beat them at this game. There are just too many of them."

"So what do I do?" the Thing growled back at him. "Pull over onto the flippin' shoulder? This ain't exactly I-95, y'know—and Blastaar ain't gonna be content givin' us a speedin' ticket!"

"Nonetheless," his friend insisted, "it's our only chance."

Ben didn't like the idea of baring their throats to the Living Bomb-Burst. He had a feeling they were only postponing the inevitable.

On the other hand, Reed didn't make too many bad calls. If he thought discretion was the better part of valor in this case, the Thing couldn't just ignore him. Scowling, he cut their speed to nothing.

And prayed the gods who ruled the Negative Zone had a soft spot for rock piles named Ben.

• • • •

With Tjellina standing before him, protected from the vagaries of the void by a cocoon of cosmic energy, the Surfer glided through the Negative Zone at a speed an Outrider could only have dreamed of.

"I was wrong," Tjellina said.

The Surfer looked at her, unable to see much of her face past the sweep of her hair. "Wrong? About what?" he asked.

She turned to look at him. "Back on Prodigion's ship, when I was running those tests on you, I called your abilities amazing. But they're more than that. A great deal more." She glanced at the stars that streamed by them. "You can do things even Prodigion can't. And as far as I knew, he was the most powerful being in the universe."

"What Prodigion does is more amazing to me," the Surfer replied. "And more important as well. With your help, I can find a place where his labors might prove fruitful. But the miracle of life he brings forth . . . that is something I can only admire."

For a time, they sped among the stars in silence. Then Tjellina spoke again. "There is something else I was wrong about."

"And that is?" he inquired.

As he waited for an answer, her hand slipped into his and drew his arm around her. The Surfer didn't resist in the least. In fact, he reveled in the nearness of her.

"I thought my work was enough," she explained at last. "I thought I was fulfilled. But the moment I saw you, I knew there was an emptiness that had never been filled. Nor could it be, except by you."

Tjellina turned in the Surfer's arms and gazed into his eyes. Her fingers touched his chest lightly, like raindrops.

"I wouldn't have asked you to stay," she told him. "With you on one course and myself on another, it wouldn't have been fair of me to make such a request. But when you offered to remain with us, to scout out worlds where Prodigion could sow his seeds . . ."

Tjellina never finished her sentence. Raising herself on her tiptoes, she leaned closer to the Surfer and brushed her mouth against his. And like a man who had thirsted all his life, he quenched his thirst.

When he was done, he leaned his lips against her golden forehead and stroked her raven hair. It was soft to his touch, so soft.

"I love you," Tjellina whispered.

It had been a long time since the Surfer had known the love of a woman. Or, for that matter, known a woman he might love. But the Outrider dredged up in him emotions he had felt only once since his days with Shalla Bal—with Nova, another of Galactus's Heralds. Emotions that, since Nova's death, he had never expected to feel again.

Perhaps part of it was the empathy he felt for her, since she performed a function similar to the one he had performed for Galactus. Perhaps part of it was his admiration for her courage and her selflessness.

But not all, the Surfer told himself. Not all.

"I love you," he said in return.

The Surfer had never expected to find companionship or fulfillment again as long as he lived. And now, it seemed, in a stroke of great good fortune, he had found both.

"We have work to do," Tjellina reminded him.

"Work," he echoed, as if he'd never heard the word before. Gradually, he released her. "It pains me to let go of you."

Tjellina chuckled. "A romantic. Is there anything about you that is not perfect, Norrin Radd?"

"I am far from perfect," the Surfer assured her. "But with your help—and Prodigion's—perhaps I can approach that state."

She turned away from him then, to better focus on the job ahead. He tried to do the same, but it wasn't easy. He couldn't help thinking how bright the future suddenly looked for him.

He had found a like mind in a previously empty and lonely universe. He knew how rare a gift that was. How precious.

The Surfer didn't know what kind of relationship he would have with Tjellina. He didn't know if they would complement each other the way he and a young Shalla Bal had complemented each other. But more and more, he was eager to find out.

In time, their search was rewarded. They found a star system with several planets, at least one of which was parched enough to satisfy Prodigion's criteria. Their mission accomplished, they turned around and sped back to make their report.

The Surfer trusted it would be the first of many such missions. For there was much he could accomplish in this fashion—and each life he saved was like a balm to his soul.

Seventeen

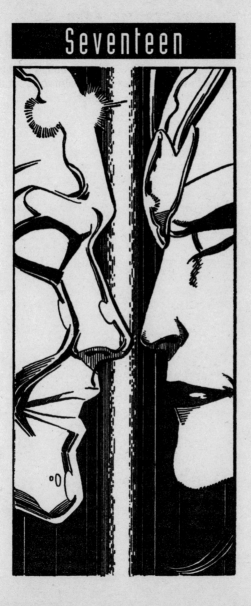

As Ben cut their engines and they drifted through the void, and Blastaar's forces surrounded them like hungry jackals, Reed wondered if he'd made the right decision after all.

Then again, there hadn't been a great many options open to them. Not the kind they would survive, at least.

Of course, they could have used their harnesses to slip out of the ship and work their way through the fleet. With the help of Sue's force fields, they might even have made it in one piece.

However, that would only have delayed the inevitable. They were a long way from the portal back to Earth—and given that much time, Blastaar's minions eventually would have landed a knockout blow.

The Torch, with his ability to soar at high speeds, was the only one with a legitimate shot at escape. But Reed didn't believe the boy would've left his teammates behind.

Besides, Reed told himself, *it's too late now to have second thoughts.* Blastaar's flagship was already nudging its way into the first ring of vessels, looking every bit as belligerent as before.

"We're cooked now," Johnny breathed.

"The hell we are," Ben rumbled.

Reed just frowned. By then, Blastaar's flagship and its bristling armaments had come almost nose to nose with the Outrider vessel. But it just hung there in space, as if waiting for something.

"Why doesn't he fire and get it over with?" Johnny asked.

"He's not going to fire," Sue told him.

Her brother looked at her. "He's not?"

"That's right," Reed agreed, smiling at Sue's perceptiveness. "If he was going to fire, he would have maintained his distance. At this range, the repercussion from an energy blast would damage his ship almost as badly as it would damage ours."

"No one ever said Blastaar had all his marbles," the Thing commented.

But Ben had been a fighter pilot. He, too, must have suspected the Baluurian had something else in mind.

Suddenly, Blastaar's gray, bestial face filled the confines of their monitor and his voice grated at them over the vessel's speakers.

"Why?" he demanded, spittle flying from his savage mouth. "Why did you see fit to betray me?"

The question was almost humorous, considering the source. But the Fantastic Four weren't in the mood to laugh.

"We didn't betray you," Reed responded. "All we did is prevent you from destroying the one you call the 'planet-eater.' "

"And is that not the same thing?" the tyrant raged.

Reed shook his head. "It's not the same at all. You were operating under the assumption that Prodigion was a threat, as the legends said. But we had a chance to meet him—to inspect his ship and his data logs. And everything we learned about him refutes that assumption."

Blastaar's tiny, black eyes narrowed warily. "Prodigion, you call him?"

"That's his name, yes."

"And what is he, if not a destroyer?"

Reed met the Baluurian's anger as calmly as possible. "As far as we could tell, he's just the opposite. He appears to bring nourishment to parched, shriveled ecosystems—establishing life where the natives have nothing to look forward to but death."

The Baluurian grimaced. "And you *believe* this drivel?"

Mr. Fantastic felt something stiffen in him. "I'm a scientist," he said. "That means I'm skeptical by nature. But I couldn't let you destroy Prodigion until I'd seen his results with my own eyes."

"And where can one see such marvelous results?" Blastaar snarled.

"On a planet Prodigion visited recently," Reed replied. "A place called Nicanthus Prime."

The Baluurian shook his shaggy head at what he obviously

considered the Fantastic Four's stupidity. Turning away from the monitor, he barked an order at one of his functionaries.

A moment later, Reed felt their ship lurch beneath them. He exchanged glances with Sue.

"Tractor beam," she concluded.

Mr. Fantastic nodded. Then he turned back to Blastaar, who was glaring at him again. "Where are you taking us?" he asked.

The tyrant leered. "You wanted to see Nicanthus Prime, Reed Richards? Then see it you shall. In fact, I'll provide an escort."

With that, Blastaar's image vanished from their monitor. Then his flagship came about with the Outrider vessel in tow and made its way through the ranks of his armada.

Reed couldn't conceal his surprise. Judging from his teammates' expressions, they'd been caught off guard as well.

"Ya see?" the Thing said. "All we had to do was ask nicely. The guy's got a heart as big as the whole Negative Zone."

Johnny grunted. "If he does, it's someone else's. And knowing Blastaar, it's on a stick."

Clearing the armada with the Fantastic Four still dragging behind, the Baluurian's ship accelerated into the immensity of space. One way or the other, Reed observed, it seemed they would see Nicanthus Prime and have a chance to inspect Prodigion's handiwork.

And in doing so, obtain the answers they needed.

As the Surfer glided through the cosmos of the Negative Zone, his arm around Tjellina, he knew that he had never been so happy.

Not even when he was Norrin Radd, winding his way through the sunny, perpetually blooming gardens of Zenn-La with a beautiful companion like Shalla Bal on his arm. Not even then.

For he had been young in those days, young and innocent. He had never imagined the tortures Fate had in store for him. He had yet to know guilt or self-loathing or the stark gray emptiness of despair.

Norrin Radd hadn't dreamt how far a man could sink. Indeed, he'd had no reason to explore such territory.

But the Silver Surfer had lived a waking nightmare, without respite or quarter. Year after year, he had searched the galaxy for hope, for absolution. And he'd found it in the last place he would have expected.

The Surfer was older than Norrin Radd, older and a great deal wiser. Having again found happiness, he knew how precious it was, how utterly rare. And he would never again let go of it.

Up ahead, he saw Prodigion's ship. "We're almost home," he told Tjellina.

She looked at him. "I don't see a thing."

"You will," the Surfer assured her.

And in time, she did. Tjellina smiled at the sight. "Your eyesight is amazing," she told him. And then: "You see? Even with all the tests I performed, you're still capable of surprising me."

The Surfer smiled as well. Looping his way around Prodigion's ship in a sort of victory lap, he melted Tjellina and himself through the molecular structure of the hull and into a corridor.

Then, his knowledge of the vessel having improved since he first entered it, he made his way directly to Prodigion's chambers. The giant was intent on one of his monitors, but he turned to acknowledge their approach.

"Surfer," Prodigion said, his voice booming through the high-ceilinged space. "And Tjellina."

"We're back," the Outrider confirmed, stepping off the Surfer's board. "And we've located what you need. In fact, no Outrider has ever found a better place on her own."

The giant nodded his massive head. "That is good to hear," he remarked. He eyed the Surfer in particular. "I am indebted to you."

"No," the Surfer told him, descending from his board as well. "It is I who stand in debt. By conferring this responsibility on me, by making me your scout, you've given me something more valuable than I can repay—even if I served you for all eternity."

Prodigion considered him. "Then I am doubly pleased." He turned to Tjellina. "I will need the pertinent coordinates. The urge to sow my lifeseeds is upon me."

"Of course," the Outrider replied.

Striding across the room to a smaller console, she programmed the data into Prodigion's system. Then she returned to the Surfer's side.

"The stardrive has been given a destination," Tjellina said. "All you need to do is activate it."

"Thank you," Prodigion told her.

He reached out with his mighty hand and touched a square shape in his console. A moment later, the Surfer could feel a vibration in the deckplates that told him they'd changed course—and perhaps accelerated as well.

Tjellina turned to the Surfer. "Would you do something for me?"

"Anything," he told her.

"Would you take me outside again?" she asked, her eyes dancing with anticipation. "So we can soar beside the ship?"

He regarded her. "Was that your practice as an Outrider?"

Tjellina shook her head. "No. But I would like to make it a practice from now on. After all, I enjoyed our journey as I've enjoyed little else."

The Surfer shrugged. "As you wish."

Together, they mounted his board and left Prodigion to his labors. Then they melted through the hull of Prodigion's vessel and regained the star-studded immensity of space.

Later, there would be time for quiet moments and intimacies. For now, the Surfer was content to shepherd the great ship as it negotiated Negative Zone space, seeking the destination he'd provided.

And to bask in the knowledge that Tjellina was at his side.

On the monitor in front of Reed, a series of green and red graphics told him they were approaching Nicanthus Prime. "We're getting close," he notified his teammates.

"Which one are you," the Thing grunted, "Huntley or Brinkley?"

Again Blastaar's savage, lion-maned visage leered at the Fantastic Four from every monitor on their control board.

"We have arrived at our destination," the tyrant announced with a snarl.

"Yeah, yeah, we heard," Ben grumbled.

He tried to adjust the controls, to free them up so he and

his partners could see what was going on. But it wasn't working.

"Nuts!" he growled. "That beady-eyed Baluurian slob is on every flippin' station we got—even PBS!"

Ignoring his comrade's remark, Reed stretched an arm around him and ran a diagnostic program. In a matter of seconds, he got the results.

"Looks like Blastaar's slaved our comm system to his own," he announced.

"But why?" Sue asked.

Blastaar chuckled grimly. "You wanted a look at Nicanthus Prime, did you not? Well, have a *good* look."

A moment later, the Baluurian's face disappeared—to be replaced by a host of other images. And each of them, it seemed to Mr. Fantastic, was a view of the planet's surface.

A view of something horrible.

"Jeez," said the Thing, the green glare of the monitors reflected in his narrowing eyes.

Johnny's face screwed up in sympathy as he peered at a screen over his friend's shoulder. "You can say that again."

These weren't the sort of scenes their stay with Prodigion had led them to expect. They weren't idyllic images of life aborning, but life overgrowing. They were glimpses of something ghastly—a nightmare of mind-boggling proportions to which Reed could hardly stand to bear witness.

Where Galactus would have starved a planet of life-giving energy, Prodigion had gorged Nicanthus Prime with too much life. Like crops overinfested with weeds, eventually the planet's native life would choke and wither and die.

Sue turned to him, her eyes full of anguish. "Isn't there anything we can do?" she asked.

Reed shook his head sadly. "Not for these people. It's too far along for them." The muscles in his jaw fluttered. "But we can make sure it doesn't happen elsewhere."

Abruptly, the scenes from the planet's surface disappeared—to be replaced by the image of Blastaar they'd seen earlier. The tyrant looked intolerably smug.

"I take it you've seen enough," he said.

"Quite enough," Reed confirmed. "And I don't imagine you towed us all the way here just to make a point. You still want our help."

The tyrant shook his shaggy head. "No," he said, "I don't want your help. But unfortunately, even with all the firepower I've accumulated, I may yet need it."

The leader of the Fantastic Four looked to his teammates. "Once again, we and Blastaar appear to have a common purpose. Except this time, we needn't be observers. We've seen all we need to see."

Johnny grunted. "If you're asking what I think we should do, I think we should take Prodigion down. But then, I've been saying that all along."

The Thing sighed noisily. "I'm with ya, Stretch." He tilted his head to indicate the image of Blastaar on the monitor beside him. "Much as I hate the idea of teamin' up with Maggot Face, I'll make an exception."

Reed glanced at his wife. "Sue?"

She looked steely eyed, resolute. "It's unanimous," she replied.

Mr. Fantastic turned to Blastaar—or anyway, one of the many Blastaars he saw peering at him from the control console. "Looks like you've got yourself some allies," he told the Baluurian.

Blastaar scowled. "It's about time," he said. And then his image was gone, replaced by a different graphic on each monitor.

"He's released us from his communications lock," Sue observed.

Ben worked his controls. "From his tractor lock too, Suzie. We're free to go anywhere we want . . . as long as it's where he wants us to go." He turned to Reed. "Hey, Stretch. Just promise me one thing, all right?"

"What's that, old friend?"

"That this is the last time we'll be changin' sides in this donnybrook. My head's startin' to hurt."

Reed glanced out an observation port, where the too-lush, blue-green sweep of Nicanthus Prime was starting to drop away. Then he looked at the Thing again.

"I promise."

Eighteen

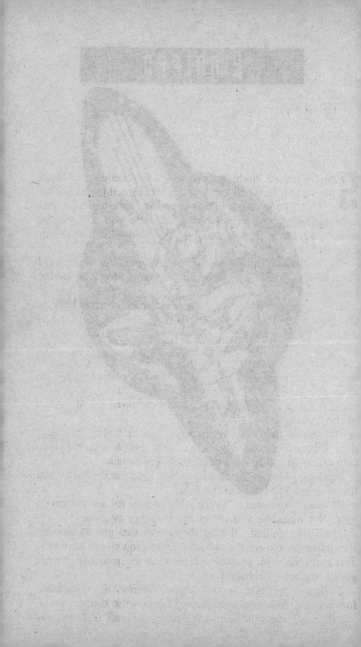

Shortly before Prodigion's vessel was scheduled to reach the system they had located, Tjellina turned to the Surfer.

"I'd like to return to the ship now," she told him. Her eyes suddenly grew vulnerable. "It's time you and I spent some time alone. I wish to"—she smiled—"celebrate our success."

The Surfer nodded, pleased at the prospect. Veering toward Prodigion's vessel, he used the Power Cosmic to penetrate the hull.

They came out in one of the myriad research chambers on the ship. A single monitor was working. The image on it was that of a thriving cityscape, blessed with waterfalls and a cornucopia of thick, rich foliage.

As the Surfer watched, the image changed. The monitor showed a parklike scene, in which individual beings could be seen interacting. The beings, a slender, dark-eyed people, seemed happy, healthy, and thoroughly amused by the antics of their young.

The Surfer didn't know these people well enough to say their situation was an idyllic one. But that was the obvious conclusion based on the evidence he had at hand.

Suddenly, Tjellina interposed herself between the Surfer and the monitor. She held out her hand.

"Come," she said. "There's no reason for us to remain here. Not when the solitude of my chamber awaits us."

The Surfer smiled. "I look forward to that just as you do. But those people on the monitor have piqued my curiosity. Tell me," he said, craning his neck to see past her, "what planet might they inhabit?"

Tjellina didn't turn to look at the monitor. She just came forward and embraced him. Kissed him on the lips.

"Please," she told him. "We have done all that was expected of us. It's our time. Time for us to enjoy each other's company."

"Of course," the Surfer assured her. "But . . ."

As he caught sight of the monitor, he saw that the scene had changed again. It showed him a planet hanging in space, illuminated on one side by its sun, its other side in darkness.

It was a green world, not unlike Earth. A thriving world. As he looked on, it loomed larger, closer, as if it were their destination.

The Surfer knew that world. He had seen it from afar, but he remembered it. It was the third planet in the system they had located—the system they were approaching so Prodigion could sow his seeds.

But it wasn't the world they were supposed to be heading for—the world that needed them. That was the sixth.

"Something's wrong," he said, feeling his throat tighten. "That planet . . . it's green already. It's full of life."

The energy Prodigion bestowed on a planet was designed to spur a proliferation of flora and fauna—an explosion of fecundity that would otherwise take millennia. But on a planet already full of life, that proliferation would leave no room for existing species.

They would be overrun. Trampled in the rush of new species.

The Surfer turned to Tjellina, horrified. "There's been a mistake. We've got to do something."

"There's no mistake," the Outrider told him, her tone strangely flat and distant. "Prodigion's function is to plant the seeds of new life where they're most likely to survive."

The Surfer shook his head, perplexed by her answer. "But what about the life that exists there already?" he asked, indicating their target with a gesture. "Won't it be destroyed by so much unfettered growth?"

Tjellina shrugged, strangely untroubled. "That's irrelevant, I'm afraid. Prodigion's mission is to create life. What existed there before is of no importance—either to him or to us."

He stared at her. "You can't be serious," he whispered.

The Outrider returned his stare. Her eyes were no longer warm and full of humor, as he had known them, but cold as space itself.

"Can't I?" she replied.

The Surfer wanted desperately not to believe what he was hearing. However, one look at Tjellina's expression told him it was the truth.

She meant to doom the sentients on that world and every other life-form on the planet as well. What's more, she meant to do it without a second thought, like the dutiful Herald she was.

And what of Prodigion? If Tjellina was intent on murder, he had to be equally guilty, equally to blame. Certainly, his methods were vastly different from those of Galactus. But the results seemed much the same: fear and misery, death and destruction.

Worst of all, the Surfer had been a part of it. Of his own volition, he had mapped out a path to this system for Prodigion. Intentionally or otherwise, he had made himself a pawn in a civilization's doom.

After he had sworn never again to serve such a master, or to hurt another living soul. How could he have been so blind? So trusting? How could he have allowed this to happen?

No matter, he told himself. There was still time to make amends for his gullibility. That world he had seen could still be saved.

Turning away from Tjellina and her treachery, he called his board to him and tucked it under his arm. Then he headed for the bulkhead. His intention was to melt through it, as he had on other occasions.

But before he could get within a meter of the smooth, metal surface, he felt himself ensconced in a field of naked, pulsating energy. Surrounded by it on all sides. He reached out to touch it and a confusion of white-hot plasma sparks sizzled beneath his silver palm.

Tjellina spoke to him from across the room, where she stood beside a control console. "You will find it's useless for you to try to free yourself. Even the floor is charged with the energy barrier, although it's a couple of millimeters below your feet."

She paused, her face a mask. It was as if she were someone other than the woman he'd known.

"Remember the experiments we conducted? The tests I put you through? The data went to good use."

The Surfer needed no further explanation. "You designed this force field with me in mind."

The Outrider nodded. "It was my objective from the beginning to harness your power on Prodigion's behalf. However"—and here her voice softened and the mask fell—"matters didn't proceed exactly as I'd planned. I hadn't expected to fall in love with you."

He lifted his chin. "More lies, Tjellina? For what purpose? You've gotten everything you wanted."

"No," she told him, approaching his energy prison, her eyes suddenly as soft as he'd ever seen them. "Not everything, Norrin Radd. Not you."

The Surfer frowned, knowing exactly what she meant. "You did have me—when I was your dupe. But no longer."

Tjellina reached for him, her outstretched fingers falling just short of the energy barrier. There was longing in her face, naked and unmistakable. "My affection was real," she insisted. "It still is."

He didn't answer. He just turned away and touched another spot on his prison. There, too, a sizzling of plasma grew under his hand.

"Was it so wrong," she asked, "to want to share my mission with you? To bestow life on planet after planet? Despite your misgivings, it's a noble mission. A *necessary* mission. There's a balance, Norrin Radd. Without Prodigion, without the seeds he spreads, that balance would be lost."

It was the same with Galactus, he reflected. But that didn't mean he had to be a party to it. Death, too, was part of the balance—but that didn't compel him to become a murderer.

Tjellina circumnavigated the force field until she was standing in front of him again. "We could still serve Prodigion's needs," she said. "You and I—we would be good together. After all, we're so much alike."

The Surfer looked at her. "No," he replied softly. "You and I are not at all alike."

"We're powerful," she argued, "each in his or her own way."

"That is where the resemblance ends," he argued back. "You are clever, conniving, and I've been a fool—allowing myself to be deceived by you and by Prodigion as I was once deceived by Galactus. Because of that lapse, that lack of judgment, I've doomed an entire planetary population to a horrible competition for survival." He grimaced with disgust—mostly for himself. "Far from reducing my burden of guilt, I've added to it."

Hurt and disappointed, the Surfer focused on the forces surrounding him. There didn't seem to be a flaw in them he could capitalize on, but he had to try. Marshaling his pain, his humiliation, he pointed at the field and unleashed the most powerful blast he could muster.

It bounded back at the Surfer with stunning effect, sending him flying backward into the opposite side of the barrier. As he got to his feet and recovered his board, he saw his effort hadn't made a dent. As Tjellina had warned him, the field was too strong for him.

Thanks to the naïveté he had thought was behind him, the Surfer was powerless to stop Prodigion from wreaking havoc on an innocent planet. In fact, he was powerless even to leave this room.

Tjellina regarded him. "I wish you could see things as I do. I wish you could see the virtue, the glory."

"There's no virtue in taking advantage of the weak and powerless. In that," he said, "there's only villainy. And madness."

The Outrider looked at him, her eyes bright and liquid. "I'm sorry you think so," she told him. "I'm truly sorry."

Then she left him to contemplate his fate.

So much for Baluur's astronomers, Blastaar thought, trying his best to control his seething anger. If—*when* he got home, he would flay them alive and then personally roll them in salt.

They'd told his councillors that Prodigion wouldn't come anywhere near his holdings. That his empire would be safe.

Yet his flagship's monitor showed otherwise. In the solar system up ahead—a system known as Sorenion, which he had claimed years ago—Prodigion had established orbit around the third planet out.

For all the tyrant knew, the planet-eater was already working his infernal magic on it, planting the seeds of destruction. If he wasn't stopped here and now, the Baluurian worlds would surely be next.

His officers turned to him expectantly. "Orders?" asked his pilot.

The tyrant leaned forward in his chair. Consulting a secondary monitor, he made sure the Fantastic Four hadn't abandoned him again.

With some satisfaction, he saw their vessel was keeping pace with the rest of his armada. He turned back to his pilot.

"Attack," he grated.

"Yes, my lord," came the response—and not from the pilot alone, but from a dozen different throats on Blastaar's bridge.

The enemy would soon be engaged. The battle was on. And its results would be felt throughout the Negative Zone, perhaps for eons to come.

Nineteen

"They're coming," Amalyn called out.

Tjellina nodded. "I see them."

Indeed, as she pivoted in her seat in the tactical center, surrounded by her fellow Outriders, she saw the entirety of Blastaar's attack force on her various monitors. But neither she nor her colleagues could ride out into space to oppose them.

After all, their ships were still in various states of disrepair—it would have been foolhardy to risk flying them in combat. Ironically, the only Outrider vessel that had been battle-ready was coming at them as an enemy. By that sign, she imagined the Fantastic Four had discovered the truth about Prodigion's agenda.

Still, it wouldn't do them any good. Just as it wouldn't do Blastaar any good to throw the remnants of his armada against them. As Prodigion had told the Surfer and his friends, his ship boasted many more defenses than his Outriders could provide.

Working her controls with all the speed and dexterity she could muster, Tjellina activated some of those defenses. At least, the ones she could deploy on short notice.

First, a force shield so powerful it wouldn't matter if Blastaar divined its frequency. Unfortunately, it would draw too much power to leave it up for long. But it would protect them from the enemy's initial attack, when they needed it most.

Next, she brought the disrupters online. According to the Outriders' scouting reports, neither the Baluurians nor their allies had ever faced such a weapon—though like the shield, the disrupters would draw a great deal of power and had to be used sparingly.

Neither the enhanced shield nor the disrupters would've been effective against Blastaar's earlier forces. He would simply have worn them out over time. But then, the Baluurian's fleet had been depleted in both size and strength.

"Ten thousand meters and closing," Amalyn snapped.

"Tjellina," another of her colleagues cried out. "They've entered optimum weapons range."

She smiled grimly. "Hold your fire for a moment. Let them think they've caught us unawares."

The Outriders, as disciplined a group as existed in the entire Negative Zone, did exactly as they were told. Finally, when their attackers were practically on top of them, Tjellina barked a command.

"Fire!"

As the Surfer watched the monitor in the room from his energy prison, he saw Prodigion's barrage obliterate the whole first rank of Blastaar's ships. There was nothing left of them, not even molecular debris. They had simply been wiped from existence.

He grated his teeth. The Baluurians were savages, but no one deserved to die that way. If he had been out there, he might have prevented it.

Instead, the Surfer was imprisoned in Prodigion's vessel, contained like a lab animal within the force field Tjellina had devised for him. He laid his palm against it as he had before. Plasma sparks crackled furiously beneath his silver flesh.

The blast of raw power he'd applied before had only backfired on him. *Perhaps*, the Surfer thought, *if I try a different tack, I'll have better luck.*

Toward that end, he pressed against the rage of sparks. Harder and harder he pushed, despite the searing pain that he felt against his palm, despite the rigidity of the field. It was resisting him as he hadn't imagined anything could, save for the constructs of Galactus.

And still the Surfer pushed, applying all of his strength, all of his pent-up fury and frustration. But the field wouldn't budge. With a cry of disgust, he pulled his hand away. He'd failed again. He turned back to the monitor, where another wave of Blastaar's ships flung itself against Prodigion's fortress. They, too, were annihilated.

Somehow, the Surfer thought, he would find a way to stop the bloodshed. Or he would die trying.

• • •

Reed shook his head. Blastaar's forces were taking a terrible beating. And every energy assault they made was turned back by an invisible barrier—one the tyrant obviously couldn't solve.

"Where's the Surfer?" the Thing wondered. "He'd crack that force shield like a piece o' cheap plastic."

The Torch nodded. "Good question, Ben. You would think he'd be out here, wouldn't you? That is, if he still believed in Prodigion's cause."

Sue frowned. "Maybe he discovered the truth and abandoned Prodigion."

"Or tried to," Reed added.

His wife turned to him. "You think Prodigion could've stopped him? Maybe imprisoned him?"

"Anything's possible," Reed reminded her. "Either way," he said, pointing to Prodigion's vessel, "we've got to get inside that ship and take out its defenses. Otherwise, our collective goose is cooked."

"Then we'll do it," Sue resolved.

"You got that right," Johnny chipped in. "I mean, we *are* the Fantastic Four, aren't we?"

The Thing grunted. "No matter what, it'll be better than sittin' in this here tin can and waitin' ta meet our maker. Let's get 'em, Stretch."

The Torch was the first one out of their vessel. Flaming on as he released himself into the void, he executed a tight loop and went hurtling toward Prodigion's fortress.

Sue came next, approaching their target a little more slowly under harness power. Her husband followed, and Ben brought up the rear.

This was it, Reed thought. Blastaar had enlisted them for just such a moment, counting on their powers and resourcefulness. Now they would see if he'd made the right choice.

The Torch slashed his way through Negative Zone space, closing with the foreboding gray surface of Prodigion's ship.

Somewhere in front of him, there was an invisible barrier. He was intensely aware of that. He didn't know exactly where it was, but he had a way to find out. Creating a sizable fireball in his palm, he reached back and flung it at the vessel.

Less than thirty feet from the hull, the fireball smashed into a dozen flaming streamers. There was no energy feedback, just the high-tech equivalent of a brick wall.

The Torch was reminded of a line from Robert Frost: "Something there is that doesn't love a wall." Well, he thought, he wasn't too fond of them either—and being a card-carrying member of the Fantastic Four, he had the power to do something about them.

The other day, when he'd encountered the Outriders for the first time, Johnny had managed to pierce their shields with a souped-up fireball. He figured the tactic was worth a shot here too.

Except he'd use something a bit bigger than a fireball to penetrate Prodigion's defenses.

Looping around in a big circle to gain momentum, the Torch concentrated on burning hotter. And hotter. And hotter still, until his flame had been fanned to white-hot intensity and he himself had become a raging supernova.

He knew he wouldn't be able to keep it up for long. But then, if all went well, he wouldn't have to.

Plunging down toward Prodigion's ship, Johnny tried to remember where his fireball had splattered. He tried to picture it in his mind. And when he approached that point, he increased his velocity even more.

Impact, he thought.

A split second later, the Torch smashed into Prodigion's invisible barrier, hitting it as hard as he'd ever hit anything in his life. There was a flare of mind-numbing force that obliterated all sight and sound.

Then he found himself drifting, his flame all but spent. Turning it up again, he looked around and saw he wasn't far from Prodigion's hull. But was he inside or outside the force shield?

Creating a tiny fireball, the Torch tossed it in the ship's direction. It didn't get very far—only a few feet—before it flew apart on impact with the barrier.

He was outside.

Swallowing his disappointment, the Torch looked around for his teammates. They were only now reaching the barrier, at a point perhaps two hundred feet down the line.

Skimming the surface of the barrier, he went to join them.

After all, he hadn't been able to accomplish anything by himself. Maybe they would do better as a team.

Sue had seen her brother's effort to penetrate the barrier. Johnny's nova flame had proven to be an immensely powerful tool in the Human Torch's arsenal, and to see it fail so miserably proved disheartening.

But the Invisible Woman was no slouch either. As she neared the force shield, she tried to estimate its location based on her brother's efforts. Then she created an invisible construct of her own.

First, she used it to more firmly establish the barrier's location. Then she probed it for weaknesses. Unfortunately, she couldn't find any. The shield seemed uniformly impregnable.

Sue swallowed, conscious that if she remained in one spot long enough, one of Prodigion's weapons stations might open fire on her. Even with Blastaar throwing everything he had at the vessel, her presence in the area of the force shield might be considered a higher priority.

Still, she was far from ready to give up. As a member of the Fantastic Four, she'd faced lots of seemingly impossible situations. To her, this was just business as usual.

"Hang on, Suzie!" bellowed a gravelly voice.

Turning, she saw Ben approaching the barrier in his harness, with Reed right behind him.

Then she remembered one aspect of her power that she rarely had the need to use. While she could render visible things invisible, the power also worked in reverse—she could make the invisible visible.

She concentrated for a moment, and then the crackling energy of Prodigion's force shield could be seen by one and all. *That should give Blastaar's fleet something to aim at.*

Then she looked over at the Thing, who was pulling his right fist back. Sue smiled. *And something for Ben to aim at, too.*

"It's clobberin' time!" he growled—and walloped Prodigion's force shield with enough power to split a fair-sized mountain. Unfortunately, it wasn't enough power to split a fair-sized force shield.

And because every action has an equal and opposite reaction, Ben went bounding in the direction he'd come from. It took Reed a moment to reel him back in.

"Fer Pete's sake," the Thing groaned. "What am I, a super hero or a blasted Ping-Pong ball?"

Nonetheless, Sue noted, his punch had had an effect. And a very interesting effect, at that.

She wouldn't have known it if she hadn't turned the field visible, but the energy pattern had momentarily changed in the spot that Ben had hit, briefly allowing Prodigion's vessel to once again be seen behind the barrier.

"Ben," Sue said, "do that again."

He looked at her. "Ya mean hit it?"

"Yes," Reed confirmed. He had obviously seen it, too. "Hit it, just as Sue instructed. As hard as you possibly can."

The Thing shrugged his rocky shoulders. "Whatever you say. But if it didn't work the first time . . ."

He pounded on the shield a second time. Once again, the barrier weakened, the temporary hole a bit bigger this time. Once again, Ben went flying backward. And once again, Reed snared his friend before he could go very far.

"Are we havin' fun yet?" the Thing asked grumpily.

"I wouldn't call it fun," Sue responded. "But I think we're getting somewhere, which may be better." She turned to Reed. "If we up the ante, I might be able to drive a force field wedge into one of those holes as it opens up."

Her husband's eyes lit up. "And we can slip something tiny through the barrier. Say, a man who can make himself the size of a straw."

"That's the objective," Sue replied.

Just then, the Torch arrived, his flame crackling around him. "No luck?" he asked sympathetically.

"Maybe a lot of luck," his sister told him. And she explained what she meant. "So if Ben hammers at the barrier— and you attack it as well—Reed may have a shot."

Johnny eyed his teammates. "Then let's do it."

The Thing nodded. "On yer mark . . ."

"Get set . . ." Reed continued.

"Go!" the Invisible Woman cried out.

Hovering in front of the barrier, the Torch blasted away with one gout of flame after the other. At the same time, Ben pummeled the shield with both fists—while Reed made a seat belt of himself and held his friend in place.

The power they brought to bear was staggering. As Sue had anticipated, it didn't put a permanent dent in the shield. But it did create several soft spots.

Fashioning as narrow a wedge as she could, the Invisible Woman drove it into one of the holes opened by Ben and Johnny's barrages, and pushed for all she was worth. To her delight, the barrier yielded, and the wedge stayed.

It was not yet wide enough for Reed to squeeze inside. But now she had a foothold—enough to spur her to an even greater exertion.

Clenching her jaw, Sue redoubled her efforts. It wasn't easy in any sense. It made her head ache and her muscles burn, as if with an oxygen deficit. It made her fingers tighten into hard, cramped fists.

But by dint of sweat and willpower, she did what she'd set out to do. She forced open a tiny access point in the barrier.

''Now!'' Sue moaned.

Reed didn't need any more of an announcement than that. Like a featherless shaft, he shot through the opening.

But partway through, it began to close on him. Reed's head, still narrow and elongated, turned inside the shield. His eyes reflected the agony he was feeling as his torso was pinched to almost nothing.

At times, it seemed Reed could assume any shape he wanted. However, even he had his limits. And at that moment, the forces working to close the barrier were squeezing the life out of him.

''No!'' the Invisible Woman grated.

She wouldn't let it happen. She wouldn't let Reed perish that way.

Pouring every ounce of strength she had into the struggle, she pried the hole open again. Wider, wider . . . fighting the darkness that impinged on the edges of her vision, battling the vertigo that threatened to overwhelm her . . . until her husband squirted through.

Then she yielded to the inevitable and felt the darkness overwhelm her.

Twenty

'm in, Reed thought.

But at what price? He turned back to look at Sue, who floated limply on the other side of the force shield—which had once again turned invisible. She looked pale and spent, as the Torch flamed off and gathered her in his arms.

"Johnny!" he called. "Is she all right?"

But his brother-in-law didn't seem to hear him. Reed cursed inwardly. Of course. If the barrier was designed to keep out energy assaults, it would keep out *all* energy—sound waves included.

Instead of speaking again, he waved to Johnny. The teenager didn't see him at first. He was too intent on his sister's condition. But the Thing saw Reed gesturing and tapped the Torch on the shoulder.

As soon as Johnny acknowledged him, Reed pointed to Sue. The boy gave him the thumbs-up. Sue was going to be all right, as far as he could tell. She had just exhausted herself.

Nodding, Reed jerked a finger over his shoulder. He was going to proceed to the ship now, to try to get inside.

The Torch made a circle of his thumb and forefinger. *Okay,* he was saying. *Go do what you have to. After all, Sue knocked herself out to give you a chance—now take advantage of it.*

Reed didn't need any more encouragement than that. Deactivating his harness's propulsion system to save energy, he kicked off from the barrier and nudged himself in the direction of the ship.

Halfway there, he saw a piece of metal he could use as a handhold and latched on to it, then pulled himself the rest of the way. As the soles of his boots hit the surface of the hull, he experienced a brief thrill of satisfaction.

The hard part was behind him. Or was it? As Reed looked around, he saw there wasn't any obvious access to the interior of the vessel. And unlike the Surfer, he couldn't just adjust his molecular structure and melt his way inside.

He compressed his lips. There had to be a way in. Unlike spacegoing craft in his own universe, Negative Zone vehicles didn't have to be airtight. In this void, there was no vacuum to worry about.

And someone like Mr. Fantastic didn't need much of an opening. The tiniest of spaces would do just fine.

Then he remembered something. In his travels throughout Prodigion's ship, hadn't he come across a system for venting noxious gases—the kind that built up when certain energy-storage technologies were in use?

As Reed recalled, the system was a complex one, utilizing a great many narrow, twisting tubes instead of several large ones. A questionable design strategy, he had thought at the time, given the incredible size of the vessel and the availability of space.

However, it wasn't Reed's intent now to criticize. Especially when there was a chance someone of his talents could use that vent network to great advantage.

Snaking his way along the hull of the ship, he searched for one of the vent endings in the flash of exploding assault vessels. It took several long, tense minutes, but he finally sighted one.

So far so good, Mr. Fantastic thought, as he propelled himself toward it with his elastic arms and legs. He knew he had a way to go before he reached his goal.

As he reached the opening, he saw how minuscule it was—but then, not much more minuscule than the one he had just come through to get past the barrier—or, indeed, than the access channels he had woven through the team's headquarters in Four Freedoms Plaza. If he could get through those apertures, he could probably get through this one as well.

Inserting himself into the hole, Reed insinuated himself along its length like some exotic variety of eel. When he came to a bend in the road, he followed it. When he saw another bend, he followed that too.

And on and on, each turning rendering him a little more disoriented than the last. He tried to keep in mind the direction in which he wished to proceed. However, it wasn't easy, especially when one was operating in total darkness and time was so much of the essence.

At one point, Reed felt a strange sort of resistance, an obstruction that wasn't part of the winding tunnel itself. Then it vanished, leaving him wondering if it had ever been there in the first place.

It was only a few seconds later that he glimpsed a light—or rather its reflection in the smooth walls of the vent. Encouraged, he followed it to its source—and found the end of his passageway.

Coming up on it with caution, Reed poked his head out and looked around. What he saw made his elongated heart beat faster against the constraints of his flexible ribs.

There was the Surfer, standing at the opposite end of a large, high-ceilinged chamber. And he was surrounded by a field of raw, throbbing energy—a field that clearly served as a prison cell.

He was watching a monitor—the only live one in the room. It showed the battle raging outside. As far as Reed could tell, Blastaar's armada wasn't faring any better.

All in all, it seemed the Surfer had run afoul of Prodigion. In some ways, Reed was grateful. He had always considered the Surfer a valuable ally as well as a friend—he would hate to have Galactus's former Herald as an enemy.

But obviously, Reed thought, the silver skyrider had caught on. He had realized the great sower of life wasn't all he was cracked up to be—that, far from being a savior, he was a genocidal maniac.

That meant the Surfer would be ready to lend a hand. Lucky for them, thought Reed. The way the combat was going outside the ship, he might be their only hope.

In fact, this was the single luckiest thing that could have happened to the leader of the Fantastic Four . . . and that was why he didn't trust it for a nanosecond. It was simply too much of a coincidence for him to have invaded a ship this size and shown up here.

If he hadn't been so concerned about his teammates, he would have approached the situation with more caution. He would have backtracked, investigated, tested one hypothesis after another until he got to the truth.

But that wasn't an option. They needed help in a big way and they needed it now. So, ignoring the possibility of a trap and the certainty of a surveillance system in the room, Reed stretched out his torso until his face was only inches from the Surfer's energy field.

Though he hadn't seemed to notice the human's approach, the Surfer showed no surprise when he turned to gaze in Reed's direction. His expression was strictly one of pain and sorrow.

"Are you all right?" the human asked.

The Surfer's voice was as soft and lucid as ever. "I am physically uninjured, if that is what you mean."

But his psyche was a mess. That much was obvious even to Reed, who'd been accused of excessive introspection in the past.

"What happened?" he asked. "Who did this to you?"

The Surfer sighed. "Tjellina. I found out we were wrong about Prodigion—I, most of all. And when I tried to undo what I had done, she imprisoned me here."

Swiveling his head on his neck, Mr. Fantastic scanned the place for a moment. He found what looked like a control console along the bulkhead to his left. Since it was the only such console in the room, it had to have something to do with the Surfer's prison.

"Yes," the Surfer confirmed, almost as if he could read his ally's thoughts. "That is the mechanism with which Tjellina created my energy prison. However, not having seen her do it, I regret I cannot describe the procedure to you."

Reed nodded. Directing the upper half of his body to the console, he took hold of it and allowed his lower half to squirt out of its hiding place. Then, reassuming a vaguely humanoid shape, he studied the layout of the controls and their accompanying monitors.

It wasn't the most confusing array he'd ever seen, but it was pretty close. Reed tried to think of it in light of the other panels he'd seen around the ship.

He was just starting to understand the logic of it when he heard a shrill clash of metal on metal. Whirling, he saw that he'd been right about a surveillance system in the room.

Otherwise, the bulkhead opposite him wouldn't have opened along a razor-thin joint he hadn't noticed earlier. And it wouldn't be releasing a pack of robotic monstrosities—vicious-looking, four-legged things with long necks and elongated heads, blood-red eyes, and pincerlike jaws.

Reed's impulse was to try to elude the robots. Unfortunately, he needed to stand his ground. The console was the key to everything. If he could use it to free the Surfer, his team had a fighting chance. If he couldn't, his team didn't. It was that simple.

Under the circumstances, his personal safety was comparatively irrelevant. Doing his best to ignore the robots' gnashing teeth and the deadly grace with which they surrounded him, he turned his attention back to the controls.

Reed ruled out half a dozen monitors and gauges in quick succession, all of them pertaining to some aspect of the ship's operation. Only two of them didn't fit neatly into one category or another.

"Watch out!" cried the Surfer.

A quick glance showed Reed what his friend was warning him about. One of the robot predators leapt at him, jaws open and ready to snap, metal skin glinting in the light from the energy prison.

Just in time, Reed moved his neck and shoulders out of the way, but left his head in place to resume his studies. Baffled by the resulting zigzag shape of its target, the robot closed its jaws on empty air and went hurtling past him, only to scrape to a halt on the deck and whirl about.

By then, a second robot was flying through the air at him. Out of the corner of his eye, Reed could see the Surfer throw a barrage of his own energy in the robot's direction—but it hit the wall of his prison and splashed back at him. Fortunately, Reed was quick enough to pull another zigzag maneuver. And as before, he kept his head in place.

The third attack elicited the same result. So did the fourth and the fifth, though the robots were coming a bit closer each time. Finally, whether it was coincidence, a programmed response, or some kind of actual intelligence, two of the metallic monsters attacked Reed at once—from opposite sides and at opposite heights.

In order to elude them, he had to fling himself away from the console—even though he believed he had finally figured out how it worked. The robots flew past each other, jaws clamping shut with terrific force.

As Reed gathered himself off the floor, he swallowed. If he hadn't evacuated his position when he did, he would have been ripped to shreds. Still, he had a problem, albeit one of a slightly different nature.

Having separated Reed from the control panel, the pack had amassed itself around him again—hunting him, backing him into a corner. But the farther he retreated, the farther he was getting from the console.

In the background, he could see the Surfer watching helplessly. If his captivity caused him discomfort before, he was now in agony. After all, Reed was risking his life to set his friend free—and for all the Surfer's incredible power, he couldn't lift a hand to help him.

Mr. Fantastic looked around. Behind him, he could see the opening through which he'd entered the chamber. It would be easy enough to slither back inside and save himself. But then, the Surfer would remain Prodigion's prisoner—and the battle outside would be lost.

Reed resolved that that wouldn't happen—not if he could do anything about it. Coiling himself up, he gauged the distance he would have to travel, set his teeth . . . and bounded across the room like a long, blue streamer.

He was halfway past the robots before they knew what was happening. By the time they leapt up and tried to take a chunk out of him he was well past them, his hands reaching for the control console.

Quickly, even before the rest of his body landed, Reed's fingers applied pressure to the appropriate pad—the one in the upper right-hand corner. At least, he believed it was the appropriate pad.

Unfortunately, he didn't have time to find out. As if they knew he'd outsmarted them, the robots came at him in a frenzy, all long, wicked-looking teeth and ruby red eyes.

Reed gathered himself into a ball and shot himself at the ceiling, but that didn't deter them. They leapt after him as he descended again, following his bounce. And before he could hit the floor, one of them whacked him with a hard metal paw.

Despite his rubbery state, the impact was devastating. It made his head spin, made him lose his concentration. By the time he slammed into a bulkhead, he had returned to human form.

And a very painful human form at that. Reed's collision

with the bulkhead had battered him badly. His head hurt as if he'd been struck by a truck.

As if encouraged, the robots advanced on him again. And this time, he was too dazed to do anything about it. He just lay there aching, the taste of blood growing stronger in his mouth, as a grisly death crept closer and closer on shiny metal limbs.

Suddenly, a stream of terrible, bright light came from the other side of the room. Like deer caught in a pair of headlights, the robots were ensconced in its glow.

Reed could feel only the faintest heat on his face. However, the robots experienced something else—something a good deal more intense. As the leader of the Fantastic Four watched, the metal predators began to melt.

Their limbs sagged and went liquid. Their snouts turned soft and ran down their chests. In a matter of moments, Reed's metallic antagonists were nothing more than puddles on the floor.

Only one being could have been responsible for something like that. As the light faded, Reed turned and saw the energy prison was gone. The Surfer stepped forward, his board tucked under his arm.

He was free.

"Thank you," said the Surfer, his voice filling the chamber. "I am indebted to you, Reed Richards."

Gone was the look of shame and despair that had gripped the Surfer earlier. In its place, Reed saw an expression of determination. Of resolve.

Approaching his ally, the Surfer bent beside him and inspected his injuries. "You have a concussion," he said. "And considerable soft-tissue damage. But not for long."

Brushing his fingertips across Reed's face, he applied the energy within him a second time—not as a destructive force, but to heal. And heal he did. Instantly, the human felt whole and alert.

Reed grunted softly. First he'd been mended by Prodigion, and now by the Silver Surfer. After this, it would be difficult to reacclimate to more prosaic medical practices.

But he had more than his health on his mind. He glanced at the monitor that showed the battle, which looked like more of a disaster than ever. But they still had a chance. They could still win this thing.

"We need your help," he told the Surfer.

Reed told him how they had discovered Prodigion's true agenda—how they had hooked up with Blastaar again and assaulted the life giver's ship. "But as you can see," he continued, "Prodigion still very much has the upper hand. That's why I snuck in—to see if I could sabotage the ship's defenses."

The Surfer thought for a moment, his normally flawless brow furrowing ever so slightly. "For one of your talents, sabotage is a logical option. But not for one who wields the Power Cosmic."

At first, Reed didn't know what he meant by that. Then he figured it out. "You're going to hit the Outriders themselves," he said. "Right in their tactical center."

The Surfer nodded. "Yes. That's my intention."

"They'll be well defended," Reed pointed out.

"They will need to be," his comrade told him.

Reed had a feeling the Surfer was right. "Mind if I come with you?"

The silver being shook his head. "I do not mind at all. In fact, I may have need of your help."

Together, they mounted the Surfer's board and exited the chamber. Picking up speed as they turned into the corridor, they steeled themselves for the fight of their lives.

Twenty-one

When Tjellina saw the blinking light on her tactical console, she couldn't believe it. "He's free," she said.

It was barely a whisper, but Amalyn was sitting only a few feet away and she had a good sense of hearing. "Free?" she echoed, her voice resonant with concern. "You mean the Surfer?"

Tjellina nodded, trying to remain calm. "The Surfer."

"He knows where to find the tactical center," Amalyn noted. "That means he's headed this way. We've got to stop him."

"We will," Tjellina assured her, her hands moving across her control board like a swarm of insects.

The Surfer had been expecting to encounter the ship's defense systems ever since he left the chamber where he'd been imprisoned. It took the vessel a long time to respond, however. Several minutes, in fact.

That's when the ceiling opened and a series of weapon turrets dropped down—and the corridor he and Reed Richards traveled filled with a barrage of fearsome purple energy beams.

The beams ripped up the bulkheads and filled the air with the smell of ozone, but the Surfer was too fast for them. With his companion hanging on to his midsection, he swung his board left and right, weaving his way through the deadly maze with uncanny accuracy.

Then they were past the beam projectors and the corridor was clear again. But only for a moment.

Suddenly, the place filled with clouds of corrosive, red gas. Enveloping himself and Reed in a protective field, the Surfer cut a swath through the billowing vapors, parting them like a clean gust of wind. Eventually, the clouds scattered and disappeared—

—only to be replaced by a spray of white-hot plasma, emitted by jets that had raised themselves out of the floor. But the same protective field kept the Surfer and his passenger from injury, the plasma spattering and eating its way through the bulkheads instead.

And before long, that peril was behind them as well. The Surfer dropped his shield and picked up the pace.

"What's next?" Reed asked.

He didn't have long to wait for an answer—as a pack of four-legged robots rounded a corner up ahead and came bounding at them, jaws clacking. These were bigger, faster, and more powerful-looking than the guardians Reed had eluded before.

But the Surfer smashed his way through them, decapitating one with his board and turning several others to slag with a gesture. Somehow, one of the robots managed to clamp its teeth onto the Surfer's leg, but he crushed its head in his hand and flung it away.

Panels in the walls slid aside and bright yellow energy barriers materialized. They weren't the kind in which the Surfer had been imprisoned, because Tjellina couldn't have had time to implement that technology everywhere—but they were powerful fields all the same.

The Surfer sizzled his way through them, one after the other, barely even slowing down. Seconds later, he had transcended them as he had all the other hazards thrown his way.

Based on his experiences of the past few minutes, the Surfer expected something lethal to take the barriers' place. Instead, the bulkheads themselves seemed to grow closer, to approach and finally slide into one another like an elaborate, interlocking puzzle.

In effect, the orderly environment of the corridor had disappeared, leaving only a confusing conglomeration of smooth, metal surfaces. But that didn't daunt the Surfer in the least.

His instincts kept him on course. And his ability to manipulate matter allowed him to pass through surface after surface, as if they were nothing more than shadows.

Both the Surfer and Reed remained unharmed. As if it realized the uselessness of its contortions, the corridor gradually reshaped itself, returning to its original form. And the two of them plunged on, getting closer to Prodigion's tactical center with each passing moment.

Closer to Tjellina, the Surfer thought. After all, she led the Outriders. It was she who would be overseeing the ship's defense.

Memories came to him unbidden—the softness of Tjellina's caress, the allure in her golden eyes, the honeyed taste of her lips. Only a few hours ago, he had thought himself in paradise.

How had things changed so quickly? How had he gone from sharing a dream with someone to vying with her for the life of a planet?

Gradually, the Surfer closed the distance between himself and the woman he had loved. As he skimmed along the corridor, nothing else blocked his path. It was as if Tjellina had given up trying to delay him, as if she had embraced the inevitable at last.

But he knew better. She wouldn't yield. Not Tjellina. She was an Outrider first and last, too devoted to Prodigion and the cause he represented to ever abandon it.

"We're almost there," Reed said, drawing on the knowledge of the ship he'd gained in the course of his excursions.

"Yes," the Surfer agreed. "It will not be much longer."

He followed the curvature of the corridor, sped down a long, straight hallway . . . and came to the great arch that served as the entrance to the tactical center. The thick, metal doors had been closed, of course, in anticipation of their arrival.

That meant nothing to the Surfer. Less than nothing. He extended his hand toward them, and a blast of energy shot from each finger.

The doors were pierced in five places. With a turn of his wrist, he connected those places like the blade of a can opener, cutting a circular shape out of the metal.

Even before the Surfer came sailing into the tactical center, the parts of the doors encompassed by the circle fell backward, exposing the Outriders at their consoles within. Eyes narrowed, senses alert, the skyrider ventured into the midst of his enemies.

There were a dozen of them, but Tjellina was the only one on her feet. She wasn't smiling.

"You shouldn't have come here," she said.

"I had no choice," the Surfer replied. "The battle outside needed ending—and not the way you would like it to end."

The Outrider shook her head. "You shouldn't have come," she repeated.

Suddenly, the Surfer found himself encased in a shell of crackling energy, created by six separate projectors set into the bulkheads. Reaching out, he touched its inner surface. It roiled and spat under his hand, reacting much the same way his prison wall had reacted.

"It's cruder than the enclosure I manufactured before," Tjellina noted critically. "Still, it should serve our purpose." Her brow furrowed as if in sympathy. "Foolish Norrin. Didn't you know I would have something like this ready for you? This is our tactical center, one of the most important places on the ship. We take our security very seriously here."

"Not seriously enough," he replied.

Tjellina's expression changed. As understanding dawned, she whirled and looked around the room. But it was too late.

No thicker than a shoelace, Reed had slithered his way along the floor to one of the consoles. Before Tjellina or any of her colleagues could do anything about it, he reached out with pipe cleaner fingers and poked at a few choice studs.

As quickly as it had appeared, the Surfer's energy prison vanished. The Outriders scrambled to override the console Reed had tampered with, but by then the Surfer had taken aim at one of their projectors.

With the slightest concentration of willpower, he used the Power Cosmic to shatter it. Then he turned his attention to another one and smashed it as well.

At the same time, the Outriders activated the remainder of the system. But when the energy beams converged, they formed an incomplete sphere—a prison only two-thirds what it was meant to be.

Emerging from it almost effortlessly, the Surfer pointed to a third projector and a fourth, destroying them as he'd destroyed the others. And with a glance at the last two, he finished the job.

He turned his gaze on Tjellina. "I don't fall for the same trick twice," he told her.

"I didn't expect you would," she answered. "That's why I took other precautions."

Even before the words were out of her mouth, she had a weapon in her hands. The Surfer threw up a shield to protect himself, but it didn't help. The bursts of energy coming from Tjellina's barrel cut through his construct and burned themselves into his skin.

"Anti-meson packets," she explained, as he doubled over in agony. "The other strategy that came out of the experiments I conducted."

The Surfer looked at Mr. Fantastic, but the human was caught up in a battle of his own. Having forced him out into the open, a half-dozen Outriders were trying to skewer him with energy beams, forcing him to snake this way and that simply to survive.

That meant the Surfer was on his own. Recognizing it even as he did, Tjellina advanced on him, pelting him with her deadly bursts, each one a hot iron searing his flesh.

"I didn't want to do this," she told him. "But you've left me no choice."

"No," the Surfer gasped. "There is always a choice."

It was the very heart of his philosophy. Despite appearances, despite the obstacles one encountered, one could always embrace good or evil. Just as one could choose to accept one's fate or strive against it.

On Zenn-La, he refused to accept his people's apathy, preferring to quest for more knowledge. When Galactus came, he refused to bow to the inevitable, choosing to abandon his old life to save his home. After Galactus imprisoned him on Earth, he had never stopped trying to penetrate the barrier the world-devourer had placed around the planet to keep the Surfer confined.

Always, he chose to strive.

Dredging up the strength still left in him, the molten core of his power, the Surfer erected another shield. Maintaining her fire, Tjellina shook her head disdainfully.

"You tried that before," she reminded him. "It didn't work."

He didn't reply. He couldn't, because of the pain that ate at him like a ravening beast. And just as Tjellina had implied it would, his shield was shredded by her attack.

But the Surfer didn't yield to her. He erected another shield.

"You're fighting a losing battle," Tjellina told him, her voice thick with what sounded like pity and maybe even regret.

Indeed, his protection was eaten away by the anti-meson packets. But this time, they didn't get through to him because he'd placed another shield in back of the first. As Tjellina destroyed the second one, he created two more—earning himself a respite, no matter how slim.

It allowed the Surfer to heal his wounds—to regain his composure. And to fight back. As he threw up another shield to replace the ones Tjellina was tearing down, he launched a bolt of pure force at the Outrider.

She hadn't expected it, hadn't believed him capable of it. But she must have had some protective aura of her own, because it didn't knock her senseless—it only sent her staggering into the console in back of her.

Recovering, Tjellina fired at the Surfer with renewed determination. But he was determined as well. Sticking to his plan of creating shield after shield, he gave himself a chance to strike again. Except now that he knew about the Outrider's aura, he put more fury into the bolt.

As a result, his adversary didn't just stagger under the impact. She slammed into the bulkhead hard enough to lose her grip on her weapon. It clattered to the floor. And before she could grasp it again, the Surfer had sent it skittering out of her reach.

With a cry of rage, Tjellina went after it. But before she could reach it, the Surfer altered its molecular structure, turning it to dust right in front of her eyes.

Next, he focused his attention on his friend Reed Richards, who was obviously tiring in his efforts to elude the Outriders' energy beams. Darting and rippling from one side of the room to the other, the human wouldn't last much longer.

But then, the Surfer told himself, *he won't have to.* One by one, he ripped the Outriders' ordnance from their hands. Then he transmuted them as he'd transmuted Tjellina's weapon.

They looked at their leader. But their leader was staring at the Surfer, disappointment and anger mingled in her expression.

"It's not possible," Tjellina rasped. "I checked the data over and over again. Those anti-meson packets—"

"Should have been the death of me," he finished for her. "Unfortunately for you, your data was incomplete. There was one thing you failed to measure."

"The size of the Surfer's heart," Reed declared as he returned to his normal size and shape and stood on the other side of the tactical center. Turning to Tjellina, he smiled grimly.

"If you'd known him as I do, you would have measured that first."

The Surfer ignored his comrade's praise. There was still a battle being waged outside—and a destructive force that had to be stopped.

"The disrupters," he said out loud, glancing around the chamber in search of the appropriate controls. "We must disable them."

"Done," Reed assured him. He pointed to one of the chamber's control panels, where a monitor showed Blastaar's ships attacking unperturbed. "I took care of it as soon as we entered the room."

Eyes wide with urgency, Amalyn looked at Tjellina. "It's true. The disrupter system is locked into a perpetual diagnostic program. To free it, I'll have to manually disengage."

"Which you will not have the opportunity to accomplish," the Surfer told her. "I will see to that." He eyed Tjellina. "You are finished. You will never again sow your seeds on an unsuspecting planet."

The Outrider returned his gaze, an ironic smile shaping her mouth. "Don't be so sure of that," she told him.

Ben Grimm couldn't believe his eyes. "Hey," he said, "Blastaar's callin' off the attack!"

Still hovering near Prodigion's force shield alongside Johnny and Sue, he pointed a blunt orange finger at the forward edge of the armada. It was peeling off ship by ship, as if it had found something better to do.

"They must be nuts," he grunted.

"I don't get it either," the Torch replied. "I mean, with those destructo-beams out of the way, they finally got to take the battle to Prodigion . . ."

"And now they're pulling out," Sue observed. She was still a little weak from her earlier effort, but not so much so that she couldn't see what was going on. "Maybe they know something we don't."

Suddenly, something else caught the Thing's eye. Turning,

he saw something bright and shiny get spit out of Prodigion's ship.

"What the heck is *that*?" he asked.

A moment later, the vessel released another bright, shiny object, and then several more all at once. To Ben, they looked like time-release capsules, the kind he might take for a headache—except they were each a million times bigger. And now that he thought about it and allowed for perspective . . .

"Oh, man," Johnny cried out, "those things are headed for the planet!" He blinked, then turned to his teammates. "They must be the seeds Prodigion uses to plant all that new growth!"

The Thing had come to the same conclusion. So had Sue, judging from the look of horror on her face.

As they looked at one another, wondering what they could do, the commlinks on their harnesses crackled with a familiar voice. "Sue! Ben! Johnny! Can you hear me?"

Without hesitating, Sue tapped the appropriate stud on her harness. "Loud and clear," she responded. "Reed, we've seen Prodigion release his globules. They're falling on—"

"I know all about them," her husband said. "But you don't have to worry. I've sent Blastaar and his ships to knock them out before they enter the atmosphere."

The Thing snorted. "Shoulda known our resident genius would be on the case."

"Are you all right?" Sue asked Reed.

"Fine," he told her. "I found the Surfer and we took over Prodigion's tactical center. The force shield's down, the disrupter banks are useless, and the Outriders are out of the picture."

"And Blastaar's on the trail of those big ol' seeds," Ben noted. "So we're in the clear?"

"Not exactly," Reed answered. "Even if Blastaar takes out all those seeds, they're only the first wave. Prodigion's ship will keep releasing them unless we stop it."

"We?" the Torch echoed.

"You," his brother-in-law conceded. "Unfortunately, that's one system I can't shut down from here."

"Figures," the Thing grumbled.

"Shush," Sue entreated him. "This isn't the time, Ben."

"Now," Reed went on, "according to the external sensor

grid, you're only a thousand feet or so from the seed emitters—those apertures we talked about when we were examining the bioregeneration chamber. And they won't start releasing new seeds for another seven minutes.''

"Waitaminnit,'' the Thing told him, gazing in the direction of the emitters. "You want us ta tear up all those apertures—like, a hundred of 'em? And we got a whole seven minutes ta do it?'' He scowled. "Why dincha give us somethin' *hard* ta do?''

"You'd better get going," Reed advised him. "Time's a-wasting.''

Shaking his head, Ben activated his propulsion system and turned himself in the right direction. Then he put the harness into high gear and sped toward the seed emitters.

Sue was right behind him. Of course, the Torch was a lot faster then they were, so he zipped on ahead, leaving a yellow flame trail in his wake.

Still, the distance wasn't great, so Johnny didn't beat them by much. When the Thing and the Invisible Woman arrived, the Torch had managed to fuse only a handful of the suckers.

That left ninety or so in operating order—and according to the chronometer in Ben's harness, the next emission was in five minutes. Not a whole lot of time even if they were the Fantastic *Fourteen*.

Even so, they did their best. Johnny poured out blast after blistering heat blast, turning one emitter after the other into a mess of molten metal. Sue plumbed the apertures with her force field until she found something she could wreck—and then wrecked it.

And the Thing did what he did best. He used his herculean strength to cave in every emitter within clobbering distance.

But with two minutes left, they'd only taken out about half their targets. When the next wave came, too many of them would still be functioning. And not knowing how Blastaar had done with the first wave, they couldn't count on him to eliminate any additional seeds.

Then Ben had an idea. Recalling what he'd learned of the emitter system in Prodigion's bioregeneration chamber, he ripped up a section of the hull around one of the apertures and dug his way down.

"Where are you going?" the Torch hollered, hovering above the mouth of the Thing's tunnel.

"I gotta date with an important gal," Ben tossed back at him. "The brains o' the operation, ya might say."

In other words, the Thing thought, the cybernetic node that processed the ship's sensor data and programmed the globules accordingly—what an average Joe might call the targeting mechanism.

Unfortunately, he didn't remember how far down it was buried, so he didn't know how long it would take to reach it—or if he had enough time. But Ben wasn't going to worry about that. Worrying never got anyone anywhere.

Grabbing huge handfuls of thick metal sheeting and circuitry, he burrowed deeper and deeper. And deeper still. His arms felt like they were on fire and his fingers were cramped, but he didn't pause for a second.

After all, he thought with a bitterness he had yet to get over even after all these years, *I'm just a Thing. And Things don't stop till their parts wear out.*

Finally, he hit the mother lode. Punching his way through what turned out to be a reinforced casing, Ben heard the whirr of moving parts. He tore away all the metal around him, then feasted his eyes on what he'd been looking for.

At least he thought it was what he'd been looking for, based on the diagram he'd seen a couple of days earlier. *Only one way to find out*, he told himself—and wrenched the mechanism free of its moorings, popping data leads and snapping power cables in the process.

Then he turned around and headed for the surface. Halfway there, he heard his commlink spout a bunch of static.

"Whadja say?" the Thing growled.

A moment later, the reception improved. It was Reed, of course, and there was no mistaking the excitement in his voice.

"—said you *did* it, old friend. The targeting mechanism went offline just seconds before the seeds were supposed to depart. Thanks to you, they're not going anywhere."

"Well, all right!" the Torch exclaimed over the commlink. "Benjy knew what he was doing after all!"

"Like ya had any doubt of it?" the Thing rumbled in response.

He was still climbing, almost within reach of the exterior

hull now. But before he could pull himself up, he felt an invisible force do the job for him.

"It was the least I could do," said a smiling Sue, lifting him out of his tunnel.

As she deposited him gently on the hull, Ben took a look at the half-illuminated planet they'd just saved. It sat there without a care in the universe, never knowing how close it had come to getting a facelift—one that would have been lethal to its inhabitants.

The Torch turned to him. "Beautiful sight, isn't it?"

"Yeah," the Thing agreed. "Big-time beautiful." Something occurred to him. "But our work here ain't done yet."

Sue's expression changed. "That's right. Prodigion is still at large."

"My thoughts exactly," Reed told them over the commlink. "Just hang on and we'll rectify the situation."

A moment later, Ben and the others found themselves sinking through the hull as if it weren't there. As he descended through layer after layer of circuitry, the Thing recognized his condition as the work of the Silver Surfer.

At last, he was going to get his shot at Prodigion.

Kabris Dorain clung to her offspring at the cave mouth and watched the spectacle in the dark, moonless sky. It was at once the most beautiful and most horrifying thing she had seen in her long, fruitful life.

The soft, shapeless younglings wouldn't even look for themselves. They would only gaze into her many-faceted eyes and see the lights reflected there from one end of the heavens to the other.

Nor did Kabris blame them for hiding their eyes. She was not a youngling—far from it—and she herself could hardly find the courage to bear witness. But she thought someone should.

After all, it might be the end of the world playing out before her. If that was so, it was her duty to watch it—to record every detail so she could share it with her ancestors in the afterlives.

It had begun hours earlier, with a simple falling star. At least, it had seemed to be a falling star, until it stopped and hovered and grew to monstrous proportions. For a time, it had shown in the sky like a baleful eye, causing all of Kabris's people to seek refuge in their caverns.

There were legends of such a thing. A predator, it was said, a predator so colossal it could swallow all existence. Kabris had heard that story from her mother and her mother's mother.

Then, as she was trying to recall all they had told her, the shining eye was joined by other, smaller lights—lights that scored the heavens with their quick and fleeting passage. Moment by moment, they seemed to multiply.

They were multiplying still, growing fiercer and brighter. Kabris sensed there was a struggle afoot, a battle between forces beyond her understanding, and it could not bode well for mere mortals. Certain that death was near, not only for her and her neighbors but for all existence, she clutched her younglings to her and waited.

She waited a long time, in fact. But the end never came.

Instead, the lights grew fainter and fewer, then vanished altogether. And just before dawn, the moon—the real moon—came up whole and unperturbed. The world was back to normal.

Kabris had the distinct feeling she and her people had been spared something terrible. She was immensely relieved to know life would go on in the universe.

But in a strange and unexpected way, she also felt as if she had missed something. Something momentous.

As the Surfer led the Fantastic Four through Prodigion's ship—presumably for a confrontation with that massive and mysterious presence—a single life-form withdrew from the field of battle. Undetected by any of the combatants since his arrival a short while ago, he smiled with satisfaction as they diminished gradually with distance.

It hadn't been a difficult thing for him to conceal himself from their sensor systems. Not a difficult thing at all. In fact, that was the least of the abilities granted him by the slender cylinder in his hand.

It had, for instance, allowed him to guide a being of remarkable plasticity through the intricate network of channels and passageways that existed in Prodigion's ship. And when that being encountered a hidden force field that would otherwise have stymied his progress—a smaller version of the great barrier he had penetrated earlier—it had been the simplest of chores to disable the field.

No matter that Reed Richards never knew he was being sent in a particular direction. No matter that he would have cursed the hand that was assisting him. The important thing was the result.

Richards had gotten through to help the creature called the Silver Surfer, who in turn had wrecked Prodigion's plans. And now, with any luck, the Surfer and the Fantastic Four would defuse the threat of Prodigion permanently.

In doing so, they would strike a blow for Prodigion's potential victims. Do-gooders that they were, that was clearly their purpose. But they would strike a blow for another as well.

For *him*. For Annihilus.

After all, Prodigion had been of concern to Annihilus ever since his gargantuan ship entered this part of the Negative Zone. He had been an unknown quantity—and therefore, to the winged one's thinking, a threat.

If Annihilus had met him head-on, he would likely have beaten Prodigion. But it would have entailed a risk, a possibility—no matter how slim—that Annihilus would have been beaten instead.

Barring something terribly unforeseen, that risk would soon be rendered unnecessary. His smile widening, the bearer of the cosmic control rod counted this a good day.

A *very* good day.

Twenty-two

"They'll be here in a moment," the Surfer announced, only a portion of his mind devoted to transporting Sue, Ben, and Johnny.

"That's good," Reed replied from the other side of the tactical center, where he was studying the monitors on one of the control panels. "And our friends here are secure. Even if the main power goes down, they'll be contained with the help of backup systems."

Behind him, Tjellina and the other Outriders were encased in an energy prison much like the one the Surfer had occupied. After all, turnabout was fair play.

The skyrider didn't look at Tjellina. He had much to say to her, but it would wait. For now, he had other things on his mind.

Despite all they'd accomplished, despite their rescue of the world below them, the threat posed by Prodigion hadn't been diminished one iota. He was still dangerous, still powerful.

The Surfer wouldn't be content until they had incapacitated him and cut him off from his support systems. Only then was there a chance they might isolate the life-giver, somehow keep him from wreaking havoc on the Negative Zone.

And what if they couldn't isolate him? What if the only option was to destroy Prodigion?

The Surfer didn't want to think about that. He had sworn never to take another life as long as he lived. He hated the idea of breaking that pledge, even when billions of other lives hung in the balance.

As he thought that, his friends melted through the ceiling and descended to the floor. Reed crossed the room to embrace his wife.

"When I looked at you from the other side of that barrier," he told her, pushing a strand of hair off her forehead, "when I saw how pale and weak you looked—"

"I know the feeling," Sue replied. "But that's ancient history. I'm okay now."

The Thing looked at the Surfer. "Somethin' keepin' us?"

The skyrider shook his head. "No. Nothing."

Calling his board to him, he allowed the Fantastic Four to step onto it. Then he joined them.

"Next stop," Ben quipped, "the end o' the line—fer somebody."

Without further discussion, the Surfer whisked them out into the corridor and turned in the direction of Prodigion's quarters.

Despite the distance involved, the journey took only a few minutes. But they were long minutes, filled with introspection and soul-searching. After all, the Thing's gibe had been an ominous one—and rightly so.

Like Galactus, Prodigion was a force as much as a being, a phenomenon as much as an intelligence. There was no way of gauging the extent of his might—or of knowing whether they'd all survive this battle.

The Surfer was certain of only one thing: they would find a way to beat Prodigion. They had to. The alternative was simply too horrible to contemplate.

Before he knew it, before any of them were really ready, they reached their destination. As the Surfer melted them through the massive doors, he steeled himself for what was ahead.

As he had expected, Prodigion was standing by his control console, intent on something he saw there. Colossal, aloof, and inscrutable, he made no move against his adversaries as they entered his inner sanctum. In fact, he didn't even seem to notice they'd returned.

"Lookit him," the Thing rumbled, his blue eyes narrowing. "The picture o' confidence, ain't he?"

Eager to do battle, the Torch circled overhead. "Not for long," he vowed. "Ol' Planetsucker's about to get a lesson in table manners."

"Be careful," the Surfer warned them. "If his power is anything like that of Galactus, he can reduce you to stray atoms without blinking."

"The Surfer's right," Reed joined in. "Play it smart. Work as a team."

Even before he'd finished his admonition, his wife had erected an invisible barrier around Reed, Ben, and herself. She did not include the Torch, since the force field would impede both his flying ability and his flame.

The Surfer, of course, wasn't in need of her protection. Of all of them, only he could have absorbed Galactus's fury and lived. He didn't imagine it would be any different with Prodigion.

"Destroyer!" the Surfer cried, his voice nearly lost in that expanse. "Murderer! Turn and face your accusers!"

Prodigion turned his massive head. His eyes fixed on the silver being who had challenged him. He pointed to him.

"Careful," Susan rasped—like her teammates, ready for anything.

"You," Prodigion said, his voice a roll of thunder that reverberated wildly from the bulkheads. "The one called the Silver Surfer." His brow furrowed as he scanned the Fantastic Four. "And you others. I saw you on my monitors."

"What of it?" the Thing threw back at him, oblivious to the danger.

"You have thwarted my will," Prodigion went on. "Defeated my Outriders. Wrecked my defenses."

"Your will was a destructive one," the Surfer retorted. "There was a thriving civilization on the planet you tried to seed. We could not allow it to become a victim of your so-called bounty." He straightened up. "No matter what drives you, no matter what hungers plague you, what you do is evil. It must end. And we five have come with that purpose in mind—to end it for all time."

"In other words," the Thing added, "go pick on someone yer own size!"

The Surfer braced himself for the storm of devastation he imagined would follow—the indignant crackle of untamed energy, the hideous force of Prodigion's rage.

But moment followed moment—and nothing happened. Nothing at all. Prodigion didn't vent his wrath on them. He just stood there, brow creased, staring at the insects who dared to oppose him.

"What's going on?" Susan asked.

"Yeah," said the Torch. "What's the big blowhard waiting for?"

The Thing grunted. "Maybe we didn't insult him enough."

But the Surfer didn't think invective had anything to do with it. Prodigion was looking at them as if seeing them for the first time. As if he recognized what they'd done but couldn't formulate a response to it.

"There's something different about him," Reed concluded, echoing the Surfer's thoughts. "He seems lost somehow."

Summoning his board, the Surfer ascended to the level of Prodigion's eyes and hovered before him. "Have you no response to my charges?" he asked the giant. "Have you no defense?"

Prodigion seemed to consider the question. Then, in a shockingly childlike way, he shrugged his immense shoulders. "I did not wish to cause anyone harm. That was never my purpose."

Suddenly, the Torch cut a blazing swath between the Surfer and Prodigion. "Don't give me that innocent act," he told the life-giver, pointing a flaming finger at him. "Don't tell me you didn't know what you were doing, 'cause I'm not buying it."

"Yeah!" the Thing roared, pressing against Susan's force field and shaking his craggy fist. "What he said!"

"Hang on," said the Invisible Woman. "I think Reed's right. It looks like all the fight's gone out of him."

Prodigion held his hands out, palms up. The Surfer recognized it as the universal plea for peace.

"I have no wish to oppose you," the titan declared, "or to dispute the truth of what you say. If there is another way for me to exist, I will be happy to do so." His mighty head slumped as if it were too heavy for his shoulders. "I only want to rest. To sleep. To look at the stars."

"What?" the Thing blurted. "Ya mean ya don't care that we beat up yer ship? Or stopped yer seeds from conquerin' that planet?"

Prodigion looked at him. "None of that matters to me. It was not my doing." He turned to the Surfer, who was still hovering in front of him. "You believe me, don't you? I just want it all to end."

The Surfer gazed into Prodigion's huge, pleading eyes—and found, to his surprise, that he believed him.

Not because he felt qualified to detect deception in such a being—or indeed in any being, after Tjellina's betrayal of him. But because he couldn't think of a reason for Prodigion to lie.

If the giant had wished, he could have unleashed tremendous forces against them—forces that would have shredded

Susan's invisible shields and maybe the Surfer's as well. He could have lashed out at the tiny beings who'd dared to invade his sanctum.

But he hadn't done any of it. He hadn't so much as lifted a finger against them. Instead, he was pleading for absolution.

It was something Galactus would never have considered. But then, clearly, Prodigion was not Galactus.

Certainly, Prodigion towered over them as Galactus had towered over them. He commanded the kind of power Galactus had commanded. But that, apparently, was where the resemblance ended.

As the Surfer watched, the Torch came to hover beside him. "Don't let him psych you, Surf. He's up to something. It's just a question of what."

The skyrider shook his head. "No, Johnny Storm. He is telling the truth. What happened on Nicanthus Prime was not his doing."

"Then whose doing was it?" the Torch demanded.

"My Outriders," Prodigion replied simply, without guile. "They guided me via a mindlink. But the link is silent now."

"A mindlink," the Torch echoed. "Yeah, right."

"It's easy enough to determine that," Mr. Fantastic noted. "I can cobble together some equipment and check Prodigion's brainwaves."

The Surfer glanced at the human. "Perhaps you should do so. Then we can agree on how to deal with him."

Prodigion glanced from the Surfer to the Torch and back again. "I just want it all to end," he repeated with childlike simplicity.

It didn't take Reed long to put a brainwave scope together. Knowing what he did of Prodigion's vast stores of equipment, he simply modified one of the devices Tjellina had used on the Torch.

Of course, Prodigion's brain was a little different from any Mr. Fantastic had ever come across. Still, there were enough similarities for him to be confident in the results.

"Well?" the Thing prodded, as they all stood there in Prodigion's quarters, surrounding Reed and his portable monitor.

The scientist looked up at the life-giver, who hadn't complained a bit when a series of leads was attached to his head.

Prodigion seemed as eager as any of them to hear what Reed had to say.

"He's just what he claims to be, Ben—an innocent, whom the Outriders used as a puppet. As powerful as he is, as driven to seed life throughout the Negative Zone, he's got the intellect of a three-year-old. And not a very bright three-year-old at that."

"In other words," Johnny commented, "pay no attention to that man behind the curtain."

The Surfer looked at him. "I beg your pardon."

"Nothin'," the Thing rumbled. "Just a line from a movie with a lotta crazy monkeys in it."

"So what do we do with him?" Sue asked.

Reed grunted. "That's the sixty-four-thousand-dollar question, isn't it? Even without his Outriders, Prodigion's still got the urge to seed planets with new life. And his ship is sophisticated enough to repair itself. In time, he'll be back to his old tricks, albeit with a marked drop in efficiency."

"He'll go on destroying civilizations," the Surfer observed.

Reed nodded soberly. "The same way Galactus does."

The Torch jerked a thumb over his shoulder at Prodigion. "But he said he didn't want to do it anymore. He said all he wanted to do was rest."

"He won't," Sue noted. "It's not in his makeup."

Reed thought for a moment. "It could be."

His wife looked at him. "What do you mean?"

"I mean we can get rid of Prodigion's itch. With the same sort of equipment I used to make this brainwave scope, I can make a brainwave restrictor. It would suppress the big fellow's urge."

"No more planet-seeding?" Ben asked.

Reed looked up at the titan. "If that's what he wants."

The Surfer elevated himself to a point level with Prodigion's eyes. "Do you desire that? To be free of your crusade? To live out your life in peace and contentment?"

The massive head nodded. "More than anything," Prodigion said.

"Then it's a done deal," the Thing concluded.

"Okay for Prodigion," Johnny said. "But what about the Outriders? We can't just leave them here on the ship. They'll find a way to take over again."

"True," Reed acknowledged. He turned to the Surfer, knowing how sensitive a subject it was for the skyrider. "What do you think?"

The Surfer didn't respond right away. "I think," he said at last, "there is but one option." He described it to them.

Reed had to admit the Surfer's plan made sense. It was just. It was humane. In fact, he thought, the Outriders might even like it.

The land was sparsely foliated as far as the eye could see. In fact, the Surfer thought as he made his descent, the whole planet was sparsely foliated. It would not be easy to make living things flourish here—but if anyone could do it, the Outriders could.

It was what they were motivated to do, what their duty demanded of them. And here, cut off from the rest of the Negative Zone, they could do it without harming others.

The closer the Surfer got to the ground, the easier it was to see the force field generators set up around the Outriders' encampment. They would protect Tjellina's people from revenge seekers—Blastaar among them.

After all, the point of bringing the Outriders here had been to prevent them from resuming their activities, not to make them easy prey for others.

As he thought this, Tjellina turned and looked up at him. With her raven hair and her golden skin, he had no trouble discerning her among her colleagues. Landing apart from the group, he stepped off his board and waited for her to approach him.

Tjellina didn't disappoint him. At least not this time, and not in this respect. Without a word or a gesture, she walked across the space that separated them.

The Surfer didn't say anything either. At least, not at first. He just watched the wind blow her hair around. It was Tjellina who finally marred the silence by speaking.

"I wouldn't blame you if you hated me," she said.

"I would be justified in hating you," the Surfer agreed. "Nonetheless, I do not."

Her brow furrowed. "I used you. Like a tool. Like the recalibrator I asked you to hold when I was gauging your power."

He nodded. "You used me, all right. And in your cleverness, you placed me here or there, depending on what you needed to hide from me. I see that now, as I see everything else. But you also loved me, Tjellina." He paused. "Or do you deny that?"

The Outrider looked into the Surfer's eyes. Slowly, tentatively, she raised her fingers to his face and stroked his cheek.

"No," she said softly. "I would never deny that."

The muscles in his jaw fluttered. "You never met Prodigion the way you said, did you?"

Tjellina shrugged. "I was recruited and accepted, as I told you. But the rest was a fabrication. Our world wasn't in need of anyone's help; Prodigion's seeds were the beginning of the end for my people."

"You knew that," the Surfer observed, "and still you joined the Outriders?"

"I put the death of my civilization behind me," she explained, "for the sake of a greater principle. For the sake of Life."

He shook his head. Tjellina's thinking was so alien to him. So diametrically opposed to his own. If he tried for an eternity, he would never understand her.

For a moment, neither of them spoke. Then the Surfer looked to the heavens, where his friends were waiting for him.

"I must go," he said.

"I know," Tjellina responded. "And with you goes all that's left of me." She swallowed. "Everything, that is, except hope. Because I believe the day will come when you'll return for me."

The Surfer considered her—her long, raven black hair and her painfully intelligent eyes. He considered the beauty and the bravery of her. And his heart, or what was left of it, melted.

But not to the point that he lost sight of what she was. Or what she had done.

"I will never return," he told Tjellina.

The Outrider's jaw dropped. Clearly, it was not what she had wanted to hear. It was not what she had expected to hear. But it was the only thing he could honestly say to her.

As gently as he could, the Surfer removed her hand from his cheek. Then he summoned his board to him and tucked it under his arm.

"Good-bye," he said.

Then the Surfer left Tjellina and the earth she stood on and soared into the sky. As he climbed the rungs of atmosphere, the Outrider and the suffering she had brought him fell away beneath him, until he could barely make her out against the barren landscape.

But he felt her gaze, her longing. And he imagined he always would.

Twenty-three

Reed Richards frowned as he watched the stars of the Negative Zone zip past him through his observation port. He still didn't know who or what had guided him to the Surfer on Prodigion's ship—and he was convinced it wasn't just a coincidence.

Mr. Fantastic hated the idea that there was a mystery he had yet to solve. Unfortunately, he doubted he would ever get to the bottom of it.

"Look at him," Johnny said, leaning past Reed and pointing to the Surfer, who was traveling well ahead of their good-as-new black needle. "He looks so lonely. Maybe we ought to get him in here with the rest of us."

Sue, who was sitting behind Ben, shook her head. "He needs to be alone with his thoughts for a while."

"Maybe a *long* while," the Thing chimed in from the pilot's seat.

Abruptly, a light began blinking on his control panel. He checked it out. "It's Blastaar," he reported.

"Really," said Reed. "Well, let's see what the man needs to talk about."

Opening a communications channel, the Thing eyed his monitor with distaste. "Whaddaya want now?" he demanded of the Baluurian.

Blastaar's lips pulled back in his savage face. "Only this, Ben Grimm—to tell you we have escorted you as far as we intend to. And to warn you that our alliance has come to an end. The next time we meet, I'll forget we fought side by side. And I'll destroy you."

The Thing grunted. "You're welcome to try. I mean, it's not like ya need our permission or nothin'."

"What's more," the Baluurian went on, a thread of spittle stretching from his top teeth to his bottom, "it'll happen sooner than you think."

"We'll be ready," Reed assured him.

But even he was surprised when Blastaar's flagship jettisoned a half dozen ruddy metal globes, each a good two meters in diameter. The second the globes were free, they took off in pursuit of the Fantastic Four.

Ben peered at his monitors. "Hang on to yer hats," he advised. "Those babies are loaded. We get hit and we're space debris."

He tapped out a command and they accelerated. But so did the globes. Johnny headed for the escape hatch.

"No!" Reed barked, restraining the Torch with an extension of his arm. "They may be heat seekers. Evasive maneuvers, Ben."

The Thing was about to comply when one of the globes exploded—far short of its goal. Then another. And another.

Turning to one of the observation ports, Reed saw why. It was the Surfer, cutting and slashing his way among the globes, skewering them with devastating energy blasts.

Ben took out a couple of the things with a barrage of his own. Then the Surfer finished off the last of them.

Johnny gazed at the silver figure on his surfboard. "I guess he didn't need to be that alone. Lucky for us."

The Thing eyed him. "Whaddaya sayin', squirt? That I couldn't've gotten us outta here on my own?"

Sue put her hand on Ben's craggy shoulder. "Let's just be glad you didn't have to try." She eyed her brother. "Or you either, Johnny."

Something occurred to Reed. The Thing seemed to notice it, too.

"Uh-oh," he said. "Looks like Stretch is doin' some fancy thinkin'. I can see smoke comin' outta his ears."

"You know," said Reed, scratching his chin, "I think Ben could have handled those globes. They weren't designed to kill us—just to send a message."

"A message?" the Torch echoed.

His brother-in-law nodded. "That's right. So Blastaar could make a point in front of his troops. So he could salvage some of his reputation for ruthlessness."

Sue grunted softly. "Maybe you're right. I mean, he wasn't exactly impressive as a military strategist."

''No,'' Reed said, ''he wasn't. If not for us, he would've absorbed the biggest disaster of his career.''

''Yeah,'' Ben sighed. ''If not fer us. Ya think ol' Blast-face'll send us a thank-you note?''

The leader of the Fantastic Four looked back at Blastaar's armada, which was diminishing with distance. He chuckled dryly.

''I think he already has.''

As his friends looked on, the Surfer knelt and picked up the creature whose life he'd saved days earlier. It looked healthier now, stronger for its stay in Fantastic Four headquarters.

''How about Spot?'' the Thing suggested.

Johnny rolled his eyes. ''Jeez, Ben, y'think? I mean, it hasn't got any spots. It's got lumps, bumps, tentacles, and little wriggly things. But no—and I underline that—*no* spots.''

The Thing shot the teenager a dirty look. ''So we should call it Lumps? What kinda name is that?''

Reed sighed and put his hand on the Surfer's shoulder. ''No matter what we call it—or him, or her—we'll be glad to take care of it for you. You can rest assured of that.''

The Surfer looked into the creature's eyes. It seemed happy, he thought. As if it had found a home. At least one of them had.

''Thank you,'' he told Reed. He glanced at the others. ''Thank you all.''

''Thank you,'' Sue insisted. ''If not for your help, we might never have survived.''

The Surfer regarded her kindly. ''And vice versa.''

He put the creature down and watched it squirm. He would see it again, he resolved, on his next visit to Earth—whenever that might be.

''I should go now,'' he said.

The Surfer's friends wished him well. But Susan wanted to do more. ''I'll walk you up to the roof,'' she offered.

Together, they negotiated a short corridor, then a flight of stairs. As Susan opened the door at the top of them, he saw that the sky had become a mighty conflagration of reds and purples and golds.

Soon it will be dark, he thought, *and the stars will come out.*

The Surfer longed to soar. To run away. To escape his pain and lose himself in the vastness of the heavens. But for Susan's sake, he restrained himself.

"You wish to speak with me?" he asked her.

She shrugged. "I just wanted to make sure you're all right."

The Surfer gazed past her, at the colors blazing in the western sky. "All right?" he echoed.

How was he supposed to respond to that? What words could he use to describe his disappointment? The terrible depth of his loss?

"I am unimpaired," he said at last. "I will go on."

"But not as you had hoped," she noted. "Not in the company of someone like Tjellina, with whom you could share your hopes and dreams."

The Surfer regarded her. Clearly, she was trying to encourage him to share his feelings. *For all the good it will do*, he thought.

"Not in the company of anyone," he said at last. "But then, that appears to be my lot. To be forever unique, forever apart."

Susan shook her head. "No. Not forever, my friend. Though right now, I know it must seem that way."

He grunted. "You don't understand, Susan Richards. You speak with one who has traveled the length and breadth of many galaxies, who has seen all manner of being and becoming. I have been worshiped, revered, even desired. But since Nova's death, I had despaired of finding anyone who could truly love me—not as a god or an idea, but simply as an equal."

"Then you found out what Tjellina was up to," Susan replied. "And your sense of justice was too strong. You couldn't let yourself remain in love with her, knowing the evil she was perpetrating."

The irony hadn't escaped him. "In all of existence, only one being managed to stir the embers of my heart. And by virtue of her ideals, she became my mortal enemy."

The Surfer thought of Tjellina's hair, of her skin and her darkling eyes. And of her touch, so strong and yet so gentle. And just as quickly, he put the image away.

"A lousy state of affairs," Susan conceded. "But that

doesn't mean the situation's hopeless. Far from it. You may not have scoured the universe as thoroughly as you think. And there are other galaxies, other frames of reference.''

He frowned. ''I know you wish to cheer me,'' he told her. ''But you see reality through a veil of emotion.''

''So do you,'' she told him. ''Only your emotions lean toward the melancholy end of the spectrum.'' She folded her arms across her chest. ''You may be the Silver Surfer. You may wield the Power Cosmic. But deep down, you're not as different from us humans as you'd like to believe.''

He pondered that for a moment. ''Perhaps there's some truth in what you say,'' he decided.

''There's quite a bit of truth in it,'' Susan insisted. ''Now go, if you like. But remember you've always got friends here on Earth. And we're pulling for you to find another Tjellina. A better one.''

The Surfer almost smiled. ''Thank you for your good wishes. I'll try to be worthy of them.''

She smiled back. ''You'll be worthy, all right. Of everything I've known or ever will know, I'm more sure of that than anything.''

He considered her. Despite her powers, she was still intrinsically human. Still optimistic beyond any reasonable expectation.

But then, perhaps that was what it took to find love in the universe. A certain optimism. A certain trust.

The Surfer envied his friend—envied her as he envied the aliens he'd found dead in their damaged starship, even before he'd heard of the Negative Zone. For Susan had found the partner fate intended for her.

He wanted to do the same. He wanted to believe it was possible. But it wasn't an easy dream for him to embrace.

''Good-bye,'' he told his companion. ''You have given me much to think about—as always.''

''Good-bye,'' Susan echoed. ''And don't stop hoping.''

He didn't answer her. He merely stepped aboard his surfboard and ascended into the sky. Higher and higher he rose, until his friend was the size of an insect, until the entire city spiraled away beneath him and was lost in a layer of clouds.

Ahead of him, the stars beckoned. The galaxy unfolded like a dark and mysterious flower.

Maybe someday, he would be as fortunate as Susan Richards, he told himself. But for the time being, where the Surfer soared he would soar alone.

When roused from one of his frequent and enduring daydreams of a world where baseball players never go on strike and White Castle hamburgers grow on trees, **Michael Jan Friedman** will admit to being the author of more than a score of science fiction and fantasy books, among them a great many *Star Trek* and *Star Trek: The Next Generation* best-sellers. When he's not writing—a condition that lately occurs with the frequency of Halley's Comet—Friedman enjoys sailing, jogging, and spending time with his adorable wife, Joan, and two equally adorable clones . . . er, sons. He's quick to note that no matter how many Friedmans you may know, he's probably not related to any of them.

George Pérez, one of the most renowned artists in the comics field, was born in the South Bronx in 1954 and started his comics career as an assistant to Rich Buckler. He has worked on virtually every character at both Marvel and DC, including memorable stints on team books *The Avengers*, *The Fantastic Four*, *The Inhumans*, *Justice League of America*, and *The New Teen Titans* (which he also co-wrote and co-edited with Marv Wolfman). He co-plotted and drew DC's landmark *Crisis on Infinite Earths* miniseries and wrote and drew the revamp of *Wonder Woman*. Recent work includes *The Avengers* for Marvel, *Isaac Asimov's I-Bots* for TeknoComix, *Sachs & Violens* for Epic, *Superman/Silver Surfer* for Marvel & DC (as writer), *The Incredible Hulk: Future Imperfect* for Marvel, and the chapter heading illustrations for the hardcover novel *The Incredible Hulk: What Savage Beast* for Putnam/Byron Preiss Multimedia.

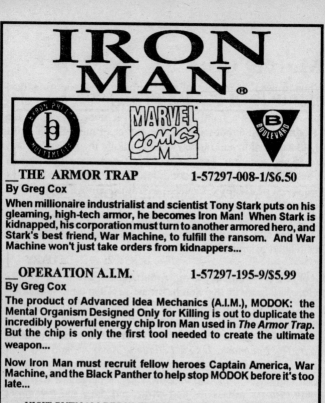

SPIDER-MAN®